RITA HAYWORTH'S SHOES

A novel

BY FRANCINE LASALA

Diversion Books
A Division of Diversion Publishing Corp.
80 Fifth Avenue, Suite 1101
New York, New York 10011

www.DiversionBooks.com

First Diversion Books edition May 2012.

ISBN: 978-1-938120-17-6

1 3 5 7 9 10 8 6 4 2

*For Shawna and the delightful
summer afternoon of shoe shopping,
swank cocktails, and evading cholera
that inspired it all.*

RAVES FOR RITA!

"What fun! This novel has it all—romance, laughs, a dollop of mystery. I was entertained from start to finish... And I want those shoes!"
—*NY Times* bestselling author Eileen Goudge

"Like hanging out with your funniest friend over a glass of champagne, *Rita Hayworth's Shoes* is both hilarious and thought-provoking. LaSala knows how to combine humor and romance for a story the reader can jump inside and enjoy."
—*NY Times* bestselling author Patti Callahan Henry

"If I had to describe this book in one word, I would choose 'magical.' I felt almost like I was reading a fairytale—an urban fairytale complete with a princess, prince, a few witches, a fairy godmother and a happily ever after. But not a syrupy sweet, predictable happily ever after—a perfectly satisfying one. I loved this book!"
—Meredith Schorr, author of *Just Friends With Benefits*

"I love the book! Congrats. I lived in New York for several years when I was fresh out of college and married a man from there. It reminds me of the many characters I knew and know. So great!"
—Dr. Natasha Janina Valdez
author of *A Little Bit Kinky* and *Vitamin O*

STEP RIGHT UP...

1

How Amy Got Ditched by David in a Dive Deli—
While Wearing a Wedding Gown

With astounding agility, Amy Miller sat down on the floor on the rolled up clump of paper towels she'd finally managed to wrangle free from the bathroom dispenser. This was a surprising, if not acrobatic, feat for a big reason: She performed this maneuver in a densely crinolined, Scarlett-O'Hara-in-the-parlor-drapes-wide wedding gown. And if that wasn't impressive enough, she pulled it off in the tiny ladies' room of one Katz's Delicatessen in lower Manhattan. That she had forgotten to wipe down the wall before she sat would become apparent later. Right now, there were more pressing matters to ponder.

It was her wedding day, after all. Or so she had thought.

Ever since Amy was a very little girl, she had big dreams for how this day would unfold. All her life, she had imagined swooshing down the aisle of an ancient church in a sweeping white gown, while glorious streams of sunlight beamed through exquisitely crafted stained glass windows. Of family and friends, shielding their eyes from the heavenly rays bouncing off her goddess-like visage as she sashayed to the massive altar. Of the man of her dreams trembling at the amazing luck he had been blessed with to have made this ethereal being gliding gracefully toward him actually have agreed to marry him.

Instead, she was stuffed like a bag of marshmallows into a shot glass, in a room that had no windows at all, while outside, her confused family and friends waited for the same thing as her. And that thing was David.

David was late. In fact, he was very late. In all the years she'd known him—and this year it would be seven—David had never been known for his promptness, so at least for the first half hour or so, there was no cause for alarm. But now, after nearly two hours more had passed, Amy was starting to doubt him—which she hated. Amy had never doubted David, ever, even if all her friends had. No, there must be something wrong. Maybe he had a car accident? Was run over by the crosstown bus as he tried to get across town? Was swallowed by an alligator that had emerged from the sewer and...

"Amy? Sweetie, can I come in?" It was her best friend, Jane.

"I'm kind of busy in here. It's not really a good——"

Jane shoved her way through the door. "Oh, Amy," she sighed. "How you doing, kiddo?"

"I'm okay. I'm fine," she lied. "I'm just having a little rest."

"On the bathroom floor?"

"Not many more places I can fit," she smirked.

"Come on, let me help you up. You look ridiculous down there."

"Yeah, what else is new?"

Jane reached a hand down and pulled her friend to a standing position.

"So how's it look out there?" Amy asked.

Jane ran a hand through Amy's fallen mousy brown bangs. "Oh, you know. It's fine. Heimlich's chugging down what must be his thirtieth Jack and Coke—and I think I may have seen him hitting on..." Jane stopped talking when she glimpsed the back of Amy's gown. "Hey, sweetie, you know you have something stuck—" Jane grabbed the clump of paper towels off the floor and started to wipe off the grease Amy had wiped off the wall with her dress. "Yeah. That's gonna stain." Amy craned her neck to look at the mess. "What else could go wrong?" she sighed.

"So *why* are you doing this again?"

"Come on, Jane. We've been through this before."

"It's just that—"

"That what? That I could do *better*? You don't think he's *right* for me? No offense, but you're not exactly in the position to be judging other women's men."

Jane's face turned bright red at this, and Amy instantly felt guilty for opening up what should now have been a very old wound, but wasn't. Elliot and Jane had been married seven years when she discovered he had a lover on the side. They divorced quickly, when their daughter was just a baby, and Jane had not so much as had even a first date with another man. She denied still being in love with Elliot, but everyone knew she was lying.

"I'm sorry about that. That was totally uncalled for. You know I didn't mean that."

"Yeah, whatever," was Jane's terse reply.

Amy tried to make it better. "Hey, without him there would be no Zoë—right?"

And Jane's face lit up at the thought of her daughter. "That's true. Zoë just wouldn't be Zoë without a dose of Elliot, would she?" Jane half laughed. "Of course it's better for her and me both that it stopped at 'nature' and that 'nurture' isn't part of that equation."

"You can say that again," Amy said a bit too emphatically, annoying Jane once again.

"I know you never liked Elliot. Believe me, he never liked you either. And I'm not just saying that to be unkind," Jane said, raising her hand in front of her face. "It's just that sometimes friends know better. It's not always easy to see things in the haze of love."

"Everyone's relationship is different. I don't have to tell you that. My relationship with David is what it is and it's not for me to explain to you or anyone else. I know you guys don't exactly get along, but give it time. I know you're going to grow to love each other. Eventually. In time."

"Right. Maybe in seven more years. Look, any guy who makes you—"

"I know what you're going to say, and stop it. Love is all about compromise. You of all people should know that. And this," Amy took a breath and looked around, "...this is my way of compromising for him."

"But you're *always* compromising for him."

"Now, that's not true. He compromised. He didn't even want to get married. But he finally gave in, didn't he? Just so long as we did it here. Here. In his favorite restaurant. Really, who's making the bigger compromise here? A few hours in this shit hole greasy dive, or a lifetime?"

"You don't even hear yourself, do you?" Jane shook her head. "You're the *bride*. It should have been *your* decision—"

"Listen, you might think this is ridiculous, but it isn't your wedding, is it? So it's not traditional. David's not a traditional guy," Amy assured, avoiding eye contact with Jane. She opted instead to watch herself twist, point and twist her foot in a pleather pump that looked worn from wear, even though this was the first time it had ever been worn. "David is special. He does things *his* way," she decided. She now looked up to the mirror to push her drooped-down updo out of her face. "And I like his way. So, what time is it anyway?"

"Four thirty-five..." she said, and trailed off. "Amy, do you really think he compromised about—"

"Jane, please. You're stressing me out. Don't go there, okay? You don't know him like I do. He'll be here. He loves me. And I love him. We're *meant* to be together. I don't know why you just can't see that."

"It's just that divorce is very hard on kids and—"

A knock at the door preempted Jane's lecture. "Mama?" The little voice broke the tension and both women smiled. "Hurry up in there. Pappy's stuffing pastrami in his pockets again. He said to me that it was okay because it's kosher, but I don't know. I don't think so."

"Now Zoë, good little girls don't tell on others," Jane called through the door. "I'll be right out. In the meantime, run and tell Nana what he's up to." Jane turned back to Amy. "See what divorce did to Zoë? It made her a raging tattletale."

"Right. The divorce did that."

"Mama? Won't Uncle David *ever* get here? I'm sooo tired of waiting for him," Zoë whined, banging on the door with a tiny fist.

"Are you back already? That was fast—"

"Mama! Come on! I'm soooo hungry."

Jane shot Amy the desperate, part embarrassed, part murderous glance of a mother approaching the end of her rope. "I think I have some Cheerios or something in my bag out there," she offered.

"Don't worry. I'll be right out."

"You okay?"

"I'm great. I have perfect faith that everything's going to be just fine."

"Okay, see you later."

Amy turned back to the mirror and blew up pesky fallen strands of hair away from her nose. She reached into her bag for a comb and the small bottle of hair spray she brought for touch-ups and went to work on her starchy bridal hair. Within seconds, she had managed to snag and break the cornerstone bobby pin, and the $150 fiasco plopped down into her face in one piece.

"Shit!" Amy frantically tried to fix it, but only succeeded in creating what could easily have passed for a bad toupee. Just then, her cell phone began to ring. She desperately extricated her hands from her hair/nest and retrieved the call just before it went to voice mail.

"Hello?" she breathed.

"Scruffy. Hi, it's me."

"David! Oh, my God! Has there been an accident? Where are you?"

"No, no. It's nothing like that, Amy. Oh, Scruffy. I'm so sorry."

"What? What is it?"

"Amy, I'm not going to make it today."

"David—what do you mean? Where are you?"

"Oh, Amy. You're such a beautiful girl. And my very best friend in the world. But I'm afraid… Oh, God. I'm so sorry."

"What is it? I don't understand."

"Amy, I've fallen in love with someone else."

Stunned, Amy hit the wall with her back and began to wipe clean another streak as she slid to the floor. "Oh dammit!"

"Amy?"

"No—no. Not you. Never mind… Wait a minute. Yes. Yes you! What do you mean you're in love with someone else? David, you're just scared. You know how you deal with commitment—"

"No, Scruffy—Amy. It's not that. It's really never been that. I *do* want to get married. I really *do* want to commit. I just don't want to commit to *you*. I'm sorry I never realized that before…"

Amy responded with silence.

"Amy? Come on, Amy. Talk to me. Amy? Please…"

"You can't mean that. You just can't. You're just having a crisis, David. Cold feet. Where are you? Let's meet. Let's talk about this."

"No, Amy. No. I never meant to hurt you," he said, and Amy could hear some humming, what she could swear was muffled speech, on his end of the phone.

"What was that?" she asked.

"What was what?" he replied, and the humming started again.

"That. That droning noise?"

"Droning," he stalled. "I don't hear any—"

"Oh, God. You're with her right now, aren't you?"

David was quiet, but the droning endured.

"You are, aren't you? Oh, dammit, David! At least tell me who she is."

"Amy, this isn't going to help…"

"TELL ME!"

"Okay, okay. It's Liz French.

"Who?"

"Liz French. You remember—the liberal arts professor? From last year's party?"

Amy thought for several seconds as a wave of nausea began washing over her. In her mind's eye, a shapeless, troll-like being bounded up to her in the grand ballroom of the Garden City Hotel with a Diet Coke in one hand and a chicken leg in the other. David heard a crashing sound on her end of the phone. "Amy? Amy?!?" There was no answer.

The crash was not heard in the main dining area of Katz's Delicatessen, a brown wood-paneled space on the Lower East Side, reminiscent of someone's never-remodeled-since-the-1950s-basement. Here, ancient salamis hung from the ceiling and vomit-colored linoleum coated the floor under the feet of sixty or so well-heeled guests, who had been discreetly picking away at the long-cold buffet as they waited for the main event, desperately trying to pretend the situation wasn't all that awkward.

Make-believe time was over when into the uncomfortable fray walked one Amy Ann Miller—bride, completely dazed, a slight trail of blood drizzling down her chin from her bottom lip and right onto her hand-embroidered silk bodice. (The shock of exactly for whom—or more like for *what*—David left her had sent her reeling forward into the sink with her face, or rather her lip, breaking the fall.)

Amy grabbed a glass of champagne from a stunned-to-a-stop waiter. She downed it in one gulp.

"Sancerre! Stat!" cried Jane, as she snapped her fingers and rushed to Amy's side. "Amy? What happened?"

A voice Amy didn't recognize, but she guessed was the horrible Hannah from her job, piped out of the growing-more-tense crowd. "That bastard!"

At last, the tension was too much for the guests to bear, and with Hannah breaking the dam came a flood of whispered observations and even some obscenities from the other guests.

"Oh no," gasped Lauren Austen-Rabinowitz, Jane's mother, as she clutched her husband Joshua's arm. Joshua could only shake his head.

"Not coming," Amy mumbled.

"That boy is trouble," said Aunt Clarabelle, as she twirled away at the long strands of hair that had sprouted from her chin in recent years, and which she had decided not to remove as she rather enjoyed twirling them.

"A travesty, this is!" agreed the massive mammoth of a woman known as Aunt Enid.

"I knew it, I knew it, I *knew* it," spat Grant, Enid's son, who had yet to get over the demise of his own marriage, and who would often—painfully and annoyingly to anyone who had to listen—refer to himself as "half a man." He viewed all weddings, whether the couple went through with them or not, as disasters waiting to happen. Enid looped her massive arms around his elbow, and began to comfort him with a soft litany of "there, there's." Jane rolled her eyes at them.

Amy's boss, Professor Fredreich Heimlich, who suffered equally from acute hearing loss and apparently severe inappropriateness, pushed in front of tiny Jane, nearly knocking her over, holding a hand up to his ear with Band-Aids wrapped around each finger.

He asked Amy, "What's that you say?"

Amy's Sancerre at last arrived, and this too, she downed in one gulp. "I said, he's not coming."

The din of speculation instantly quieted.

"I always knew that guy was a jackass," said the gnarly professor, waving a beige-plastic-wrapped finger in her face. "You just can't trust these herpetologists. Reptiles? As if that's really science," he scoffed, and took a swig of his drink. "Bunch of goddamned devil worshippers, that's what they are," he offered, putting his arm around Amy's waist, and slipping his hand down to rest on her rear end.

Amy whipped herself away from the professor and began to wail. Jane threw her arms around Amy, who, because she stood a head taller than Jane, snotted and bled into her best friend's hair. Jane was a forgiving friend.

Always a sensitive child, Zoë ran up to her favorite aunt, squirmed her tiny six-year-old body between Jane and Amy, and threw her arms around Amy's waist. "Oh, Auntie Amy! This is simply unconscionable!" she screeched.

Jane, ever-impressed by her young daughter's precociousness, joined her daughter in the hug as she kissed Zoë's downy-soft blonde head.

The angelic and wise Zoë lifted her tear-soaked face and stared meaningfully into her mother's eyes. "So, does this mean we can eat now?"

2

How Amy Ruined Her Dress, Got Drunk in the Diner, Passed Out Cold, and Lost Her Shoe

everal hours later, rumpled and intoxicated, Amy stumbled into the apartment she had lived in since her early twenties and which she had shared with David for the past several years. She dropped her keys on the floor by the foyer table and tried, unsuccessfully, to pop herself out of the ten thousand buttons that comprised the back of her gown. The realization that a bride wasn't supposed to be doing this for herself stung. But just for a moment.

Because even tonight, even after the harshest humiliation imaginable, she was forgiving. In all the years that Amy had been with David, waiting for him to finally realize that she was indeed "the one," she had somehow managed to twist in her mind the way he had treated her into what she believed was the way he expressed his love. She had accepted all his humiliations like lover's kisses. He was so magnificent. So perfectly formed. So beautiful to behold. And these were what steered her heart.

Through the years, he had eventually, well, "loved her down"— and not just emotionally. But she was just as blind to the physical changes in herself as she was to the psychological ones. Once a striking-looking girl, David's "love" had transformed Amy from fabulous into frump—well, never truly fabulous and not exactly frump…But her life with David had certainly had made a difference.

She'd let her once honey-blonde hair grow out to mousy brown, keeping it that way because David never believed in "tampering with nature"—a philosophy extended to the unruly, unshaped eyebrow hairs that revolted against each other over her large blue eyes. Eye makeup was certainly out of the question, a shame because it would have nicely brought out what could have been her best asset.

She was a mess tonight and she knew it. But she also knew that love, true love, was everything. And what she had with David was real. She felt it was. As she had told Jane, if it meant making compromises, so what? Of course you have to give up something to have something real. Didn't you?

Amy staggered across the room and squeezed herself between the tiny couch and ratty old coffee table in the living room before collapsing into the cushions in a worn, white heap. As she sat there considering the events of the day, the past and the future, she knew in her heart only one thing: That she still loved David. Her beautiful David. And that when he came back to her, she would forgive him.

"Well, babies…things didn't turn out quite as we had expected today," said Amy, seemingly to no one, but anyone who'd ever been to her apartment knew exactly who she was talking to: Her pets. Or David's pets? *Their* pets. Their *babies*. Now it looked like these were the only babies they were ever going to have together. No. It couldn't be true. She knew it couldn't be over.

She lay out on the couch like a corpse, which is what she felt like and, the truth be told, wished she was. Would God be merciful and take her that night? She wondered. She hoped. And then she thought about the babies. No, she had to live, at least for the babies.

"Don't worry. Mommy's not going to leave you," she said out loud, as if they had been worried. "Daddy will be back. Soon everything will be okay again."

She looked down at the coffee table, covered in layers of David's favorite magazine, *Reptiles*, with a couple of issues of Hannah's top read, *National Geographic*, somehow also in the mix. On the cover of one of these was a headline that beckoned: "Rainforest: Discover Our Treasures." She shuddered and knocked the magazines off the table. What other reminders did she need that her life was a mess, and that it was all pretty much her fault?

Except under the magazines was a treasure—for her at least. It was her worn-out old copy of Voltaire's *Candide*, a story pretty much now lost to time for everyone but literature freaks like herself, and one that had been lost to her for weeks under the stack of science magazines.

She smiled as she picked it up. She must have read this book about thirty times and she never got tired of it. She'd even let Jane drag her to see the musical on Broadway one year. As much fun as it was, she couldn't help but think the musical comedy buffs weren't quite getting it. Though, if she had to be honest, she had to admit that whenever she read it, no matter how many times she read it, she couldn't help but feel that she really didn't quite get it either. It was like something was missing somehow. Or that maybe what was missing was just something missing in her. She didn't know now. She didn't know anything anymore.

She opened the book. Her whole life, Amy had escaped into books. Other worlds where she didn't have to face the madness of her own. Her constant companions. Characters she understood better than the people she knew. Plots that made sense. Predictability, even when the plots were unpredictable. There would always be resolution, good or bad. And when she was done she could take the book and shelve it and start over again with another book. So not like her own life...In her life, where was the resolution? Where was the closure? So, Amy had made books her life. At least she had wanted to make them her life and she'd completed all the schooling she needed. She'd even written her thesis. But her defense seemed undoable. David and she had agreed about that. David and she had agreed about so many things. Until now...

Amy tried to read the first page, tried to bury herself in its mad absurdity and tried to forget the day, but her eyes still burned so badly from all the crying she had done that she just couldn't focus on the words. So she closed the book and lay out on the couch.

She was tired. Much too tired to lift her wedding-gown weighted self to her bedroom, and she started dozing off right there in the living room. "Yes, babies. Everything will be just fine," she slurred. "Daddy will be back before you know it." And with that, she drifted into a dreamless sleep.

Three days later, after much prodding, Jane finally got Amy to agree to meet her and Zoë at a diner around the corner from where Amy lived. The Omega Diner, while not original in name, was an original establishment of this Eastern Queens neighborhood. This was apparent mostly in the never-renovated fixtures and finishes, and the ancient desserts that sat behind the greasy glass under the countertop where the cash register sat, probably petrified by this point, museum pieces that they were.

It was only as they waited for Amy to show that it became obvious to Jane what a terrible idea it had been to have also invited Hannah. Yes, Hannah was a friend of Amy's, but she had a tendency to be overbearing and self-righteous, not to mention a bit boring with her obsession over primitive peoples—and she kind of got on Amy's nerves.

Zoë, the ever-wise Zoë, seemed already to know that it had been a bad idea for Hannah to be there, but it wasn't truly cemented for Jane until from their window booth, they all watched Amy spot them from the street and smile. And then freeze. And then make a mad dash for home.

"I'll be right back," Jane said across the table as Hannah and Zoë watched Amy run the other way.

"I *told* you not to invite Hannah," said Zoë, not taking her eyes off Amy. "She doesn't like Hannah."

"Zoë, that's not polite. What did I tell you about *telling*?" she blurted, instantly embarrassed about confirming the child's speculation. "I mean, about *lying*," Jane now lied with a nervous chuckle. "You know that good little girls don't lie."

"Do good *big* girls?"

Jane smiled meekly at Hannah. "Sugar," she explained, pointing to Zoë's nearly full glass of chocolate milk. "You know... It makes them kind of..." she demonstrated just what it made them by twirling a finger in the air around her ear.

"It's not a problem," Hannah smirked. "I know Amy has her issues. But Zoë likes me. Don't you, Zoë?"

"Whatever," the child mumbled. Through her straw, she began to blow bubbles in her milk.

After another quick moment of uncomfortable silence, Jane raced out and Hannah and Zoë pressed themselves up against the window to watch. They saw Jane catch up to Amy at the traffic light. They watched the women argue back and forth for several moments. They watched Jane grab Amy by the arm and drag her back to the restaurant.

Zoë shook her head. "Wuss," she hissed under her breath.

"What's that, sweet one?" Hannah asked.

"Oh, nothing," Zoë replied. "Look—here they come."

As they entered the diner, Amy again froze. But a quick elbow shove from Jane set her racing at an unnatural speed toward the table.

"Hannah! Hi!" said Amy through the most authentic smile she could muster. "I'm *so* happy to see you!" she beamed, as Jane and Zoë exchanged worried glances and Amy slid into the booth directly opposite Hannah, who also looked a bit worried herself—even more so when Amy grabbed both Hannah's hands in her own and exclaimed in a much too excited tone: "Tell me—how's everything at work?"

Zoë looked to Jane in horror, begging with her eyes for her mother to make it all stop, nodding wildly as she crossed her neck with one of her tiny fingers in the manner of slashing.

Jane did not get the message.

"Well since you asked," Hannah began, nervously at first. "Well, as I was just telling Jane..." and then gaining confidence, "...since you've been out, I've had to deal with Heimlich for you," and then with annoyance... "...and you *know* what a pain in the ass he is."

"Okay," Jane interrupted protectively. "But weren't you going to take over some of Amy's stuff anyway when she left for her—" this last thought lodged in her throat.

"You mean my honeymoon?" Amy asked coolly.

"Sorry, sweetie," Jane said sheepishly. "I was just trying to help."

"Oh, no. Don't worry. It's not a problem," Amy said, still with a deranged look in her eyes. "Believe me, Hannah, if I were you, I'd be annoyed at me, too. But don't worry. I'll be back at work on Monday."

"Really? That isn't too soon?" Jane asked, worried.

"Wow. I guess that was pretty bitchy," said Hannah. "Forgive?"

"Don't worry about it," Amy waved, with a smile so saccharine, you'd probably get cancer if you licked her face.

"So big girls *are* allowed to lie!"

"Zoë!" Jane and Amy chided in unison, and then turned to Hannah. "Sugar," they both smirked, each twirling a finger in the air around their ears as Jane had earlier.

"Yes. Sorry, Hannah," said Zoë, pulling out a book and opening it to read. "Apparently, sugar makes me…" she dropped her voice to a whisper, "…crazy."

"Hmmm," said Hannah. "Charming child."

They were all silent for a moment. Then Jane spoke. "So, I was thinking after this we could maybe go to the salon for makeovers," she said breathlessly, nodding at Hannah for support.

"Why, yes," she gushed, nodding at Jane. "What a wonderful idea——"

"I don't think I'm really in the mood for all that primping and doting. You know? I really don't think…"

"Auntie Amy, please," said Zoë, in a most angelic voice. "You just can't walk around like that anymore. Your eyebrows," she looked away, shaking her head in despair. She dropped her voice to a loud whisper. "It's like caterpillars are sitting over your eyes…"

"They're horrifying," scoffed Hannah, as Jane nodded helpfully.

Amy paused for a second to look at her friends. She seemed to consider their words carefully. And then she brushed them off. "So, do they have anything stronger than coffee here?" Amy blurted, flipping though her menu. She looked up at the others, who looked back at her, except for Zoë, who'd gone back to her book. "I've been having a little trouble sleeping lately. Don't need the caffeine, you know."

"So order a cocktail."

"Zoë! Good little girls don't push cocktails on their friends. Right?" Jane asked, unsure, looking to the others for confirmation.

"You know what?" Amy nodded. "I think one would help. Thanks, kiddo."

"No problem," said Zoë, not looking up.

Amy waved down the waiter and ordered a vodka and cranberry, while the others ordered lunch.

"You're not going to eat?" asked Jane.

"Not hungry."

This did not sit well with Jane. "But if you're going to drink in the middle of the day you really should—"

"Not. Hungry."

"Oh, she'll be fine," snapped Hannah.

Jane looked to Zoë, who looked up for a second, regarded the women with a blank, bored stare, and went back to her book.

"So, I found out something interesting about Amazonia this week, a lead I'd been sniffing out about some of the tribes that live in the rain forest over there," said Hannah, and Amy rolled her eyes at Jane. Jane tapped Hannah gently on the arm and shook her head apologetically. "Perhaps another time?" Jane offered.

Hannah was crestfallen. "Sure," she said, and looked away.

Amy's drink arrived, along with an unsweetened iced tea for Jane and a carrot juice for Hannah. She gulped hers down in seconds and ordered another.

Hannah and Jane exchanged another quick glance as Jane urged Hannah, by raising and lowering her own well-shaped eyebrows, to speak. Hannah shook her head. Then Zoë nodded to Hannah. So, Hannah took a deep breath, looked around, and opened her mouth. "So, when I was in college, I loved this guy named Joe," she said. "Man, I would have done anything for this guy. In fact, I once sucked him off—"

"Ahem," said Jane, nodding in Zoë's direction. "Don't you mean that you," she cleared her throat, "'lucked his dwarf'?"

"Right," Hannah said, looking at Zoë. "Sorry," she mouthed to Jane. "Anyway, the point is, there was nothing I wouldn't do for this guy. But it didn't matter. Three days later, I found him in the library having his, um, *dwarf* lucked by some bimbo from our physics class."

"Oh, that's horrible," Jane gasped, now looking to Amy. "Isn't that horrible?!"

"What?" said Amy, seemingly to her drink. "Yeah, terrible."

Amy pulled the paper off a straw lying on the table and added it to her drink. So delighted was she with the speed the drink now went down with two straws, she ordered another. And proceeded to add yet another straw. It seemed the more straws she sucked her drinks through, the faster they went to her head, and the less she actually had to hear what was going on around her. Her friends didn't seem to notice what she was up to. They had other things to think about now.

"We all have a story like that," Jane mused.

"Really?" asked Hannah as the waiter placed another drink in front of Amy and she tore open another straw. "What's yours?"

"Well, my ex, Zoë's father…he ran off with the UPS delivery woman."

"He didn't!" Hannah gasped, clearly enjoying the scandal.

"He didn't—"Amy interrupted.

"He *did*!" Jane insisted.

Amy shrugged her shoulders and went back to her drink.

"Well, I for one am glad he didn't go through with it, personally," Hannah suddenly blurted, and Amy glared at her.

"On second thought, maybe this isn't the best conversation to be having right now," Jane deflected.

"Appropriate or not," scoffed Hannah. "You can't say it isn't true."

"I think we should get off the topic," Jane said noticing that Amy was starting to look a bit wobbly. "It's really none of our business, and I think it's making Amy uncomfortable."

"Look, all I'm saying is that Amy's got a twisted view of this thing—of her whole relationship with David. You know it and I know it. Even Zoë knows it." Zoë didn't look up, but a quick wave of her right hand confirmed her position.

"Well, just because she hasn't fucked everything she could wrap her legs around," Jane snapped before catching herself. "I mean ducked every goose—oh God, whatever! That's no reason—"

"He never did anything for her, and you know it," she said firmly, shaking her head. "He never did anything, I don't know, *special*—"

"Liz. Lizzie. Fizzie Lizzie. Dizzie Lizzie," Amy slurred as she slurped around the ice melting in her glass.

"Oh, for goodness' sake," said Jane. "Honey, maybe it's time we got you home?"

"Lizzie Borden. Lizbeth Borden. Lizabeth Borden took an axe—"

"Waiter—check, please!" Jane called out.

Amy ignored Jane, now sucking only air through five straws. "Lizabeth. Elizabeth. Queen Elizabeth! Elizabeth Taylor. Lizabeth… Elizabeth… Eliza- " she slurped, "Bitch! Eliza-bitch!"

Jane lunged across the table to cover a squirming Zoë's ears with her hands.

"Eliza-BITCH! ELIZABITCH!" Amy squeaked as Hannah and Jane exchanged looks of bemused horror. "ELIZAPHANT!" With that, Amy snorted and passed out on the table. "At least now she'll sleep," Zoë remarked.

The waiter finally brought the check, which Jane paid, and they set about getting Amy home. Together they maneuvered Amy out of her seat, sliding her out of the booth as one of her blue denim clogs slipped off her foot. Jane bent down to get it.

"No. Let it go." said Hannah, dead serious.

Jane looked at Hannah, annoyed.

"Really. I hate those shoes," Hannah said. "I'll take her shopping tomorrow if I can revive her. But she can't wear those anymore. She just can't."

Jane shot Hannah a sharp look out of loyalty to her friend. But she knew Hannah was right.

"She's right, Mama," said Zoë. "Those shoes suck."

"I know," Jane said, shaking her head sadly at the shoe. "I know you guys are right. But Zoë, I don't think—"

"Yes, Mama. I'm sorry. Those shoes are not suited to Amy's sparkling personality and are certainly worth replacing. Better?"

"That'll do."

"Freamy-manna-hotta-cown-flewn-buck," Amy murmured as they lifted her arms over Hannah's ample shoulders.

"I'm sorry, honey. What was that?" Jane tried.

"Freakish-mannish-husky-corn-fed-flab-bucket!" Amy managed to utter before slipping off Hannah's shoulders and falling in a clump at the exit.

Amy opened her eyes, now startled. Was it morning? Where was she? Why was her head pounding and her throat so painfully dry? *Oh. Right.*

Remembering the diner and the drinks, she reached over to her night table where she hoped she had at least had the sense to leave herself a glass of water. Upon leaning over, she fell right out of the bed. The night table wasn't there. This woke her right up. Realizing she was nearly naked (and without even the vaguest memory of how her clothes had come off) she spotted something white poking out from under the bed and she grabbed it. It turned out to be one of David's dirty T-shirts.

Amy pulled the shirt up off the floor and clutched it to her face. She breathed in the scent that still lingered in the fabric. A mix of musk and Old Spice. The smell of David. The smell of her love. She pushed the T-shirt up closer to her face and tried to take it all in, tried to breathe the scent right off the material.

Her beautiful David, with his deep brown eyes, his eyelashes so long they spread like fans over his eyes when they were shut. His chiseled cheeks and chin. His exquisite skin. His bow-shaped mouth—a mouth she would never kiss again. She sighed, pulled the T-shirt over herself, and headed for the kitchen.

But she didn't get any further than the living room. Everything in her apartment was gone. No tiny couch. No ratty old coffee table. No wool rug that David had had since college and refused to replace because it was still useful. No TV. And all her books. Her precious books were gone. She realized that he must have come in while she was out and taken it all. In a panic, she whipped her head around to the opposite side of the room and breathed a great sigh of relief. At least he had left the babies. Thank God he had left the babies.

Amy headed into the kitchen to make herself a cup of coffee, but the coffee pot was gone. For the first time, she considered it a good thing that David had never liked tea. She had always loved it, drinking full pots of it from the delicate antique china cups she collected. She had hoped David would join her—if for nothing else because of the joy it gave her. But that would not have been David's style.

So Amy made a pot of tea and poured some into her favorite little cup, the one with the green flowers. She headed into the living room and sat cross-legged on the floor as she looked around. She tried to feel something. *Anything*. She wanted to shake but she didn't have the energy. She wanted to cry but she was simply too numb. So she sat there and sniffed, trying to force the tears to come.

It was through this sniffing that she detected the scent of something unusual. That scent...great memories of summer washed over her and began to calm and soothe her as she began to think about her parents and how much she missed them, of eating fried chicken with them at the carnival before they disappeared...

Amy sniffed harder. That smell. That now-stale odor of chicken. Did she detect the presence of—she sniffed harder—was that *artificial sweetener*? Oh, God! *She* had been there. Elizabitch. Elizaphant! That blobby gnome had been in *her* apartment. Her home.

As Amy breathed in the toxic fumes of the man-stealer, nausea erupted in her like a geyser. She threw up all over David's shirt, which she'd now have to wash or throw away.

And now she cried.

3

How Amy Returned to Work and Killed Her Boss

Monday morning arrived quickly, but Amy was ready for it. Or at least ready to escape her empty apartment. After a quick shower, she dressed in a gray sweater and loose-fitting black pants. She slipped her foot into one of her favorite shoes, her blue denim clogs, and searched everywhere for the other. It was nowhere to be found, but it was too late already to care. She settled instead on a pair of Chuck Taylor low tops, swung her improbably large bag over her shoulder, and headed out the door.

As she exited her building, she was stopped, "Yo baby!"

"Dammit," she whispered under her breath before plastering on a polite smile and turning to face the group of white-T-shirt-wearing, gold-chain-donning, twenty-somethings who lived in her building with their mamas, and who spent most of their time hanging out on the front steps.

She knew them all, of course. Having lived in this building since they were in middle school, she'd even watched them grow up—from pre-adolescent boys who had occasionally needed her help with their English homework, to these men standing here. These sexy young men. She felt a shudder, not unpleasant, course within her.

"Hi, Tony," she waved. "Hi, Mario and Frankie. And hello there, Angelo."

They each nodded their hellos as they looked her up and down. "Where you off to, Miss Amy?" asked Angelo.

She held up her bag. "Work. You know?" From the looks they gave her, it was clear they did not.

"Saw your old man the other day," said Mario, puzzled. "Looked like he was moving?"

"Here with his aunt or something," added Frankie.

"A little chummy for an aunt," sneered Tony.

"*Chum* being the key word there," Angelo said, and they all burst out laughing. Except for Amy. A fact of which they were soon painfully aware and which silenced the mirth.

"Who was that broad?" Frankie wanted to know.

Angelo laughed again. "*Broad* being the key word…"

Now Amy burst into tears and Tony immediately threw his arms around her. He held her a bit too close as he glared at Angelo. "Whatsa matter with you? Show some respect."

"Uh, sorry," said Angelo.

Amy cried in Tony's young, strong Italian arms, and she felt a stirring of something like lust. But she quickly shook it off. Truth was it had been so long since she and David had done it, a shrub scratching up against her legs would likely have had the same effect. But still, there was something so gentle, yet manly about him. Something so unexpected about his touch that she looked up at him and smiled for a second.

He smiled back. "You okay, toots?"

She pulled herself away and took a deep breath. "Long story," she said.

Tony pulled her back again and she stirred again, this time with a little more intensity. "We gonna have to kick someone's ass?"

She smiled. "Thanks, but I don't think…"

"I never liked that guy," said Tony, shaking his head. "Total dick." Though the *way* he said it, full of manliness and rage and sex, made Amy even hotter than before. She pulled away again, and this time took a few steps out of his reach.

"Thanks, guys. But it's just a temporary thing. David will be back and everything will be back to normal before we know it."

Mario shook his head. "I sure hope not," he said, undressing her with his eyes.

She shuddered, but not with disgust. "Gotta go!" she gasped and ran off.

An hour later, Amy was sitting in her cubicle outside Professor Heimlich's office in the English department of Stratton University, chatting with Jane on the phone instead of dealing with the pile of files mounting on her desk as she tried to make sense of things. Including the strange new stirrings her young neighbors had sparked.

"But they're barely *twenty*," said Amy, cradling the receiver between her shoulder and chin as she shuffled through stacks of unopened mail.

"And what? You haven't done it since they were all in middle school?"

"Oh, come on. It hasn't been that long."

"Really?" Jane paused. "How many years were you with David?"

"Seven."

"And how many times did you do it in the past five years?"

Amy was silent.

"How many?"

"Uh," she stammered. "I dunno. Maybe seven?"

"Not even close. In the first two years *maybe*."

"David just wasn't that into—"

"*You*. I'm sorry to be so harsh about it, sweetie. But that's what it comes down to."

Amy looked up briefly to see that Hannah was standing over her desk. "The sooner you—"

"I gotta go," Amy snapped and hung up the phone. She looked up at Hannah. "Can I help you?"

Hannah started down at her for a minute without speaking. She then produced a giant box of cookies, which she handed to Amy. "Peace offering?"

Amy took the box, screwing up her face as she read the package. "Almond biscotti?" She looked back at Hannah. "For what?"

"Well, for your shoe. For one."

Amy cocked her head. "My shoe?"

"What? Oh, nothing. Just forget about that. So, how was your weekend?"

"Horrendous," said Amy, looking away. "*She* was in my apartment, you know. That woman. And David." She shook her head. "They took *everything*."

"I know," said Hannah, in the same nonchalant manner someone might acknowledge a crumb on a coffee table.

Amy narrowed her eyes. "What do you mean, you *know*?"

"David told me." Again, in the same irritatingly casual tone.

"You spoke to David?"

"Well, I wasn't planning to talk to *him*," said Hannah. "I was trying to have a conversation with Liz and——"

"With *Liz*? Liz French?"

"Uh, yeah. We're, um...we're kind of friends," Hannah looked away guiltily. "I mean, we're not *friends*, friends. We just know each other. We both worked——"

"I don't think I want the details, thanks," Amy said, looking away.

"Look, I wanted to tell you the other day. I just didn't know how——"

Amy shook her head. "I don't understand. Why didn't you *say* something." And then the realization burned through her. "Holy shit, you *knew*. Didn't you? You knew there was someone else!"

"Well, yes. And *no*. I mean, I knew Liz was involved with *someone*. I just didn't figure out that it was David until just a few days ago." She put up a hand, "After the wedding," she offered, helpfully. It did not help.

Amy took a deep breath and tried to suppress the urge to scream. "How long has it been going on?"

Hannah looked away. "You don't want to know."

"How long?"

"Oh, come on, Amy. What good is this going to do anyone?"

"*How long*!?"

"About six months."

"What?"

"I said about six——"

"I heard you. I just don't understand. How could it have gone on that long?" She slinked down into her chair. "Right under my nose."

"It wasn't serious all that time. I mean, of course they were sleeping together the whole time but..." Hannah stopped talking for a while when Amy let out a noise not unlike a yelp. "You know, she's also kind of into reptiles."

"As a food source," Amy jabbed.

"Say what you will but it's not *her* fault he's with her. Surely you can't blame her for what happened. I mean, she's actually a really nice girl. Once you get to know her you might like her..."

Amy stared at Hannah a few moments and then stood.

"Where are you going?" asked Hannah.

"I am going to have a word with him," said Amy, pushing around the side of her desk.

Hannah grabbed her by the shoulders. "You can't do that."

"I can *do* whatever I want."

"No, I mean you *can't*...."

"Look, I don't think you're really in the position of playing the friendship card right now. I don't see why I need to look out for your best interests when you couldn't give a crap about mine," said Amy, growing ever more determined to extricate herself from Hannah's iron grasp.

"No. It's not that."

"What is it then?" "Well...he's not here."

"He's not here?" she asked, confused for a moment. "Okay. So I'll go have a word with her." And she wriggled away from Hannah.

Who clamped right back down on her. "She's not here, either."

"What do you mean?"

"They...uh..." Hannah let go finally and looked away. "They went...out of town."

Amy realized immediately what Hannah meant. "They went on my honeymoon," she whispered, deflated.

"Well. Yeah."

Walking backward to her desk, Amy slammed square into a filing cabinet. "Shit!"

"Language!" shouted Heimlich from his office.

"Sorry," she said.

Doctor Heimlich emerged from his office, dressed in his professorial tweeds and khaki pants, and hobbled over to Amy's desk. At seventy-two, he didn't look a day over seventy-eight. "So, you're back now, are you?"

"It was time."

"You get those notes I left here typed yet?" he snapped, noticing the mountain of yet-to-be filed papers on her desk.

"I guess I forgot," she said.

"We're back at that one again, eh? And who's this?" he asked pointing to Hannah with one of his Band-Aid wrapped fingertips.

"I've been filling in for Amy all week—"

"Never mind," he cut her off. "Don't care."

"Professor, I'm so sorry for all the noise," said Amy. "I just learned some disturbing news."

"What? That snake boy took off to the Bahamas with his new girl?"

Amy looked away, choking back tears. "Well. Yes."

"A damn shame, that," he said, shaking his head. "Talk of the whole damned campus." Amy felt herself flush with color. "Bahamas, eh?" She nodded. He shrugged his shoulders. "Would have been a nice trip."

"Yes, I suppose it would," she said.

Heimlich stared at her for a while, then gave her a playful punch in the arm. "Ah, but you're here with us now," he smiled. "Now back to work," he added, businesslike, tapping her twice on the tush. "Chop, chop."

"Okay...well...let's see. Messages." She took a deep breath as she held up a stack and began to read. "Dean Cornish called about—"

"Ah, screw old Cornish," Heimlich said, talking over her. "How about some coffee?"

Amy was shocked at the thoughtfulness of the craggly old man. "Why, thank you. I'd love some."

"Not for you, silly girl!" he laughed, shaking his head at Hannah as if he and she had been involved in some kind of private joke over the coffee. Hannah laughed back and Amy glared at her.

"How about that new hazelnut over there in the lounge," he said. "Grab me a cup of that."

Amy fought to keep her composure. "But you're allergic to nuts."

Heimlich regarded her like she was an infant just discovering that she had hands. "I can't eat *PEA*-nuts," he cooed. "But to humor your silly little simple brain, just make it regular this time." He giggled to himself as he sauntered off down the hallway.

"Speaking of nuts…" Hannah tried.

Amy ignored Hannah's attempt at levity as she headed down the hall in the other direction.

Later that day, Amy received a disturbing phone call. It seemed the ice sculptor that had been hired for her wedding felt his business would now be irredeemably hurt by his association with her abysmal affair. He was demanding restitution. As Amy argued the finer points of getting jilted in a dive deli and understanding better than anyone alive the meaning of "irreparable social disgrace," Professor Heimlich entered her workspace in search of a snack.

Spotting the new box of treats Hannah had gifted earlier, he craned his neck around the increasingly agitated Amy, reaching behind her as he tried to get to the biscotti. To spare herself further humiliation, perhaps of having the old man land in her lap, she handed the box to Heimlich, who happily snatched it away and ran off.

Even later that day, just as Amy was wrapping her conversation with the ice-hearted ice sculptor, Professor Heimlich began dancing wildly around in his office. Amy didn't notice Heimlich dancing and she didn't notice as he began gesticulating wildly, flopping about back and forth, this way and that. And at the very moment that she slammed down the phone, she did not notice Heimlich's dramatic crash to the floor. The loud clamoring his fall generated got her attention, to be sure, and she looked back at the phone for a moment in pure disbelief that she had slammed it down so hard as to make such a sound. Then she realized that it had emanated from Heimlich's office. So loud was the crash, in fact, that it had attracted everyone in the English department to Heimlich's door, and also some anthropologists. Including Hannah.

Amy ran into Heimlich's office to find him lying on the floor, a half-eaten biscotti clutched in his wiry, Band-Aid-wrapped fingertips. She wasn't even aware that Hannah had followed her in until she spoke.

"This is bad," was all Hannah said as they pondered what do next over Heimlich's prone and lifeless body.

4

Amy Has a Most Unusual Day

From the outside, the Aberdeen Funeral Home looked like your typical old-time funeral parlor—a "home" complete with a wraparound porch and cheery gingerbread. It had once been the home of the Aberdeen family, who had converted the downstairs into a funeral parlor, and for generations, it had hosted numerous mourned and mourners in the many "Rest and Reflection Chambers" that could be found in the sprawling Victorian space.

Except there were no Aberdeens here anymore. Gus Aberdeen, son of the third-generation owner of the facility, who was also named Gus, had never been able to muster much passion for the preservation and showcasing of the dead. So, the day his father passed away, Gus placed a call to The Bloomquist Group, the nation's leading purveyor of all things funerary, and asked them to make an offer on the business. Before the body of the elder Gus had itself been preserved and showcased, the younger Gus had accepted their offer. The day after his father's funeral, Gus and his wife and three kids packed up and headed to North Carolina.

Now, thanks to the "vision" of the Bloomquist Group, the Aberdeen Funeral Home was a bustling business, known to boast: "We Host the Most on this Coast!" In an effort to remain true to the home's original condition, actually a mandate of the local zoning board, the outside of the home had been left pretty much intact. The inside, however, was left to Bloomquist to do whatever they chose. And they became mad with the freedom of all of it.

Now gone was the sweet flowery wallpaper, the soothing pastels of matching walls and carpets. The Aberdeen of the twenty-first century, instead, featured special rooms themed to the passions and proclivities of the deceased, including among others, a Winter Wonderland Chamber, a Stadium Chamber, and the one in which survivors of one Dr. Fredreich H. Heimlich now gathered: The Graceland Chamber.

True to the spirit of the Memphis mansion of Elvis Presley, The Graceland Chamber featured floor to ceiling green shag carpeting, exotic plants, animal prints, and even a working waterfall on the far wall. The room wasn't an exact replica of the Jungle Room, however; the furnishings had been reorganized to suit the specialized needs of the space. So, while many of the pieces that appeared in Bloomquist's version of the room were close copies of those featured in the actual Jungle Room, Bloomquist's version also included rows of folding chairs lined up to face the casket, which rested low on a replica of the famed kidney-shaped stone table.

It was, in a word, hideous.

Yet not quite as hideous as Amy Miller's present mood as she sat in the third row of chairs, watching as mourners filed in and out. The wake was surprisingly crowded, yet not a single person had opted to occupy the two empty chairs on either side of Amy. She had never felt more alone.

But while alone, she wasn't unnoticed. Several cops, uniformed and plainclothes alike, scoped out the space—and one detective in particular kept glancing in her direction, twirling the ends of his handlebar moustache. She thought he was sizing her up for a motive. Every time she looked at him, he seemed to be looking at her. And once she was sure she saw him and a uniformed cop point at her while they whispered to one another. She didn't realize it was because her legs, usually carefully hidden, were really quite stunning in her short black skirt and black tights. She could only feel guilty as she looked away.

"Who knew the old coot was such an Elvis freak?"

"Jane," Amy smiled for the first time that day. "You're here."

"And what's with," Jane pulled on her fingertips, "these?" She sat down next to Amy and lifted her giant bag on top of her lap.

"He's wearing the Band-Aids?"

"Yep," she said, matter-of-factly and she looked around the room.

"I'm so happy you're here," said Amy.

"Like I was going to miss Graceland?"

"Pretty incredible, isn't it." Amy shook her head.

"It almost makes me want other people I know to start kicking it so I can get a look at some of these other rooms." Jane turned to Amy. "Did you know they had a Paris Chamber?"

"I didn't, no."

Jane sighed. "I've always wanted to see Paris," she said, wistfully before turning her attention back to the crowd. "I can't believe this turnout. You always made Heimlich seem like such a pariah. But look at all these people."

"Again. Who knew?"

At that moment, a child a little older than Zoë ran up to the coffin in the front of the room. Amy winced as the child leaned over the casket and squealed. "Oh, Poppy! Oh, no. What have they done to you!"

Amy buried her face in her hands. "Oh, my God. I killed him. Oh, God. I'm so cursed."

Jane embraced her shaken pal. "You didn't kill him, Amy. He was old."

"*They* think I did it," Amy whispered as she subtly nodded to the officers across the room. Jane whipped her head around dramatically, apparently not getting the hint, and nearly shouted. "Who? What? You mean those *cops* over there," she pointed with her thumb. The detective with the handlebar moustache smiled at Jane and she smiled back.

"Just like I killed my parents," Amy gasped.

Jane turned back around to face Amy and shook her head. "First of all, you did not kill your parents."

"I encouraged them to take that trip."

"You mentioned it might be cool if they checked out the rain forests of Brazil. You did not make them go. And you did not—"

"Still."

31

They sat in silence, watching the child as he continued to rant. "Oh, Grandfather! Oh, how could this happen! How could this *be*?" he shook his small head in despair as he beat his own chest with tiny clenched fists. "Just as we were starting to put our differences aside."

The child began to cry as a woman around Jane's age took him into her arms. She led the boy away from the casket and they glowered at Amy as they passed.

"Not your fault," insisted Jane. "Not your folks and," she nodded toward the coffin, "not this one, either."

"Tell that to that child."

At that very moment, Zoë appeared. "Dead people are weird," she said, not taking her eyes off the coffin, where Heimlich's Band-Aid wrapped fingers "clutched" a book of Shakespearean sonnets and a *Blue Hawaii* DVD. "But living people are even weirder," she said, and darted off after the little boy.

Amy was astonished. "You brought her to a wake? *Really*?"

"She's going to have to face it sometime," said Jane. "Better it be someone she doesn't know up there."

Amy gave Jane a blank stare, which Jane didn't notice. Jane was too busy beaming at Zoë, who was now embracing the hysterical boy. Zoë pulled away from the boy, producing a Smurf figurine from behind his ear! The little boy delighted in the magic trick and began laughing wildly. Jane took it all in, beaming with pride, and finally turned back to Amy. "What?" she said.

Amy shook her head and went back to sulking and Jane said, "I guess I better go make sure Zoë doesn't take him outside and show him the trick of the vanishing pants again." And then Jane was gone, but quickly replaced.

Amy hadn't noticed that a man had been watching her since she'd come in and now that man was standing over her. "It's amazing, isn't it?" the man said, cheerfully, in a deep, thick baritone. Amy didn't look up.

But if she had looked up, she would have seen right then and there that these inappropriately cheery words actually came from a gigantic hulk of a man, who also happened to be completely bald. Not just on bald on the top of his head, mind you. He had no hair *anywhere*. Neither eyebrows nor eyelashes. Nary a whisker on chin or cheek. She may even have noticed that there was no hair in his nose, his ears, on even on his arms or legs. But she wasn't paying attention.

So maybe if she had been paying attention, his next words—spoken as he helped himself to the seat that Jane had vacated—may have shocked her just a little bit, "How some people's passing is surprisingly easy to take."

The giant bald man looked at Amy for a reaction and she didn't react. So he sat a few moments and looked around. He looked at Heimlich. Then he looked down at his watch, and then back again at Amy.

"So how does it feel to have killed a man?" he asked, in as matter-of-fact a tone as someone might wonder about the performance of a sports team or the recent weather.

That got her. She turned her head to retort and then let out a large gasp at the sight of him. As stunned as she was by what she saw, however, her anger at what he'd said won out over shock. "I beg your pardon?" He let out a deep, throaty laugh. "Aren't you the assistant?" he taunted. "The one who slipped him the tainted biscotti?"

"For your information," she began, but he didn't let her finish, cutting her short again with that laugh of his.

"I know, I know," he said. "Detective Franks is an old friend of mine," he smiled, nodding at the detective. Franks, noticing them looking at him, crossed his arms over his chest, shook his head and turned away. "He said the old guy choked—that he had some kind of nut allergy, but it was actually chomping the thing down without chewing that got him."

"Oh..." she said, and she looked at him again. Terrifying as he appeared, he had nice eyes and this relaxed her a bit. Until he spoke again.

"Don't you find it even a little hilarious that a guy called Heimlich choked to death?" he teased.

Amy felt anger rise up in her, then mysteriously disintegrate into humor. She couldn't help but let a smile escape. "I guess it's kind of ironic, yes."

"It's ridiculous. I mean, talked about predestination," he said.

"'Abandon all hope'," she mused.

"'All ye who enter here,'" he smiled. "I didn't take you for a Dante person."

"What did you take me for?"

He looked at her, pretending to size her up. He smiled. "Dunno. The Brontës maybe?"

"What's that supposed to mean?"

"Maybe all the black. It's kind of gothic," he said, a twinkle in his eye.

"It's a wake."

"So it is," he said, and pursed his lips.

Amy shook her head, although she was not as annoyed as she felt she should be as she folded her arms across her chest and sighed. "Honestly."

The man did not leave. Instead, he drummed his fingers on his lap and started humming, of all things.

"Are you humming?" she asked, aghast. "Is that Duran Duran?"

"Just a little levity. I'm sure he doesn't mind," he nodded to the coffin. "Although I guess Elvis would be more appropriate." He smiled at her. "You're a fan, then?"

She shot him an incredulous look. "Just how *old* do you think I am," she replied. "Just because I recognize a song doesn't mean—"

"Hey, Duran Duran is timeless. Liking Duran Duran does *not* make you old."

She warmed. "You're right," she said. "I may not be as old as you but I do love Duran Duran," she looked off into the distance. "Wow. I haven't listened to them in years."

"Now, wait a minute. Just how *old* do you think *I* am?" he asked, slightly scandalized. "And why in God's name have you been off the Double Dees?"

"Dunno," she said, sizing him up to answer his first question. She made what she thought was a generous estimate. "Maybe forty-eight, give or take?" she shrugged.

"I'm thirty-seven, actually," he said.

She casually shrugged her shoulders and went on to address his next question, ignoring any damage she may have done. "My fiancé listened to a lot of garage bands and I—"

He now slumped in his chair. "And you're engaged."

"It's not that simple actually."

"Well," he said, ignoring her. "Cutting you off from the Taylors and Rhodes and LeBon and filling the void with that abysmal amateur crap," he smirked. "Sounds like a fun guy, truly."

"I don't think you should be judging—"

"Why?" he asked sharply, then catching himself. "He's here?" He looked around.

Before Amy had a chance to answer, Hannah swept over. "Excuse me," she said, her eyes fixed on the large, bald creature. "I need to talk to my friend."

"Sorry," Amy smiled at the man. "I'll be back." And she surprised herself by meaning it.

Hannah led Amy outside the Jungle Room, her eyes still fixed on the man. "Who's Uncle Fester over there?"

"Dunno," said Amy. "He seems nice enough," Amy said, turning around. "He just started talking to me."

"You really know how to attract them, don't you?" Hannah said, her eyes still on the man, who now waved back at her. She looked away, but her eyes returned to him quickly. "Listen, bad news."

"What?"

"Liz and David are back from the Islands and rumor has it they're headed here."

"Oh."

"Are you going to stay?"

Amy wasn't sure. "I don't know," she said. "I mean, if I leave, it will look like I still care. But if I stay…"

Just then, Jane approached. "What are you guys talking about?" she asked, then, following Hannah's line of vision, "And who's Uncle Fester?"

"David's coming," said Amy, choking on the words.

"Oh, my God!" Jane grabbed Amy by the shoulders. "Can you see him? Are you ready?"

"I don't think so," Amy said, glancing back into the Graceland. "I'm not sure." The others followed Amy's gaze, just in time to watch Zoë approach the large bald man. They observed in stunned silence as tiny Zoë chatted with him and laughed, and then as both he and Zoë looked toward the doorway. Zoë shook her head, shook his hand, and walked toward them.

"His name is Decklin," Zoë said as she approached. "Decklin Thomas. And it looks like he likes Amy," she said turning to Amy, who blushed and looked away. "He says to come back and join him when you're done over here," she said, and started walking away. Then she stopped and turned around again. "And I have no idea what happened to his hair." With that, she gave a flip of her own platinum locks and disappeared into the fray.

The women were quiet. "Maybe it's time for the 'strangers' talk?" Hannah offered.

Amy, finding herself oddly drawn to the bald man's warm smile and sparkly eyes, walked away from her friends without speaking.

"I'm back," said Amy, and she reclaimed her seat. "I'm Amy," she said, feeling strangely at ease as she offered a hand.

"I know," he smiled, and presented a meaty paw for her to shake. "Decklin. But most people call me Deck."

"It's nice to meet you, Deck."

"Likewise."

"So how did you know…" she asked, nodding in the direction of the casket, where Detective Franks just happened to be standing.

"Franks? Strange story really."

"No. I meant—"

At that moment, Zoë raced over. "Bastard and the Beast closing in at four o'clock," she said. "In case you want to split. Hannah's keeping them busy over by the front door."

Amy started to panic. "I can't stay. I can't see them. Oh, God. Oh, God..."

"I just found a back exit," Jane rushed over, out of breath. "Through the Vegas Chamber." The others just stared at her. "What? No one's in there now." They all nodded that this was okay. "Come on," said Jane, waving Amy on.

Deck reached out for her. "Wait. Can I——"

"I gotta go," Amy said. "Sorry. It was really nice——"

"Now," Jane exclaimed. "They're coming. *Now*!"

"Yeah. You, too," Deck waved. "See you around."

Jane and Amy raced through the halls of Aberdeen's and right into the Vegas Chamber, which was tastefully decorated with silent slot machines and card tables set up with real playing cards and poker chips. In the back of the room was a dazzling "stage" platform, awash in a thousand tiny lights and flanked by two six-foot-tall, sequin-clad, topless showgirl mannequins.

"Wow," said Amy, temporarily stunned.

"That way," said Jane, pointing just beyond the towering headdress of the girl on the left.

"See you tomorrow," Amy said, giving Jane a quick kiss on the cheek and then running off. She pushed through the exit door and reemerged in what she hoped would be a more normal world.

Safely on the street, Amy was a mess of emotions. That amusement park of a funeral parlor. The dead professor. The cops. And coming much too close to running into Liz and David. Not to mention that bald yet oddly compelling whackjob... Decklin. It was enough to set a girl right over the edge.

Feeling calmer with each step she took away from the freak show at Aberdeen's, Amy slowed her stride and began peering into the store windows she passed. She'd never noticed many of the small, quaint little shops that lined this street she must have walked down a thousand times. There was an antique shop and a bait and tackle store. There was a small bakery and a cheese shop.

At the end of the strip there was a second-hand store. This one she was familiar with. Smitty's. David used to buy his clothes in this store and often encouraged her to do the same. She was sure many of the gifts he had purchased for her while they were together had come from here. Yes, she had been here many times with him, dragged against her will to locate bargains. Useless used garbage at irresistible prices. So, as she looked into the window, she was half expecting to see some of the stuff taken from her own apartment up for sale here. There wasn't. But there was something that caught her eye.

Right in the center of the front window, raised above a broken-down eight-track player and a handheld video game from the 1980s, and perched on a pedestal of luscious black velvet, sat the most remarkable pair of shoes Amy had ever seen. She had never been one of those women who went gaga for shoes, but there was something about these—shiny, red leather pumps with a dramatic high heel and an embellishment on the toe that looked like a happy little daisy. She couldn't look away and she surprised herself when she leaned in to get a closer look. She could swear that the shoes had somehow...sparkled. But that couldn't be possible. Could it?

Her heart was racing. Her blood ran hot in her veins. She couldn't understand this strange sensation washing over her. She could barely breathe as she leaned in to read the card that bore the price of these magnificent specimens. So transfixed on the shoes was she, that she hadn't noticed the shopkeeper had come out of the store and was watching her from the front door. Amy leaned in further, squinted her eyes, and then gasped. "Two hundred and fifty dollars?" she shouted. "For that! For shoes?!"

"My dear," the stooped-over old woman said, walking over to her. "These are not just *any* shoes," she exclaimed, looking Amy up and down. "You may be too young to remember, but surely you've heard of Rita Hayworth?"

Amy shrugged an acknowledgment.

"She was a Hollywood legend," the woman said. "These shoes used to belong to her." She took Amy's arm in hers, and they both looked again at the shoes in a state of reverence. "A lot of people don't know the real story of Rita Hayworth," she sighed deeply, as she looked at Amy. "Do you?"

The spell was broken. "You know what? I don't care if Michael Jackson was buried in them," Amy scoffed. "That price is ridiculous!"

The shopkeeper seemed unfazed at the accusation. "Can you really put a price on what makes you feel good, Amy?" she asked. "Can you really attach a limit to what you're worth?"

"H—How did you know my name?" She could not remember ever seeing this woman before any other time she'd been here , and had no idea how she would have known her name. "I don't think…" she started, suspiciously. And she quickly ran off.

As Amy turned the corner of her street, she spotted the Building Boys firmly planted on their stoop. She took a deep breath and put a smile on her face, trying to pass them as quickly as possible.

"Hello, sexy Amy," cooed Angelo.

"Where did you come from, looking all hot like that?" asked Mario.

"Heh. Who's the skirt?" teased Frankie, and they all laughed.

"Hi, guys," she choked out. It was all she could muster.

Tony seemed to sense her unease and he raced to her side. "What's wrong, Miss Amy? Another bad day?"

"Something like that." She smiled weakly.

He moved closer to her, the magnetic Italian machismo of him way too intoxicating as she began to fall under his spell. "Why don't you let Tony take you upstairs?"

She was breathless. "Uh… maybe…" she said.

He was insistent. He licked his full lips and looked her straight in the eyes. "I think Tony knows how to make it all better."

She paused momentarily and without being too obvious about it, took in the shocked looks on the faces of the others. Jazzed up by the madness of the day, especially the last mind-bending moment at the second-hand store, she felt all of it could only be explained one way: She'd gotten herself trapped in a looking glass world and perhaps the only way to make sense of all the "crazy" that surrounded her was to dive right in... Or maybe...

"Maybe another time," she panted, and she darted inside.

5

How Amy and Her Extended Family Celebrated the Holidays

Lauren Austen-Rabinowitz, Jane's mother, had once worked at the same publishing house as Shirley Miller, Amy's mother, which is how the Austen-Rabinowitz and Miller families had become acquainted. But it was Shirley's admission to Lauren that the Millers had no extended family which brought their two families together when Amy was in preschool and Jane a preteen. Since then, the families had become inseparable. Until Eric and Shirley Miller's ill-fated vacation several years before, that is. Now it was just Amy and a mishmash of other random family members who really had no place else to go for holiday events, such as the one Amy was about to attend.

"Hello, Amy," said Carlos, the doorman, as she entered the building.

"Hi, Carlos."

"They are waiting for you," he seemed to chide.

"Yes, I know. I'm late. Thanks." She darted into the elevator and pressed the button for the seventeenth floor.

She didn't know what she had expected to find when the front door of the apartment swung open, but it certainly wasn't what had greeted her: Zoë outfitted in a quasi-Playboy Bunny getup, wearing a set of oversized bunny ears and an expression that could only be described as humiliated. "No. Not Elijah," Zoë called back into the room and then added just for Amy: "Only Vashti."

"Oh, very funny," Amy smirked, as she leaned over to give Zoë a giant hug and kiss.

"I have to find the humor in all this somehow, Auntie Amy. Do you *see* what they have me in this year?" she asked.

"What's wrong? I think you look cute."

"If I was sixteen and decided to wear this myself, my mother would ground me until I left for college. I mean, look at this," she said as she turned around to give Amy a look at her perky cotton tail. "Seriously," she said. Then she looked Amy up and down. "What are *you* wearing?" she asked.

"Why? What's wrong?" Amy asked, immediately self-conscious. "It's just a turtleneck and a jumper."

"A jumper," Zoë repeated, in a flat tone.

"A jumper," Amy replied, wondering what the big deal was.

"Auntie Amy," she shook her little blonde head. "A *jumper* is a person who's given up on life. Someone who sits on a ledge or a bridge somewhere ready to say 'good-bye cruel world' and take a leap. It isn't something you *wear*." She looked away, ashamed. "It's dreadful."

"Zoë!" gasped Jane, who had just come over to welcome the new arrival. "Nice little girls…"

"I know, I know. Nice little girls let their friends walk around looking like bag ladies if that's what makes them happy."

"That's not what I meant, young lady." Quite the opposite of Amy, Jane wore a gauzy yellow sundress with a white, loosely buttoned cardigan sweater casually tossed over it. New white espadrilles adorned her otherwise bare feet, and showcased a bright peach pedicure. She was perfectly dressed for a spring celebration; Amy, on the other hand, was dressed more along the lines of…

"It's Urban Amish," said Zoë.

"Sorry?" both women asked, looking to the girl.

"Urban Amish. I've been trying to figure it out for years and now I know," she said, folding her arms across her chest as she nodded at Amy. "Yep. That's her look."

"Zoë, nice little girls…" Jane stammered, embarrassed, yet more than a little bit intrigued.

"Think about it, Mama. When's the last time you saw Auntie Amy wear any other color but…" she started naming on her fingers, "black, navy blue, beige, gray." She looked to her mother. "Am I missing one?"

"No. It's true," Jane said, looking pained. And then, as though Amy had ruined Zoë in some horrible way and for life, she added, dramatically, "What's wrong with having a little color in your life?"

"There she is!" came a voice from the living room. "There's our Amy!" Saved by the rabbi. Joshua Austen-Rabinowitz, along with Lauren, joined the party at the door, and took Amy into his arms. "Come on in," he said as he hugged her, taking the bottle of wine she'd brought and passing it to Lauren.

"Nice to see you, dear," said Lauren, as she planted polite air kiss on each of Amy's cheeks, and took her hand into her own, which was slightly cold and bony. "You over him yet?"

Amy, caught off guard, smiled weakly. "Oh, well. You know how it is. It takes time. I don't think I've ruled out reconciliation and—"

"I think I have the cure," Lauren cut her off, without emotion. "There's only one cure for a broken heart, you know." And then Lauren let out a boozy, uncharacteristically hearty laugh.

Amy didn't know what she was talking about, but nervously laughed along anyway.

"Come! The egg hunt is about to begin," Joshua beamed, his eyes on his granddaughter. "And our little bunny's done one heck of a job with the hiding this year! Haven't you, Zoë?"

"Sure," said Zoë, wincing as she looked down at her barely covered form.

Following an hour-long egg hunt that essentially consisted of Zoë having to find every single egg she had hidden earlier as the adults found the bottoms of their glasses again and again, the family gathered around the large, festively decorated table in the center of the dining room for the much-anticipated annual Easter-Seder feast.

A spectacular spread was laid out before them—one that celebrated both the Jewish and Christian traditions of the varied members of the Austen-Rabinowitz families assembled. There were miles of matzoh and mountains of maror. There was a rack of lamb and asparagus and roasted rosemary red potatoes. There enough brisket to feed an army. There was challah bread with colored eggs baked into it (though there wasn't a single drop of Italian blood to be accounted for here)—St. Yosef's bread, as Joshua liked to joke. And, to ensure the evening would be rich in tradition, and loose in inhibition, there were four wineglasses set at every place.

"We're at the kids' end," Zoë said to Amy, as she led them to their seats at the foot of the table. "We get to sit with the Happys again," she joked. Amy couldn't help but let a giggle slip, as this could only mean they'd be sharing their end of the table with the gloomiest people she had ever met.

As if the seating order ever changed from event to event, everyone searched out their place cards. Joshua was at the head, with Lauren to his right and Jane to his left. To Jane's left was Joshua's younger brother, Morty, who looked to be about ten years older than he. To his left sat Lauren's ancient Aunt Clarabelle, followed by Amy. On the other side of the table, there was an empty seat next to Lauren, and beyond that sat Joshua's own ancient aunt, Enid. Next to her sat her long-divorced, morbidly morose son, Grant. And next to him sat his miserable thirteen-year-old daughter, Ava, whom, Zoë had explained to Amy as they walked to their seats, she was expected to entertain. Except not even the bunny suit had sparked even a mocking smile.

The doorbell rang and Zoë cringed. Joshua and Lauren grinned at their granddaughter through a haze of pre-dinner wine and Zoë buried her face in her hands.

"Maybe that's Elijah!" slurred Aunt Enid.

"Go on and get it!" screamed Clarabelle, with a hint too much enthusiasm.

"But I'm really not into *any* of this," Zoë pleaded. "I'm a Buddhist."

Everyone laughed, charmed as ever by the adorable little girl. Except for Amy, who gave Zoë a supportive little hug. And except for Grant and Ava. Because Grant and Ava never smiled.

Zoë took a deep breath and slid out of her chair. "I wonder who this could be," she said, monotone as she dragged her feet to the front door and opened it.

"Hi, Zoë," came a man's voice from the other side of the door.

"Oh. Hi, Brendan." Zoë said, bored, as she turned back to the table. "It's just Brendan."

Amy didn't know a Brendan and immediately turned her head toward the front door when she saw how excited the other woman at the table appeared at the mere mention of his name. She nearly choked as he entered, as the man—whom Zoë had dismissed as *just Brendan*—was the most beautiful man Amy had ever seen. Brad Pitt would have looked like a pile of vomit next to this strapping, sandy-haired, green-eyed Adonis. Amy must have been staring, for when Zoë came back to the table, she leaned over and whispered loudly in Amy's ear, "Stop staring." Amy promptly took a sip of water and tried to refocus on the dinner party.

"You can't fall in love with a body," Zoë said pointedly to Amy.

Jane quickly jumped up, urging Uncle Mort to take the seat next to Lauren on the other side of the table. "Come. Sit here," she gushed to the new addition, tapping the seat next to her. "How *are* you, Brendan?"

Lauren stood. "No, dear. He'll sit by me," she said. Jane glared at her mother. "Not for you," Lauren mouthed, as Jane crossed her arms and sulked and Brendan made his way over to Lauren.

Amy leaned toward Zoë. "Who is he and why haven't I met him before? I mean, he's here in your house for the holidays. He must—"

"He's no one. Believe me," Zoë said, letting out an exasperated sigh.

"Seriously. He must be someone special. An actor?"

"He's just a guy Nana found lurking around at Starbucks one day. Some college dropout." Zoë looked at Brendan, who began schmoozing with the others. "He's one of those 'strays' New York liberals like to bring to these kinds of events. You know, just some loser with no family and nothing else to do."

"Oh." Amy looked away, embarrassed.

"Oh, God—I didn't mean *you*, Auntie Amy. Of course you're one of us."

She smiled. "Thanks, Zoë."

"Gooble gobble."

"Huh?"

Before Zoë could explain the reference, Joshua lifted his wineglass and stood. "Now that we are all present and accounted for, we may begin our celebration. The glorious union of centuries-old traditions that could only be possible *here*."

"Cheers, everyone," said Lauren, raising her glass. Everyone drank. And then drank some more as a long, uncomfortable silence followed.

Impatient, Joshua nodded to Zoë. "Come on, child. You should know this cold by now."

Zoë signed deeply and then began. "Right. Sorry," she cleared her tiny throat. "Why is this night different from all other nights?" she said in what had become her trademark monotone this evening.

As the ritual unfolded, Amy tried to sneak a quick inconspicuous glance at Brendan, mortified to find he was staring at her. He waved, throwing her for a bigger loop. She turned her head to make sure no one was standing behind her, causing him to chuckle and shake his head. He waved again and mouthed a small "Hello." She waved back and quickly looked away as the four questions ended.

"Bon appétit," said Lauren, and everyone dove in.

"So, Amy," said Joshua. "Tell everyone how you killed your boss."

"Joshua!" Lauren gasped.

Clarabelle shouted across the table at Enid. "What did he say?" And then to Morty, "What did he *say*?" Morty leaned in and whispered to Clarabelle. "She did what?!" Now Clarabelle gasped.

"Dad! Honestly," said Jane, shaking her head. "Amy didn't *kill* anyone. Her boss choked to death on a cookie."

"How do you choke on a cookie?" asked a puzzled Enid.

"It was a biscotti," Amy chirped, thinking this would help somehow.

"Oh," said Enid, as if it had.

"Pappy, come on," laughed Zoë. "Amy's not a killer. I mean, seriously. Just look at her outfit." Now Ava looked Amy up and down, and nodded in agreement when Zoë added, "Doesn't exactly scream 'femme fatale'."

"Zoë Mary-Alice Austen-Rabinowitz!"

"I kind of dig a chick in a jumper," said Brendan from across the table. "Seriously," he said, as if no one believed him.

"I still don't see how you could choke to death on a cookie," said Enid, looking worriedly at Grant, who had just taken a large bite of a macaroon. Sensing his mother's displeasure, he immediately tossed the macaroon back onto his plate. When she turned away, he picked it up again, considered it, and shoved the rest of the cookie into his mouth.

"I'm Brendan," Brendan waved to Amy. "I think I was invited here to meet you, right?" he asked, now looking around. Lauren pretended to be looking at her fingernails when his eyes fell on her. He smiled again at Amy. "You know, I've hated every boss I ever had. So I have to say, it's especially nice to meet you."

Amy flushed bright red. "Well, thanks. But I didn't kill—"

"You never did like that Heimlich, did you?" asked Joshua.

"And those shoes," said Ava, out of nowhere, and miraculously now smiling at Zoë. "Yes, I see. I think I know exactly what you mean—"

"Speaking of shoes," said Amy, coughing as she desperately tried to change the subject. "I had the strangest experience yesterday with a pair of shoes."

"Really," said Zoë, now enjoying an audience with Ava. "Because I—"

"Zoë!" shouted Jane.

Amy cleared her throat and continued. "I was walking by Smitty's—you know, that second-hand store down on the strip?"

"Yes!" exclaimed Clarabelle. "Such bargains. I bought this scarf there and for such a bargain," she nodded to Enid, who looked crossly at Clarabelle. Clarabelle looked away and absently tugged at the hairs on her chin.

"Right. Well, anyway," Amy continued. "There were these shoes there, shoes like I'd never seen before. They were red and so shiny and..." she drifted off. "I can't explain it."

"Did you buy them?" Ava craned her neck to look under the table.

Zoë joined her. "Those aren't them, are they?" asked Zoë. "Because you know those aren't *red*, right?" Zoë taunted, and Ava actually laughed.

"I don't get it," said Brendan.

"What? No." said Amy, getting annoyed that Zoë was entertaining Ava at her expense.

"Well *did* you?" asked Grant. "Did you buy them?"

"That's the ridiculous part," Amy said. "They were two hundred and fifty dollars. *Used.* I mean, could you imagine?" she looked around for support from the other women, but not even Jane would look at her. "You don't think that's just a little ridiculous?"

"What price can you put on what you're worth?" asked Morty, seemingly to the air.

Amy was amazed. "That's so weird," she said. "That's kind of what the saleslady said," and she looked around for a response. She got none. "Anyway, she also said that the shoes had belonged to Rita Hayworth, like that was supposed to decide it."

"Rita Hayworth," mused Joshua. "Now that's a name you never hear anymore. Big in my day, but—"

"Dad, you're in your sixties," said Jane. "Were you even *born* when *Gilda* came out?"

"Well, in my father's day maybe. But, oy. What a knockout she was. Hair red as fire. And the most gorgeous set of—"

"Pappy!"

"Sorry. Well... Anyway, tragic story. Tragic girl," he shook his head. "Started out bad," he said, draining the wine from the bottom of his glass. "Drunken horrible parents," he said, and poured himself another. "Ended badly."

"What happened?" asked Amy.

"Drank herself crazy," said Clarabelle, grabbing another bottle from the table and filling her glass. "Alzheimer's and a slow death."

"Abusive childhood. Bad marriages," said Joshua. "Divorced five times," he said, looking right at Grant.

"And here I thought one was a pain in the ass," Jane smirked.

Grant was not amused. "Sometimes once is enough," he chortled, and looked as though he would burst into tears at any moment. "It's like being cut off at the waist. Every day a new struggle. I just don't—"

"Oh, are you still sensitive about that? Sorry." Jane said snidely. She collected some dirty plates from the table as Grant glared at her.

"Let me help you with that," said Brendan. She blushed and as he followed her into the kitchen.

Zoë looked at her grandparents and then back at Amy. And then at her grandparents. And then back at Amy.

Joshua reflected for a moment and stood. "I have to agree. Two hundred and fifty is too much for a pair of shoes," he said, as Lauren coolly looked the other way. She stood, collected more dirty plates, and headed for the kitchen. Joshua dutifully piled up the plates in front of him and followed.

Zoë waited for her grandparents to be out of earshot before she leaned in and said, "Except he didn't tell you the important part."

"What do you mean?" asked Morty.

"The legend," said Zoë. "About the shoes?"

"I don't think I know anything about the shoes," said Enid.

Now they all looked to Zoë, as they often did. "Well, from what I read," she began, and looked around.

Clarabelle leaned over to Morty, "That child is always reading," she nodded. "She would know."

"From what I read, Rita Hayworth was kind of plain and boring when she was young," Zoë said. "A little like you, Auntie Amy."

"Thanks."

"But then she made a decision that would change her life. She fell in love with a pair of shoes. A very *expensive* pair of shoes. And, after passing them in a store window day after day on her way back and forth from her job in a factory during the height of the Great Depression, she decided she just had to have them."

"But how could she afford—"Grant started to ask.

"She always had to give all her earnings to her father on payday, it's true—"

"So he could drink it!" growled Enid, in disgust, and then swallowed down the rest of the wine in her glass.

Zoë smiled. "That's right. But this one week, she decided *no*. That it was *her* money and that she would spend it the way she wanted to. So..."

"So?" Ava wanted to know.

"So she stopped in the store and bought the shoes."

A collective gasp came from the group.

"And her father?" asked Clarabelle. "What did she tell her father?"

"She pretended she got mugged," said Zoë.

"Did he believe her?" asked Amy.

"Oh, no," said Zoë.

"Then what?" asked Morty.

Zoë looked around before speaking. "Then he beat her, of course."

Another gasp.

"But it never mattered again, because after that, everything changed," said Zoë. "Margarita, her real name, went out in the shoes the very next day, and she met Darryl Zanuck."

"You mean the big Hollywood producer?" asked Enid.

"The same," said Zoë. "He offered her a role in his latest film, and she left for Hollywood two weeks later."

"I heard that story!" said Clarabelle. "I remember that!"

"I don't quite remember it like that," said Morty, looking a little confused.

There was a moment of silent reflection, but only a moment.

"Are you going to buy the shoes, Amy?" asked Clarabelle.

"They could be the ones!" gushed Enid.

"Buy the shoes, Amy!" urged Ava.

Amy tried to make sense of it all, while trying to pull herself out of the spotlight. "I don't think I knew any of that, Zoë. Thanks. But two hundred fifty dollars for shoes. I mean, *come on*."

"Some people just don't understand the power of shoes," Lauren said, catching the end of the conversation.

"Personally, I don't think all that much of it," said Zoë. "Yet I can't scientifically rule it out."

Brendan returned with Joshua. Jane, looking annoyed, walked a few steps behind them.

"So who's taking over for Heimlich?" Joshua asked.

"Right now? His classes are being covered by a few of his graduate students and some other members of the department. But going forward—"

"What about you?" Lauren asked. "Are you taking on any of them?"

"Me?" Amy blushed. "Oh, no. I couldn't possible teach his classes."

"But don't you have a Masters degree in English Lit?" asked Lauren.

"All she has to do is defend her dissertation at this point and then it's PhD all the way."

"Jane!" said Amy, horrified.

"Well, I'm sorry, Amy. But it's true. She downplays how far she's gotten, and how brilliant her paper was. All she needs to do now is defend it."

All eyes were now on her. "I have a little, uh, stage fright."

"Perhaps if you had the shoes…" mused Clarabelle.

"What's that?" asked Joshua.

"Oh nothing, Pappy," said Zoë. "Don't worry about it."

After dinner everyone moved into the living room for coffee. Jane sat down on the couch next to Amy and tucked her feet under her as she sipped her tea. She reached out and gave Amy a gentle stroke on the arm. "How are you doing?" she asked.

"I'm okay," said Amy.

"Hey, I'm sorry about before. About your dissertation. I didn't mean to throw you under the bus like that."

"I think that was the least of my problems at that dinner, honestly."

"I know," she said. "But I was serious about what I said, Amy. Not everyone makes it as far as you have, and it kills me sometimes that you don't just go and finish it up already."

"I've been busy," said Amy. "I mean, until about a couple of weeks ago or so."

Jane gave her a gentle hug. "I know, I know. How are you feeling about all that?"

"Dunno," she replied. "I guess it takes time. Honestly, I still don't believe this thing with Liz is real. And I know in my heart of hearts that he will see that and he *will* come back and—"

"Your heart is lying to you, Amy. It's only holding you back. And has been for some time."

"I don't think you understand—"

"Don't I? Look, kiddo, sometimes men leave. And sometimes they make shocking choices when they do."

"We really never saw that coming, with Elliot. Did we?"

"I'm sure there were clues along the way. And hey, stranger things have happened. Right?"

"Even Jabba the Hutt couldn't beat—"

"Let's just say his working at home wasn't the best idea for that marriage and leave it at that."

"That and running a business that involved daily deliveries."

"Dirty deliveries," Jane mused. They looked at each other and laughed. "It's tough, you know. Getting past having a life with someone. But once you start to see the difference between the person who you actually are and the one you were trying to be, it does get easier. Unless you're Grant," Jane added, watching Grant as he stared out the window onto the street, his mother repeatedly tapping his back and whispering "There, there."

Amy gave Jane a puzzled look. "I'm not sure what you mean," she said. "I think I've always been the same person."

Jane smiled. "You'll get there. It takes time, but you'll get there." She gave Amy a gentle squeeze. "So what are you going to do about the shoes?"

"Huh?"

"The shoes. Clarabelle told me the story Zoë told you guys."

Amy shook her head in astonishment. "Tell me, how does that kid know so many things? I mean, how could she possibly have so much information in that little head?"

"God only knows. She comes from a long line of intellectuals is my only guess."

"Except for Elliot."

"Oh, definitely not Elliot," Jane laughed. "Speaking of intellectuals," joked Jane as Brendan walked by the girls and smiled. Then she got serious. "He likes you, you know," she told Amy. "Brendan does. He told me. In the kitchen. In front of my parents even," she smirked. "Sorry you missed it."

"Sounds like it was a real moment," Amy teased.

"Oh, you bet," she chuckled. "Unforgettable. I guess you can have this one."

"Oh, thanks. But I don't think I'm ready…"

"Then don't *think*," said Jane "The Universe is offering you a gift. Just take it."

Now Brendan approached.

"I'll see you later," said Jane, and she stood up and walked off.

Brendan took Jane's place on the couch next to Amy, and the charge of attraction she felt nearly caused her to faint. "So did you really kill your boss?" he asked, and she was sure starlight shone out of his eyes.

She had to look away. "No, not really."

"Did you want to?" Brendan asked, flirtingly.

"Sometimes, I guess," she said, and smiled nervously. "I mean, really. Who doesn't want to kill their boss sometimes?"

"Can I take you to dinner some time?" he asked.

Amy looked over at Lauren, Jane, Clarabelle, and Enid, who were all standing together and nodding her on.

"Give me your address. I'll pick you up on Friday at eight?" he said.

Now Zoë and Ava had joined them and they were all nodding so wildly, she thought their heads might pop off at any moment if they kept it up any longer. (In fact, Zoë did nod her bunny ears right off.) So she turned back to Brendan. "Sure," she smiled, and reached into her bag, where she rifled around a while for something she couldn't find because, as usual, it wasn't there. "You have a pen?"

Very full and slightly drunk, Amy took the long way home so she could pass Smitty's. The shoes were still in the window, majestic on their velvet pedestal, though the eight-track player and the video game had now been replaced by an aquarium with a crack in the frame and an ancient Mr. Coffee, respectively. She didn't see the shopkeeper watching her from inside as she paused before them.

Sure enough, the feeling was still there. It burned and gushed and tingled within her when she looked at the shoes. It was a feeling of euphoria. Of magic. Of falling in love, but more special somehow. More pure. She leaned in hoping the price had changed, but it hadn't. She stood a while longer, admiring, contemplating. And then she walked on, never noticing the other woman's eyes on her, or the shock of coarse, tangled, reddish-silver hair that had escaped the kerchief the shopkeeper wore.

6

How Amy Got a Surprising New Boss

As she cleaned out his office after the weekend, Amy wondered what had happened to all the so-called loved ones who had attended Heimlich's wake and funeral. Not a single soul had volunteered to come in and sort through his personal effects. Perhaps it was all part of an elaborate penance devised for her, she reasoned, as she trudged through mountains of files and books, a lifetime of literature lessons.

Well, if it was a penance, she was glad for it. As she opened each file and read the scrawled, sometimes scathing notes he made about his students, their papers, even the works of some authors she admired and cherished, she felt a small pang of relief that Heimlich wouldn't be scrawling notes anymore. With each file she tossed, the weight of Heimlich's death seemed to lighten for her. And when she found her last employment review, in which he referred to her as "overqualified," "scattered," and "underachieving," with one "well-meaning", a couple of "earnests", and even a random "cute" thrown in for no good reason, she felt the smallest pang of remorse that she hadn't played a more active role in his demise.

She was just topping off another blue recycling bin when Hannah barged in. "This looks like fun," she said, pushing a stack of books aside to sit on a corner of Heimlich's desk.

"Someone has to do it."

"I guess you're right." Hannah said. For a second Amy thought Hannah might have come to help, but Hannah continued to sit and watch as Amy pulled open another drawer and began sifting through its contents.

Hannah's hovering presence soon became irritating and Amy looked up at her. "Do you need something?"

"I was just wondering, um, what was the name of the tour company your parents went to the rain forest with?"

"You mean Jungle Jimmy's? Why?"

"No reason. Just making conversation."

"Huh," said Amy, and she went back to her task. Hannah didn't leave.

"So you wouldn't happen to know where they were located or anything? You know, like in Brazil, or in—"

"Uh, I don't think so."

"No, I don't suppose you would." Hannah continued to sit at on the edge of the desk, now swinging her legs back and forth, kicking the side of the desk every few seconds or so. Amy tried to ignore her. "So…"

"What?"

"I found out they just hired someone to replace Heimlich."

"Who?" Amy asked.

Hannah was quiet for a minute, which made Amy incredibly nervous. She was terrified that she may possibly have remembered that at some point a long, long ago, Liz French had been a professor of English…

"You'll see," said Hannah as she darted out.

Amy took a deep breath and went back to her task. If Liz was her new boss, well, she'd just have to jump off that bridge when she got to it.

She moved the two-drawer filing cabinet she had just emptied to make sure nothing had fallen behind it. Nothing had, but there was something there, strangely enough. A small door—not unlike the first door Alice encountered when she landed in Wonderland, Amy thought.

Amy tried turning the knob and found the door was locked. So she reached up onto the desk for a letter opener, and began prying away at the lock. At last it clicked open and she pulled at the door, only to find another mystery: a small steamer trunk. She pulled it out and, saw that it too was locked, so out came her trusty letter opener again.

As she tried to pick open the lock, the tip of the letter opener slipped and stabbed her in the finger. "Shit," she said, and opened Heimlich's top drawer, where she knew he kept his stash of Band-Aids. She opened one and wrapped it around her fingertip. "Huh," she said, realizing she may have just solved the mystery of Heimlich's Band-Aid wrapped fingertips.

She sat back down on the floor and tried the lock again. This time, it clicked open and the lid flipped up, revealing the contents: a sequined Elvis costume, a black Elvis wig, what seemed like hundreds Elvis of CDs, and then, underneath these, a collection of six antique bisque dolls. Under the dolls, there was another locked section that she was just about to start picking when she got interrupted.

"Now that's shocking."

Amy looked up, shocked herself for a moment to see the hulking bald guy from the funeral parlor standing over her. "You mean the dolls or the secret stash of CDs?" Nothing seemed to make sense anymore.

"Not really either," he said, joining her on the floor. He pulled a couple of dolls out of the trunk and made them dance with each other. "I just would have thought vinyl. For both."

"Good point," she nodded, and then caught herself. "Hey, wait. What are you doing here?"

"Me?" he smiled, his eyes still as warm as the other day. "Oh, I'm just on an errand for my old pal, Detective Franks. He wanted to know if you'd return to the scene of the crime. It seems you…"

Amy froze, and Deck let out a hearty laugh.

"Oh, very funny," she said, snatching back Heimlich's dolls from him and stuffing everything back into the trunk. She closed it, pushed it back into its hiding spot, and slammed the little door. "Seriously, what are you doing here?"

He stood and offered his hand to help her up. "I work here, actually," he said. "Turns out, I'm replacing old Heimlich," he explained, with a glint of mischief in his warm, somewhat wonderful eyes. "Which I guess makes me your boss."

Amy relaxed slightly, thinking this would have to be better than working for Liz. "Small world,'" she said, and she pushed the filing cabinet back in front of the door.

"Most things are small to me."

"You are kind of tall, aren't you."

"Not that tall. Not *freakishly* tall," he said, and she had to look away on the word "freakishly."

"Not going to give the trunk to the family?"

"Dunno. It seems too weird, you know? I say let Heimlich have his secrets."

"If you say so. Oh, which reminds me..." Deck reached into his pocket and pulled out a folded sheet of paper. "Here," he said, handing it to her. "You're going to need this."

She took the paper from his enormous hands and began unfolding it. "What is this?" she asked.

"Oh, just a list of things I may be allergic to," he smiled.

She smirked at him. "Ah," she said, as she scanned the list. "Well I'll be sure there's always plenty of cantaloupe around here then."

He smiled. "So all his stuff's still here, huh?"

"Yeah," she sighed. "No one contacted me about what to do with it and I'm not sure who to call."

"So you're not tampering with the crime scene then?"

"Are we back to that now?"

He laughed. "If you're going to work for me, you're going to have to lighten up."

"I don't think I do 'light' all that well."

"What do you mean? You must be, what, ninety pounds. Just look at you," he smiled. "I bet if I blew on you I could make you fly."

"I don't think anyone should be blowing anyone around here," she said, embarrassed at the realization that the double meaning she had not intended had indeed been interpreted by Deck as such.

"Too bad," was all he said with an impish grin. She wanted to die.

"That reminds me of something that came up at Easter Seder," she blurted out, trying desperately to change the subject.

"Sorry?"

"Easter Seder," she said, now a little impatient. "Oh, forget it. It's a long story."

He was intrigued.

"I have time," he said, and sat in Heimlich's chair, elbows on the desk and leaning forward, his square chin resting in his massive hands. She hadn't noticed he had a dimple on his chin before. Very John Travolta. John Travolta made up to play Daddy Warbucks.

She relaxed. "Okay, well, remember my friend from the wake?"

"Not the tall, frizzy-haired girl?"

Amy shook her head. "No, not her. I'm not exactly sure I'm friends with Hannah. I meant the mother of the girl you were talking to."

"Oh, right. The little one. The little woman, I mean."

"She's not that little," Amy snapped defensively. "She's more than five feet tall. I mean, just over five feet..."

"Everything is small to me, remember?"

"Fair enough," said Amy. "Anyway, that's Jane. Jane Austen-Rabinowitz, actually."

"Interesting name."

"I suppose," she replied. "Anyway, we've been best friends since we were kids."

"Okay..."

"Her mother, Lauren, is your classic textbook WASP. The whole Martha Stewart-Connecticut-holiday-traditions-are-sacred type. When she told her family she was marrying Joshua, it was a total scandal. But Joshua—"

"The Rabinowitz?"

"Yes. Well, he's Jewish, as you can imagine. But he was never religious. And before they married, he was fine to go along with whatever Lauren and her family wanted. He would ignore all his traditions and his Judaism and be whatever she wanted him to be.

All he asked was that she promise to love him until the day he died," she trailed off.

"Still in love?"

"So in love. Like my parents were. Joined at the waist really."

"Huh."

"What?"

"I'm just going to let that one go," he flashed another mischievous grin.

"Okay," she smiled in spite of herself. "Anyway, one day he was rushing off to work and he got hit by a bus."

"Holy shit."

"Holy shit is right. Because after that, he had what he calls his 'epiphany.' When he woke up in the hospital, tubes coming out of everywhere, he realized he had forsaken his faith and did a total one-eighty, wearing his tallit and yarmulke around like they were accessories, lighting his menorah on Christmas Eve. You know, crazy stuff like that."

"A born-again Jew?"

"Exactly," she said.

"And his wife?"

"Well, you can imagine this didn't sit well with Lauren and her family. It wasn't what she signed up for, you know?"

"Sure."

"But she loved Joshua, desperately, and she wanted to stay married to him. So she devised a way to make his new overt Jewishness slip right into their lives."

"I think I'm starting to understand..."

"She created all these new traditions that combine elements of what they each like from each other's holidays, and made the holidays as they thought they should be."

"Easter Seder."

"They think they're very progressive about it all."

"So what exactly do they do on holidays? Sit around and read passages from *The DaVinci Code*?" "They're very really nice people," she said. "Like second parents to me." "So what are your own parents? Muslim Wiccans?"

"That's just weird," she smiled. "Actually, it's not something I like to talk about."

"Sorry," he said. "Perhaps another time."

"Perhaps."

"So was all that just an elaborate smoke screen or does something in this story remind you of 'blowing people over'?" he teased. She looked away, annoyed that he wouldn't just let it go.

An uncomfortable silence fermented between them, and Deck opted to make it worse. "What about your fiancé? How did he—"

"You mean my ex-fiancé?"

"Yes. How are you doing with all of that, by the way? I kind of pieced together that—"

"I'm not sure that's any of your business."

"I guess it isn't. Sorry. I guess I just know how it feels to have your heart ripped out and run over. I didn't mean anything by it."

Now she felt bad. "Why? What happened to you?" she asked.

"Don't worry about it," he said, clearing his throat. "So I guess now's a good time to get down to business."

"Right," said Amy, surprised at her disappointment in him clamming up. She could swear there were tears cresting his beautiful eyes, but she decided not to press it. "So what do you expect of me."

The grin returned. "That's a heady statement."

"Oh God, here we go again," she said, blushing slightly. "For work, I mean. The job."

"Uh-huh…"

"*This* job," she said, now a bit flustered. "Can't you be serious for a minute?"

"Not really," he said.

She looked away, clearly flustered.

"I'm sorry. I didn't mean to make you uncomfortable," he said, his eyes now sparkling. "Why don't you finish up here?" he said. "I'll grab us a couple of coffees and we can talk when I get back?"

"Okay," she smiled.

Later that evening, on her way home from work, Amy walked by Smitty's and stopped in front of the window yet again. The shoes were still there on their pedestal. They were still magnificent. They were still calling out to her—and, apparently, so was the old woman inside. "For Christ's sake already," she shouted from the doorway and then hobbled outside. "I'll give them to you for two-twenty-five."

Amy didn't take her eyes off the shoes even to blink as she replied, "Deal."

7

How Amy Went Out with Brendan and Rediscovered Sex

Amy had just come out of the shower when she heard her front door open. "We're here," Jane shouted from the foyer. So Amy greeted Jane and Zoë dripping wet and in a towel. "I just used my key," said Jane apologetically. "I hope that was okay?"

"No problem," said Amy. "You know that. But what are you guys doing here?"

Jane and Zoë looked at each other, and Zoë shook her head. "Your date?" Zoë said.

"Yes?"

Jane and Zoë looked at each other again. Now it was Jane's turn to speak. "Honey, you don't honestly think we would let you get ready for this on your own, do you?"

Amy was perplexed. "Jane, just because you're a mother, it doesn't make you everyone's mother."

"Auntie Amy, you need us. You know you do."

"I think——"

"I think you could use our help," said Jane and she and Zoë looked at one another again. And then Jane looked back at Amy. "First of all, what are you going to wear?"

Zoë said, "Mama, you know she has nothing to wear."

"Right," smirked Amy. "I'm Urban Amish."

"Not that there's anything wrong with that," said Jane, looking chidingly at Zoë.

"Well for your information, I was thinking about taking a shopping trip," Amy said as she walked into her bedroom. She reemerged with a shopping bag. "So I could find something to wear with…" she said as she reached into the bag like a magician reaches into a hat and pulled out… "These!"

"Rita Hayworth's shoes?" Zoë remarked, impressed.

"Oh, my God!" squealed Jane. "They're gorgeous!"

"Worth every penny," said Zoë. "Truly."

"You really went through with it. Good for you!" said Jane.

Zoë approached and craned her small neck to examine the shoes. "You're sure they're authentic?" she asked.

Jane shook her head. "Oh, what does it matter? Put them on. Please."

Amy slipped her feet into the shoes and paraded around the living room in only the shoes and her towel.

"You look like a stripper!" Zoë gushed.

"Zoë!" Jane gasped. "Nice little girls—"

"What? Don't compliment their friends when they look hot?"

"No. Nice little girls *your age* don't know what exotic dancers are for a start," she said, and then softened. "But nice girls *do* compliment their friends, it's true."

"I've never seen a stripper, Mama. Just read about one. Promise," she waxed angelic.

"Can we take you shopping, Amy?" asked Jane. "It would be so much fun!"

"And a makeover!" exclaimed Zoë. "Mama, please tell her she needs a makeover."

"Okay, and a makeover, too," smiled Amy.

"How about for you, too, Mama?" said Zoë.

"Really? You think…"

"Mama has a new boyfriend, you know," Zoë said, smugly.

"You do?" asked Amy. "Who?"

Jane blushed. "It's nothing, really. It's no one."

"His name is Ollie and he's a cop!"

Jane shook her head. "He's a detective, actually." She looked at Amy. "I was going to tell you, but really, it's nothing."

"Not yet!" beamed Zoë.

"A detective?"

"You know him, actually," she said. "This is so embarrassing. It's the guy who was investigating Heimlich's death."

"The guy with the crazy moustache? Franks?!"

"That's him, yes."

"I don't understand…"

"I was going to tell you. It just didn't seem that significant. He came around a couple of times afterwards, you know, asking questions about you. And after that, I guess he just kept coming around."

"Like *every* day," said Zoë.

"Anyway, do you think you can babysit for me next week? Ollie wants to take me out to dinner and my parents have other plans."

"Sure," Amy smiled. "No problem. Looks like things may be looking up for all of us then, huh?"

"Looks like it," said Zoë. "But not while you're looking like this. Let's go now. Please?"

Five hours later, a blonder, more gorgeous, and saddled-with-shopping-bags Amy walked up to her apartment building. Predictably, but comforting in its way, the Boys were planted on the stoop. But instead of calling out to her as she approached, they just parted to let her pass. She was surprised to feel sad about not having their attention, especially now, but even more surprised when Angelo politely regarded her as "Ma'am."

"Ma'am?" She flipped around. "Who are you calling 'ma'am?"

"Miss Amy, it is you?" said Frankie, as he stuck out his hand and nodded to Mario. Mario shook his head and reached into his pocket.

"What's with the new look?" Angelo wondered.

"Dunno. I guess I was bored with the old one," she said. And then tentatively, "You like it?"

"I think you look great," said Frankie, as he counted the stack of bills he'd won from Mario, and slipped them into his pocket.

"I kind of liked you the way you were," remarked a sulking Tony.

65

"I have a date," she confessed, and they all nodded.

"That him?" asked Mario, nodding to a figure making its way toward the building.

"Holy shit. What time is it?" she panicked.

"Go ahead," said Tony. "We'll stall him."

She hesitated a moment, unsure of what that would mean coming from Tony.

"We got it covered," said Mario. "Hurry up."

"Okay," she stalled, and Frankie waved her in. "Thanks, guys!" she said and she darted inside.

Amy flew into her apartment, tossed her shopping bags in her bedroom, tore one open, and dressed in a somewhat clingy white and pink minidress. Then she raced to the closet to pull out the finishing touch: Her beautiful shoes. As she crossed the room, she caught her reflection in the mirror and she smiled. She stood up stick strait as she took in the new her. She was happy.

Then she remembered that Brendan was only seconds away. "Oh no!" she said, and darted around to finish getting ready.

Nearly breathless from getting dressed so quickly, she entered the living room and waited for the buzzer. *Where was he?*

As the minutes passed, she became sure he had changed his mind, that he'd realized finally that a guy that good-looking didn't date mousy girls like her. Except she wasn't a mousy girl anymore, was she? As she sat, she watched her foot tilt back and forth in its amazing shoe, and another explanation occurred to her. The Building Boys scared him away. In a panic, she flew to the window and looked outside. They were all there; Brendan was not. She slumped into a chair just as her buzzer rang. She hadn't realized she had been holding her breath until she rose to answer the door.

"Wow," said Brendan as she let him in. "You look amazing!"

"Thanks," she said shyly, quietly praying the heat she now felt in her face at the sight of him wasn't manifesting as red blotches on either cheek.

"And the shoes. You got the shoes?" he asked.

"You noticed," she said.

"Baby, I thought they'd be hot," he said, smarmily, and licked his luscious lips. "But they are *sin*-sational!"

"Uh," she paused. He smiled at her and motioned to the front door and she froze where she stood. And then that starlight shone out of his eyes again and she decided to ignore anything else that came out of his mouth for as long as she could stand it.

Twenty minutes later, Amy and Brendan entered a Japanese restaurant on Northern Boulevard where she and Jane had eaten many times before. She never came here with David, however, because she never went out to dinner with David. The restaurant was expansive and loud and decorated like a Japanese garden, with seating outside in the back in an actual Japanese garden, though Amy knew the restaurant, like most of the pizza restaurants, taco stands and sushi restaurants in the neighborhood, was Korean-owned.

"So you used to come here with your ex?" Brendan asked.

"My ex?" she replied, defensively.

"I'm sorry," he said. "I didn't mean to pry. Lauren told me some things."

"Oh," she said. "What did she tell you?"

"Not much. Just that you were in a bad relationship for a long time," he said as he reached for his menu, "and that you haven't had sex for about five years," and opened it.

"She said——"

"Don't worry," he smiled, looking up, smiling a lascivious grin that sent a crackling of electricity to her nether regions. "I know how to fix that."

Amy was horrified. Not only was this guy already expecting sex at the end of the date, she was almost positive she was going to give it to him. He was breathtaking after all, like perfection itself had been poured into a mold of sensuality and hardened into an exquisite, god-like form. Now if only he would stop talking…

"That came out all wrong. Sorry. I'm not expecting to sleep with you tonight," he said.

"Oh," she replied, relaxing a little but also feeling somewhat disappointed. "My ex never came here," she explained. "He didn't believe in restaurants."

Brendan stared blankly at her. "I don't get it."

"He didn't think it made sense to spend money on having someone else prepare and serve your food when these were things people should be able to do for themselves."

"Huh," he grunted. She could feel her clothes peeling off, piece by piece in his head, as he stared at her from across the table. He grunted. "Still don't get it."

"It's not important," she said, hoping her attraction to him wasn't too apparent. "And honestly, I'd rather not talk about him anymore."

"Fair enough," Brendan said, and the salacious grin he now wore indicated to her that the last article of her clothing had indeed been removed in his tiny mind.

"So what do you do for a living, Brendan?" she asked, admittedly breathless, as she opened her menu.

"I'm in sales. Or at least I used to be. Now I don't work."

"Oh."

"Had to get out before I killed my boss," he winked. "You know how that is."

"Yes," she said, and cringed a little. "So where did you go to school?"

"Bayside High."

"No, I mean after that."

"After? Are you kidding. I couldn't wait to get out of school. I mean, my folks made me do a couple of semesters at Queens, but wow. Not for me. I mean... I'm supposed to *pay* for that? I didn't like it when it was free."

"Oh," she said.

He leaned across the table and clasped her hand and she nearly jumped out of her skin. "But does any of that really matter?" he asked, in a tone so seductive that she began to feel that it really didn't matter at all what he said or would say ever again. Something that had lain dormant in her for so long was starting to awaken. There was a pull across the table, a pull so electric she felt like her skin was on fire. Like he was in possession of some erotic remote control device that fueled all of her most scandalous desires. It was almost too much to bear.

Then Zoë's little voice sounded in her head, "You can't fall in love with a body."

"Brendan, will you excuse me?" she said, nearly panting. "I have to use the ladies'," she said, lifting herself out of her chair and grabbing her purse.

"No problem, gorgeous," he winked. "I'll be right here, waiting for you."

Amy made it to the bathroom door, but instead of going in, she made a quick left toward the exit and darted outside. She scrambled up Northern Boulevard and onto 192nd Street, and then broke into a sprint.

Thankful that the Boys seemed to have something else to do this evening, she ran into her building and up to her apartment. Safely inside, she secured the lock, both dead bolts, and the chain. She headed into the kitchen, where she opened a bottle of cabernet and poured herself a full glass.

Twenty minutes later, there was gentle knocking on her front door. "Amy? Are you okay? It's Brendan."

She didn't say anything.

"You took off so quickly. Are you sick? Do you need me to call an ambulance?"

Still quiet.

"Babe, I know you're here. Angelo told me," he said. "They watched you come in. They let me in. Let me help you."

She opened the door. "I'm not sick."

"Then why did you take off like that?" he asked and moved close to her. Very close to her. So close, she could feel the heat radiating from his manhood.

"I'm just a little overwhelmed I guess," she breathed. "It's just been so long and I...I'm not sure..."

He pressed up against her and she felt as if all of her joints were going to give, that she was going to fall right into him, and that she was powerless to resist any of it. He kissed her, gently at first, and then in a way that spoke his full intent. She kissed him back, hungry for it—for his kiss, the feel of his body, desperate to be ravaged by him.

And even while being with him violated all common sense, *not* being with him was an outrage to her other senses. She already knew how he looked and the seductive rhythm of his voice, despite the banality of the words that voice spoke. But the way he smelled when he held her close. The bristly, rugged texture of his skin. His hot breath on her neck and the taste of him…

Her body trembled as he kissed her so skillfully. So ardently. Just the swirling of the tip of his tongue on her lips had caused a stirring down below. A tingling she had all but forgotten could exist within her. She had no other choice but to give in.

Brendan swept her up in his incredibly sculpted arms as he continued kissing her. Her entire body was alive. He brought her to the bedroom and gingerly laid her down on her bed, where he treated her to a thousand tiny, euphoric deaths before collapsing in her arms.

She held him close and nuzzled into his luscious neck and breathed him in. David seemed as remote to her now as the Congo. If only Brendan had been a mute.

"Baby, driving you is like driving a Beemer," he, well, beamed.

Feeling the best defense would be a quick offense, Amy mounted him again, pressing her lips firmly against his to silence him.

Later that night, he turned to her and said, "I gotta get going. I hope we can do this again," he said, and kissed her.

She smiled. "I don't see why not." Although she could see all the many reasons swirling around them like a swarm of mosquitoes.

He got up and she watched his incredible body as he dressed himself. All the taut muscles and perfect skin glistening in the moonlight. A Calvin Klein underwear ad right there in her bedroom. A gorgeous specimen of physical perfection.

He took up an eyeliner pencil and piece of paper from her dresser and scribbled something down. He handed it to her. "Here you go," he smiled. "I hope you'll use this. A lot."

She grabbed it from him and smiled. She read what he had written and was puzzled. "I didn't know you spelled your name with an 'i'," she said.

"Huh," he said, as he grabbed the paper back from her and shook his head. "Why do I always do that?"

8

How Amy Learned Some Interesting—and Less Interesting—Facts About Her Friends, Deck, and the Terrible Acoustics in Her Office

"So what if he can't spell his own name. Sounds like it was a miracle of a night. Just what you needed," Jane said on the other end of the phone.

"He's very sweet. Really. But he's kind of a pinhead."

"Is he small where it counts?"

"Well. No. But he hasn't read a book since high school. Even then—"

"Look kiddo, not everyone's going to satisfy you on all levels. David read all the time but he was deadwood in bed—your assessment, not mine."

"Still. I have to believe it's possible to have both."

"Sex and Sophocles."

"Something like that."

"You don't have to *love* him, Amy. Sheesh. Just *enjoy* him."

"I do enjoy him. I guess I do."

"So, are you going to see him again?"

Amy looked up to see Hannah hovering again. "Gotta go. Hannah's here. Call you later."

"What?" Amy snapped at Hannah, and actually felt bad about how harshly.

"I came to say good-bye," Hannah said. "Well, I mean not now. But soon."

"You have a new job?"

"Not exactly. An expedition," she said, her eyes lighting up. "Did I ever tell you that there are more than forty tribes in Amazonia that have never had any contact whatsoever with the civilized world? At all? I mean, who knows what kinds of peoples are hanging out down there in the jungle, just waiting to be discovered! It's…" Hannah gushed, then sensing her enthusiasm was one-sided, she shook her head dismissively. "Boring, really. You wouldn't care."

"No. Probably not," Amy said distractedly, not looking up. "So, when you do leave?"

"A couple of weeks."

Just then, Deck came out of his office. "Wow," he said. "What happened to you?" he asked Amy.

She blushed. "Just a little makeover," she said, a little embarrassed.

"Huh," he said, looking her up and down. "Nice shoes," he said, and then turned to Hannah, who was glaring at him. "Have we met?"

"You remember Hannah?" said Amy. "From the wake?"

"Sure," he said, now sizing up Hannah. "How are you?"

Hannah responded coolly. "Just fine. Thanks."

Hannah continued to glare at Deck as he eyed her guardedly.

"I guess I should go," said Hannah, not willing to break the stare-down. "Lots of arrangements. Shots and stuff."

"Me too," said Deck, finally looking away. He headed down the hall and stopped after a few steps. He turned to Amy. "By the way, I read your dissertation. This weekend."

"You did what?" Amy asked.

"It's on file here," he said. "What? You didn't know that? And here I thought you were too smart for this job."

"I know it's on file. What would make you look for it?"

"Heimlich's files. The ones you missed. His notes intrigued me so I had to see for myself."

"Creepy," Hannah whispered.

"Why didn't you finish?" he asked. "Why didn't you do your defense?"

"I don't know. Too busy, I guess."

"Really?" he asked, a twinge of sarcasm in his voice. "Too busy?"

"Sure."

A strange darkness came over his face as he marched determinedly toward her and stared right into her eyes. "I guess you didn't really want it then," he accused, the volume of his voice shockingly elevated. "Because I fought like hell for mine," he barked and walked off.

"There's something wrong with that guy," said Hannah. "I don't trust him."

"Deck? Come on. He's mostly harmless," she said, and then giggled at her own joke.

Hannah looked at her, puzzled. "Mostly harmless. Like Earth?"

"Huh?"

"Douglas Adams? *The Hitchhiker's Guide to the Galaxy*? The blip of an assessment of the planet Earth? Two words in a guidebook tens of thousands of pages long?"

Hannah just shook her head and Amy rolled her eyes. She imagined her assessment of Deck was accurate, that his size probably made him seem more terrifying than he actually meant to be. But after that peculiar outburst, she didn't fully believe it herself.

"I don't think so. I can't quite put my finger on it," said Hannah, shaking her head. "But there's something… I don't know. Missing."

"What? As in his hair? Give me a break."

"Oh, my God," said Hannah, a realization dawning. "You like him, don't you?"

"I don't."

"Yes, you do. I thought so at the wake but now it's totally obvious."

"I don't *like* him. Not like that. And for your information, I just had the most sensational weekend of my life with this amazing-looking guy who—"

"You mean the one that can't spell his own name?"

"How did you…"

"Thin walls," Hannah laughed. "See you later," she said and walked off.

Minutes later, Deck returned with two coffees and placed one on her desk.

"Thanks for the coffee," Amy said in an exaggerated tone, looking toward her back wall. "How thoughtful of you."

Deck smirked at her and looked in the same direction. "Why are you shouting?"

"What? Oh, nothing" she said.

"Were you able to pull that file I asked you about yesterday?"

"Oh, that. No sorry," she looked away. "I guess I forgot."

"You forget a lot of things."

"That's not true," she squeaked, defensively. "Just what are you trying to say?"

"The minutes of the last department meeting?"

She looked at him blankly.

"You were supposed to transcribe them? And email them to everyone?"

"Oh, right," she clicked her tongue against the roof of her mouth a few times as she looked around—anywhere but at him. "Sorry."

He laughed. "Don't worry, I know it's total mind-numbing minutiae. Why don't we do them together. Are you free now?"

She relaxed. "Let me finish up this other email and I'll be right in."

A few minutes later, Amy entered Deck's barely unpacked office to find him stooped over his desk, where a Scrabble board and tiles were set for two. "What are you doing?" she asked.

He looked up to give her a quick smile. "Scrabble. You familiar with it?"

"Duh."

"I'm in the middle of a pretty heated match."

"Oh, I'm sorry," she said, feeling awkward. "I didn't realize you had someone here."

"I don't."

"I'm confused. Then your friend just left?"

"I play myself."

She scrunched up her face. "Why? Are you that good?"

He laughed and moved to the other side of the board. "No, actually. It's because I'm that bad." He looked at her. "No one will play with me."

"But you have a doctorate in English."

"And I'm remedial at best at Scrabble. I really love this game. And I practice all the time. But alas," he shrugged, "I'm terrible."

"I don't believe you."

"Is that a challenge? Because I assure you, if you ever need a boost to your intellect, just come in and challenge me to a game of Scrabble." He folded the board and swept the tiles back into the small silver bag. "Wanna see?"

"Aren't these supposed to be *work* hours?"

"It won't take hours. It will barely take minutes."

"Okay, let's go."

Deck let Amy choose her letters first, explaining that really, it wouldn't matter. She quickly played her move. "Twenty-two points. Not a bad start," she smiled.

"So, why the change?" Deck asked bluntly.

"It was just time, I guess," she replied casually, and he placed down his tiles: NADIR.

"Now why would you do that?" she asked. "You just set me up for a triple word score! I mean, thank you. But, come on."

"You have to admit it's a pretty good word."

"But that's not the point of the game. Who cares if it's a twenty-dollar word if it only buys you six points?"

"I guess I do."

"And this is why you're no good," she teased. She laid down a Q a U and a T, using his triple word set up.

"Now that's an idiotic word."

"That's a forty point word."

He considered this. "Did I mention I was terrible at Scrabble?"

She laughed. As he played his next turn, she glanced around his office. "It looks like you're making some progress settling in."

"I'll get there eventually," he said. "Right now there are more pressing matters. Your turn."

She looked back at the board, disgusted. "How can you lay down an X and a Z and only get nineteen points for it?"

"It's zax. It's brilliant!"

"It's infuriating," she said. "I'm done."

"And this is why I end up playing by myself," he said, and folded the board.

"You are a big baby, aren't you?" she chided playfully and rose out of her chair.

"I guess I am."

"So do you need help organizing any of this or putting it away?" she asked, glancing around at things already unpacked. Among them, she spotted a framed photo of a man smiling on the beach, toned and tall, with warm blue eyes and a thick mane of shaggy black hair. She did a double take.

"Yes, that's me," he said, walking over to her. "That *was* me at least."

"I'm sorry. I didn't mean…"

He took the photo from her hands. "She took that photo. Marny. My ex," he said. "Our honeymoon."

"Wow," she said. "You looked *really* good," she nearly gushed. Seeing his expression darken, she realized using the past tense had probably been a stupid thing to do.

He placed the photo back in a box. "I know what you want to ask, so ask already."

"Ask what?"

"My, haven't you become the coy one with this fancy new look."

"I don't know what you mean," she said, evasively.

He grabbed up a marker and the Scrabble score pad from the desk, and began scribbling furiously on it. He held up the pad. It read: ASK ME.

She shrugged, nervously. "Ask you what? What are you talking about?"

He scribbled again: ABOUT MY HAIR.

Amy was mortified. "What hair?"

"Aha!" he said. "Now we're getting somewhere."

"I didn't mean..."

"This is almost too easy."

"It's not from chemo, is it?"

"That's just what you need. Two dead bosses in one year."

"Cancer isn't funny."

"No. I don't suppose it is."

"So what is it?"

"I have something called alopecia," he explained. "The latest thinking is that it's an autoimmune disease. Basically my white blood cells woke up one day all crazy and paranoid and decided my hair cells were out to get me. So they attacked them and killed them off—you know, like when you fight off an infection. Sometimes major stress can trigger it."

"Your white blood cells attacked all your hair cells?"

"What can I say? Much like the rest of me, they're not that smart. And no, it isn't contagious, so if you ever feel the urge to kiss me, you'll probably keep your hair. Though I can't promise about your heart."

"Seriously. Can you be *serious* for a minute?" He nodded. "Please tell me what happened. How did this happen to you?"

He opened his mouth to speak then shook his head. "Okay. This is seriously what happened. My wife left me."

"Okay."

"She was having an affair. I knew about it. We were supposed to be working things out. She said she'd call it off with the other person. And the next thing I know, she just disappeared. Did I tell you she was also my assistant?"

Amy blushed. "Uh, no."

"Yes. Pretty stupid, right? Anyway, I guess I couldn't give her what she needed." He paused once again. "So I filed a missing persons report and everything. This is how I know Ollie. Detective Franks. Funny story about the cops. They all felt pretty bad for me. Kind of adopted me after a while, I was at the station so much," he spoke with a faraway look on his face, which turned serious. "I was really determined to find her. She tore my heart out, but I loved her desperately."

"I think I understand that."

"Turns out, her lover disappeared, too. I guess they ran off together or something," he smirked. "Anyway, I never heard from her again."

"And then your hair fell out? Overnight or something?"

"It's not really that simple, but I guess you could say it happened that way."

"So will it grow back?"

"Nothing's grown back yet. Who knows? I'm used to it anyway. You can't imagine how much money I save on shampoo and shaving cream."

"You really don't have a single hair anywhere on you?"

"Not a one," he said. "But enough about me and my bare bum. What's your story? With the ex-fiancé, I mean. What happened there?"

"Oh, I'm not sure..."

"You now know that there isn't a single hair on me. And it's written all over your face that you've been scanning my entire body for hair in that twisted mind of yours. Now if that's not intimate, I don't know—"

"He jilted me," she said. "On our wedding day. He left me at the altar."

"Ouch."

"Not really an altar. More like a deli counter. But still. It was pretty bad," she fought back tears. "I'm surprised you don't already know about it because everyone here knows about it."

"Wait a minute. This isn't the poor bastard who hooked up with Liz French?"

"Eliza*bitch* French. Yes. Why? Do you know her?"

"Alas, Liz French. I knew her, Horatio. And Elizabitch is a pretty apt moniker."

"I'm sorry? You *know* her?"

"Such a delight she is. It takes a mighty magnificent kind of beast to be able to assault all the senses at once. Freakin' Grendel of a woman."

Amy laughed.

"Wait, it gets better."

"Do tell," she urged.

"She was dumped by the very same person my wife dumped me for."

"Come on."

"No, really. We all worked together. Made for a gorgeous scandal."

"I don't get it. How could anyone want to be with *that*?"

"I have no idea," he laughed. "But that's not even the best part," he said, a teasing glint in his eye. "After they took off, Liz kind of hit on me."

"Oh, God! That's ridiculous," Amy shrieked with laughter.

"Hey, that's not fair. I wasn't always ugly," Deck deadpanned.

"Oh, no. I didn't mean… I mean, I'm sorry. You know that's not why I'm laughing."

He smiled. "You don't think I'm ugly?"

"Oh, God no," she said. "I mean…" She looked at him, into his eyes, a glance that lasted maybe a second too long. Self-conscious, she quickly looked away.

"It's nice, by the way," he said. "Your new look. I thought you were pretty before, but this is very nice. I guess the date was a success?"

Amy was embarrassed and even felt a little guilty. "How did you know about that?"

A devilish grin turned up the corners of his mouth ever so slightly. "Thin walls."

Hours later, Amy was wrapping up her work and trying to figure out what to do with her free evening when a familiar voice interrupted her thoughts. "You're looking well."

Amy froze. She knew that voice all too well. "You don't sound very sincere," she told David.

"Well look at you," he said. "I can't believe you ruined yourself."

"I *ruined* myself."

"Do you not remember *The Beauty Myth*? I mean, my God, you're like a Barbie doll."

Amy was incensed by the comment, especially coming from someone as attractive as David was. And she was even more incensed at herself that she still felt that way about him—that he was so good-looking. She composed herself. She played it cool. "Because to be beautiful you have to plain?"

"All I'm saying is beauty is in what's natural. It's primitive. It's *visceral*."

"Like the smell of fried chicken and saccharine in the morning," she mumbled.

"What was that?"

"Nothing," she smiled to herself.

"Look, I'm only trying to help you."

She looked at him. "Oh, but you already have. More than you know."

David stormed away and Amy sat back, savoring the satisfaction of not giving a rat's ass if he ever returned.

A blip from her computer signaled an email was waiting and she rolled over to the screen:

Hi Amy,

You Want To Do Sumething Later? Ive Been Thinking, Of You All Day.

Luv,
B

While the superfluous initial caps and odd spelling made her cringe, she decided to focus instead on what was important now: More of that drug that only Brendan could give her. She typed back a quick reply and hit "send" before she could change her mind.

Sitting back, she noticed Deck had left a file on her desk and she got up to return it.

She found him perched over the Scrabble board again, which made her smile. "Do you need anything else?" she asked. "I'm heading out now."

"Another date?" he asked.

"Uh. Well, yeah." She was uncomfortable but she wasn't sure why. "Haven't you been out there yet?"

"Not ready," he smiled weakly. "I know, it's weird, right. Because who *wouldn't* want me? A socially awkward aesthetic atrocity. It's a wonder I haven't been snatched up by now," he said with a giant laugh.

"See you tomorrow," she said, with a twinge of sadness for him.

"Just be careful," he said, with a sincerity so unexpected, Amy had the sudden urge to cancel her plans. To stay with Deck just a little longer. But it was too late to cancel with Brendan without standing him up. She had to go.

It had been Brendan's idea to meet at a place called The Slot & Joystick, one of those combination video arcade, sporting arena, and restaurant establishments. The plan was to have dinner and then partake in the various amusements available—maybe even take a spin on the famed go-cart track. Amy had very little enthusiasm for the idea of any of this, and nothing but enthusiasm for the "after party." It had not been a great day, especially considering the confrontation with David and she needed some of Brendan's magic to take the edge off.

"I didn't know what risotto was," he said. "So I just ordered the rice."

"I see," she remarked, with nothing else to contribute. It becoming all too apparent that there wasn't anything at all they could talk about. The empty look on his face when she gently explained to him what risotto actually was only confirmed it for her.

"So you embarrassed me into reading a book, you know."

Maybe there was hope? "You read a whole book since I saw you last?"

"Uh, not. Not even close. But I started one!"

"Great! Fiction? Nonfiction?" he stared at her dumbly and sexily. "A true story or made up?"

"It's gotta be made up. It's too funny not to be made up. There's no way any of this could happen," he beamed.

"I'm intrigued," she smiled. "What is it?"

He folded his arms over his chest and smiled almost smugly. "Ever hear of a little book called *I Hope They Serve Beer in Hell*?"

Now the spell he held her under was definitely beginning to splinter away, evidenced by a headache that was taking hold of her brain. She rationalized. It could have had something to do with the constant beeping of the video games, the whir of the go-carts on the track that circled the restaurant. She didn't want to believe the truth of what it really was: Brendan. Sexy Brendan. With the body of a god. And not an interesting thought in his head.

"So that's when I told him what he could do with his tinted windows!" he exclaimed.

"How nice," she said. Amy picked at her spicy fries as she tried to follow what he was saying. She was hoping that he would say something, anything, that would ignite the fire from the other night. But it was just one cold splash of water in the face after the other.

When they finished eating, he took her hand in his. "How about a little Primal Fear," he asked, pulling her into the vortex of blinking and beeping and whirring that was the arcade.

"Primal what?"

He shook his head in kind of a patronizing way. "It's a *video game* where you're both dinosaurs and you tear each other to pieces. It's so cool."

"How about we skip the games?" she said, in the most sexy tone she could deliver.

And finally, the light of understanding illuminated his face. "That sounds like a great idea to me."

Back at Amy's apartment, she prayed the electricity of the other night would return. That when he kissed her, her body would light up like it had that weekend. That the same hunger to conquer him and to be conquered by him would return. But it didn't. Every kiss felt like a jellyfish was slapping at her face. Every time he touched her, she could actually feel her skin cells recoil. How could that mad attraction have transformed into repulsion so quickly? All she could think was that seeing David had flipped a switch in her. And now she really wanted to kill David.

"Is everything okay, baby?" said Brendan. "You don't seem that into this."

"Actually," she said, trying to wriggle out from under him. "I'm not. I'm sorry. I think you're really nice, but I don't think this is going to work out."

"Kind of a strange time to tell a guy something like this."

"I know. I'm sorry. But if you could just…"

Brendan shook his head. "I knew this was going to happen. I *knew* it!" He jumped off the bed and into his clothes. "Your friends told me you were bad news, you know. But I didn't listen. Stupid me."

"Friends?" she wondered. "You mean Lauren and Jane?"

"I mean those guys that hang out on the front steps," he said, pointing at the window. "They said to watch out for you because while you may seem like a big nerd, you were really pretty nuts."

"They did, huh? Well…sorry." She was torn between being annoyed at their interference but also moved at them looking out for her.

"Next time I'll be smarter," he said, and he stormed out, slamming the door behind him.

After Brendan left, Amy got up out of bed and headed to the kitchen, where she found another half-finished bottle of cabernet and poured herself a glass. Considering the amount for a minute, she grabbed up the bottle and headed to the living room. She curled up on a beanbag chair next to the wall where her babies lived.

She was sad. Conflicted and confused. She hadn't realized until much too late how talking to David today had made such an impact on her. And she was *so* mean to him. She was feeling terrible at the way things went down, about the way she had treated David. And she was sure now that if there was any chance they would get back together, she had totally blown it.

The more wine she drank, the more she missed David. She thought she was over him, getting over him. But clearly she had thought wrong. "I don't think Daddy's coming back, babies," she told them, burning with regret.

Amy finished the rest of the wine and stumbled back to her bedroom. Snuggled under the blankets, she thought of David. Of the way things were. Of how much it sucked to be alone. And of how good Deck smelled, kind of like rain. She opened her eyes for a second at that, but then chalked it up to wine-confusion as she slipped back into a deep, quiet sleep.

9

How Zoë, Jane, Lauren, and Even Deck Try to Talk Sense into Amy—and How it All Falls on Deaf Ears

"What the hell?" Amy walked in the following morning to the sound of loud guitar and trumpet music blaring out of Deck's office and she headed over to investigate. Was that Chicago? She hadn't heard that song since she was a kid. Yet, there was Deck, singing at the top of his lungs, and moving his body in a way that might be described as dancing, but only in the most indefinite terms.

Seeing her, Deck waved, took three walking spins to the door, grabbed her by both hands, and pulled her in as he continued to sing, "Only the beginning..."

"This is too stupid," Amy said, yet somehow fell under his spell, as he twirled and pulled and she allowed him to twirl and pull her again and again.

"Of what I want to feel forever..." he belted as she laughed until she coughed, yet still allowed him to lead her in the dance like he was playing with a marionette. "Only the beginning!" he screeched with so much enthusiasm, Amy actually lost her footing from laughing so hard and hit the floor—still laughing.

"My, you are a clumsy little thing, aren't you?" he smiled, righting her again, and leading her into a quick spin, and then a very deep dip. He pulled her up with his left hand and he knelt down on one knee as he pulled, so that when she came up, she was sitting on the other knee, which was bent, her face inches away from his. They sat there for a long moment, looking into each other's eyes, until

85

Amy jumped up. Deck shook his head, stood, and turned off the music.

"You get crazier by the day," she said to him, shaking off the glee and trying to get back to serious.

"Better mad as a hatter than sly as an adder," he said.

"Who said that?" she asked. "And what does it even mean?"

"Me," he smiled. "But they're words to live by. What it means is that I'd rather show you up front who I really am, crazy or not, than hide in the brush and give you a little death bite when you stumble upon it for yourself."

She thought for a moment about this, but it still didn't make any sense to her. "Huh," she said. "Well, good morning."

"Good morning to you," he parroted, and went behind his desk. "Hey, I was just looking for the notes on the Flaubert lecture in the server, but I couldn't find them. Did you put those in my folder yet?"

She looked away. "Uh, no. I guess I forgot."

"To put them in the folder?"

"Um, no. To transcribe them."

"I see," he said. "You know, Flaubert's been gone for more than a hundred years but I'm certain he's really anxious about me getting my thoughts about his life and work published as quickly as possible," he said lightheartedly, but she missed the joke.

"Sorry."

"You really are kind of a serious one, aren't you?" He squinted at her, and then tried again. "Then how about for a punishment, you go to that party Wednesday night with me?"

"Oh, I kind of already asked my friend Jane to go," she said, edging toward the door.

"Too bad," he said. "Well, how about you let me take you for an ice cream later then?"

"That's a punishment?"

"I guess it's all relative," he said, leaning forward. "So what do you say? You like ice cream?"

Amy felt a little warm and whole lot awkward. "I dunno," she said, nervously. "I don't really think we should—"

"Jesus, Amy. It's just ice cream."

"Uh, okay," she said, tentatively.

"So, yes?"

"Oh, no. I can't," she said. "I have to babysit for Zoë tonight."

"Some other time, then?"

"Maybe."

"Well in that case, please be sure to muck things up around here as much as possible going forward so I'll have another opportunity to invite you?"

"Oh," she said, unsure. "Okay."

"What's the matter, Amy? I thought we were friends."

She looked up at him. "I think… I think…"

"You sure do think a lot. Gorgeous people like you don't usually think at all, let alone as much as you do."

She was quiet for a minute. "I usually make bad decisions."

"Well, that's because you *think* too much," he said, moving off his chair and sitting down on the edge of the desk in front of her. "What do you *feel*?" he asked, looking right into her eyes, looking right through her.

"I think I better get those notes typed before I get myself fired," she said, and she ran out.

Later that evening, Jane, Lauren, Zoë, and Amy sat in Jane's bedroom as she got ready for her date. The women were sipping wine and Zoë was drinking chocolate milk, curled up on her mother's bed, immersed in a book.

"I can't believe I haven't had a date in two years."

"Three years," said Zoë, not looking up.

"No, I'm pretty sure it was two."

"Actually," Amy began.

"Try closer to five," said Lauren.

"That's true," said Zoë. "I was being nice."

"That's not possible," said Jane, genuinely surprised. "Five years?" She counted back on her fingers. Her expression dropped.

"Five years," she said. "What am I thinking about? I can't do this," she whined.

"You're going to be fine," Lauren assured. "It's like riding a bike."

"Actually, riding a bike isn't even like riding a bike," said Amy. "I was on a bike a couple of years ago after not riding since I was a kid, and there's just no way that statement is true. It was impossible to balance and I—" Lauren and Jane glared at her. Even Zoë broke away from her book to glare. "Oh. Sorry," Amy said, meekly.

"You're going to have a good time," Lauren assured. "You're going to have dinner, maybe take a nice walk—"

The doorbell rang and nobody moved. It rang again, and all the women looked to Zoë. "But the holidays are over," she whined. Seeing it was getting her nowhere, she dropped her book and jumped off the bed. "Fine," she hissed.

Lauren walked over to the bed and picked up Zoë's book. "*The Second Sex*?"

Jane shrugged her shoulders. "She's on a sociology jag."

"Women are so complicated," she sighed, putting the book back down. "But men," she continued. "Men are easy. Really all they want is a blow job now and then. Do that and you can hold on to them forever. Truly. That's the secret."

"Huh," said both Jane and Amy, both painfully uncomfortable.

"Which reminds me," said Lauren. "Be sure you bring condoms."

"Mom! Nice mothers—"

"Save the preaching for the kid, sweetie. You look gorgeous. It could happen." She reached into her purse, and much to the girls' horror, pulled out a strip of six. "Be safe."

"I can't believe you, Mother," Jane huffed. "Honestly!" she huffed.

Lauren lay the condoms down on the bed and headed for the door. "I'm going out to see what's gotten you all riled up," she said.

When her mother left, Jane snatched them up and slipped them into her purse. She stood in front of the mirror, and Amy stepped behind her. "You look beautiful," Amy said. "Truly."

Jane took a deep breath. "Let's go."

They walked into the living room to find Zoë snuggled on Lauren's lap on the couch, and Detective Ollie Franks sitting opposite them, sipping at a brown beverage in a lowball glass. "The little one actually makes a pretty terrific Manhattan," he smiled and rose. "Wow. You look terrific," he said as he walked over to Jane and planted a small kiss on her cheek.

"Where did you learn to make that?" Jane asked Zoë. She shrugged slyly.

Jane chose to change the subject. "Are you coming from work?"

"Actually," he looked at Amy. "I just saw Deck."

"What's a deck?" Lauren asked. "Is that a police term?"

Ollie laughed. "No, he's a guy. A really standup guy, actually. Amy here works for him."

"Oh," said Lauren, a little betrayed for not already knowing this.

"I just started working for him last week or so. No big deal," said Amy.

"Last week, eh?" said Lauren. "About the time you told poor Brendan you didn't want to see him anymore?" she pressed, and everyone turned to Amy.

"One had nothing to do with the other," she snapped. "If you all most know, it was because I saw David that day, and it kind of turned me off things."

"Oh?" asked Ollie.

"It was a bad relationship," she began. "I mean, no. It was a good relationship. It just ended badly." Lauren, Jane, and Zoë all shook their heads.

"Only a bad relationship ends badly," said Ollie, with authority. "Like what happened with Deck and Marny." He shook his head in disgust. "That woman was evil to him, pure evil all the way through," he said. "But Deck never saw it."

"What happened?" asked Amy. "In the end? I mean …"

"I hope we find her just so we can find a good way to punish her."

"Was it so bad?" Jane asked.

"It was terrible," Ollie said. "Crippled him. I mean, who loses their hair like that?" he shook his head. "Through it all, all he wanted to do was find her and that's all he devoted himself to for months and months. Despite the problems they were having, he really believed something had happened to her."

"Sounds like a prince," said Lauren.

"Just a very romantic soul," said Ollie. "A shitty Scrabble player, though. You really don't know any of this?" he asked Amy.

"No," she said. "I mean yes about the Scrabble. But all he told me was that she left."

He shook his head. "The day she left," he paused. "That morning they were having coffee, talking about taking a vacation, maybe even starting a family. When he got home from work later that afternoon, she was gone. Vanished into thin air without even leaving a note."

"Oh, my," said Jane.

"It wasn't until months later that we found the photo albums."

"Albums?" Zoë asked, and snuggled up to her grandmother.

"Apparently, this sick bitch—" Jane cleared her throat; Zoë rolled her eyes. "Sorry," he coughed. "She took all his photo albums—his childhood, their wedding, everything…"

"And?" Lauren asked.

"And she burned them in a ditch in the backyard."

"I had no idea it was so bad," Amy gasped, feeling a stab in her heart. "I had no idea she was so cruel."

Ollie finished his drink. "Some people are just plain evil," he said. "Beautiful, but evil all the same." He downed the rest of his drink. "And some people can't see crazy when it's wrapped up so pretty," he sighed and then looked at Amy up and down for a moment. "He thinks the world of you, as you know."

"I didn't know that, no," she blushed.

"Seriously?" he asked.

"Why?"

Ollie gave Amy a doubting glance and walked over to Jane, extending his arm. "Well, it was very nice meeting you all, but we better get going if we're going to make that reservation."

"I'll walk you out," said Lauren, and she kissed Amy and Zoë good-bye. "I haven't been home in two whole hours and I'm sure Joshua's bouncing off the walls with boredom," she said. "Has no idea what to do with himself when I'm not around."

"Bullshit," Zoë squealed.

Amy rolled her eyes at her young friend and took up the stack of cards Zoe had just called her bluff on. "I don't know how you talked me into playing this game with you." She shook her head as she appraised the contents of her hand. "Your mother would kill me if she knew."

"Just turn over that next card and let's keep it going," said Zoë. Amy sat across from Zoë at the dining room table, a bowl of chips between them.

"Anyway," Amy spoke from where she left off, "he thinks I should defend my dissertation already. He tells me every day."

"*Everyone* thinks you should you should finish, Auntie Amy," said Zoë, clicking her tongue on the back of her top front teeth. "Two sevens."

"Everyone who *loves* me, sure."

Zoë shot her a coy glance. "Are you saying he doesn't?"

"That would be a little ridiculous. Don't you think?"

"You heard what Ollie said. Why would it be ridiculous?" she asked.

"Because I've only just met him. I've really only been working closely with him a couple of weeks. "Two kings. He doesn't *know* me."

"Does it matter?" Zoë asked, clicking her tongue on her teeth again, and threw down more cards. "Three nines. You know the story of Paris and Helen of Troy."

"Of course."

"He didn't know her at all but he loved her so much and had to have her so badly, it started a war."

"And you know how that turned out. Besides, it was Aphrodite who—" Zoë shook her head. "I'm doing it again?" Zoë nodded. "Sorry."

"You don't fall in love with a body," Zoë said.

"I think you say that to me a lot. Two fours," she said, and placed down her cards unchallenged.

"You need to hear it a lot. And you also think a lot. Two sevens. Maybe too much," she said, studying the cards remaining in her hands. "Except not about things that matter."

"Bullshit!" Amy screamed out, and Zoë took up the cards. Now calmer, she asked, "What does that mean?"

"Starts with a D."

"Deck?"

"No, *d*ummy," she said, emphasizing the D. "*D*issertation. *D*efense. Two sixes." Zoë shook her head. "It could have been anything and you went right for Deck," she said, and shook her little blonde head. "And you say you don't like him," she rolled her eyes.

"Honestly, I haven't thought about that paper in years. Three nines. I haven't thought about a lot of things in years."

"Bullshit!" Zoë exclaimed, and Amy picked up her cards.

"You want to know what I think?" said Zoë, now tapping away at her tooth with her tongue.

"What?"

"I think you've totally got a thing for old baldie! Two twos."

"Bullshit," she motioned to Zoë to pick up the cards and Zoë glared at her as she added them to her hand. "That doesn't even make sense," Amy said.

"Oh, no? Because you bring him up all the time," she said, flicking the back of her teeth with her tongue again.

"I *work* with him," she snapped. "One ace."

"You *worked* with Heimlich, too," said Zoë. "Two fives."

Amy looked at Zoë, now with one card left, and looked at her own. She opened her mouth to speak, but Zoë beat her to it. "And I basically only knew about him from your wedding and his funeral."

"Two sevens," said Amy, throwing down cards as Zoë beamed.

"Bullshit, Auntie Amy," she grinned smugly. "One seven!" she shouted, and threw down her cards. "And I win!"

"Fine," Amy said, throwing down her cards. "Why don't we just drop it, okay?"

Zoë shrugged her shoulders and continued clicking her tongue against her teeth. Amy finally lost her patience with it. "Why do you keep flicking your tongue like that?"

"I think I have a loose tooth."

Amy warmed. "Wow, honey! Your first one!"

"Yep. Crazy, huh?"

"Oh, Zoë. You're growing up!"

Zoë looked up at Amy over her eyebrows. "Now why would I want to do that?"

"Why? What's wrong with being grown-up?"

"Grown-up people are nuts."

"I don't see—"

"No, you don't. None of you do. You've got this perfectly nice guy all crazy about you and somehow you're still hung up on that dipshit."

"Zoë, nice little girls don't—"

"Look, I'm not that nice. Don't tell my mother," Zoë teased. "Seriously, she's another one. Ollie's so nice and she wasn't going to go out with him."

"The moustache?"

"You *know* how she feels about men with facial hair. Anyway, she gave it a shot, but she wasn't going to—and just because of that. Crazy."

Amy mentally weighed a moustache against having no hair at all, and Zoë continued.

"The point of the matter is I think that when you grow up, you go crazy and you stop being able to see the obvious. That's just my opinion," she said, now tapping her tooth more aggressively than ever before.

"Then why do you keep trying to wriggle that tooth out?"

"Because it's annoying me."

"Really because it's only just started to come loose."

"Let's not talk about it anymore."

Jane got home at eleven-thirty, a little tipsy and more than a little giddy. Amy greeted her at the door. "Looks like it went well."

"You have no idea," she gushed. "I had no idea I would go for a man in uniform."

"He's a detective. He doesn't wear a uniform."

"He could if I wanted him to," she teased, a mischievous glint in her eye.

"I didn't need that visual."

"Oh lighten up," she said. "What about you? When are you going to give poor Deck a shot."

"Seriously?"

Why not?"

"I didn't tell you before. But I think he wanted to kiss me today."

"Kiss you?" Jane gushed. "What happened?"

"Well we were dancing around..."

"At work?" Jane said, smugly.

"Kind of," Amy replied, feeling slightly embarrassed but also warmed by the thought of it. "Anyway, there was a moment when I landed on his knee that seemed..."

"You landed on his knee?"

"Just forget it. Anyway, the point is, he's really nice. A little quirky, too.," she said with a warm smile. "Except he really likes Chicago."

"Chicago's a nice city."

"The group."

"Oh," she said. "And why again is that one for the no column?"

"He's a little goofy," Amy said, almost wistfully.

Just then Zoë poked her head out of her bedroom. "I told you she liked old baldie!"

"I thought you'd be sleeping, monster," Jane said, and she motioned Zoë over. Zoë ran to her mother, who took her in her arms and lifted her off the ground. "How's the dangler?" she asked.

Zoë clung to Jane like an orangutan. "Still dangling," she said.

"Don't rush it. It will come out when it's ready," Jane assured, giving Zoë a couple of Eskimo kisses.

Amy smiled at the tenderness between mother and daughter, and felt a pang of longing for her own mother as she watched them together. "So are you still coming to that party with me?"

"Of course. Will *he* be there?"

"Sure."

"Good. I look forward to getting to know him better."

"Whatever, but he really isn't my type."

"So what *is* your type?" Zoë asked.

"I don't know. Less big? I mean Deck's got be six-foot-five or something."

"So you're looking for *less* of a man," Jane shot back. "Like the girly men you've always dated."

"They aren't girly."

"Please," Jane scoffed. "All David needed was lipstick and a dress and he'd be a woman." Zoë giggled. "And I apologize to women everywhere for saying that."

"I don't see——-"

"No, you don't. You need a man, a real man. Someone who really cares about you. Someone who would do *anything* for you," she mused. "Someone who could be a real hero. A prince. I think Deck could be that guy…"

"Look, Deck's a nice guy and everything. But there has to be *some* physical attraction for it to go somewhere. Doesn't there?"

Zoë shook her head. "Now you sound like Charlotte in *Sex and the City*—but see how that turned out!"

Both women turned their heads to look at Zoë; Her mother was not amused, which the sharp little one picked up on instantly.

"I mean, not that I ever watched that show. But seriously, you'd have to be living under a rock if you don't get the reference," she said, now a little defensive. "But I don't watch it. I have never seen that show or know who any of those women are and I've never seen any of them naked." The women now raised their eyebrows at her.

"At least, I don't watch it anymore. But that's not the point, really, is it? The point is Charlotte fell for Harry who was bald, when her horrible, handsome husband with all that hair was bad to her. It's just like with you, Amy. Don't you see it?"

Amy shook her head. "Harry was missing hair on his head. This guy doesn't have a hair on his body. Like a frog."

"Come on, Amy. You never kissed a frog?"

"You're thinking of the wrong story."

10

How Amy Came Face-to-Face with David and a
Sea Monster, and How She Learned Some
Monstrous Details of Deck's Past

The Stratton University annual gala was held every year at the Garden City Hotel on Long Island, New York. Why is was held there had always been a mystery, as it wasn't particularly easy for anyone who worked at Stratton to get to, and it seemed an uncharacteristically opulent venue for a school which was generally casual. One rumor holds that the party was held here because Dr. Phil Nickerson, the one-time president of Stratton, once an all-men's college, had a thing for the then-president of Adelphi, Dr. Lindsay Frost, who headed the then-all-women's college. He believed hosting the event at the hotel, which was located mere blocks from the women's school, would win both the attentions and affections of Dr. Frost. But he never quite succeeded at winning either of them.

Years later, the event was still being held at the Garden City Hotel, because Stratton prided itself on being strong on tradition and altering the location would have violated that. Or something like that. In any case, anyone paying the tuition bill at Stratton, and thus footing the cost of the event, would probably not bat an eye if this particular tradition was chucked.

This year, the party was being held in the main ballroom, where a grand buffet offered everything from carved meats to an assortment of pastas and salads to an Asian station complete with sushi. Two bars at either end kept the guests feeling festive. A band played at the front of the room as various members of the Stratton

University faculty and staff, and their guests, bounced and bobbed and bopped on the dance floor. But not Amy. She, instead, found herself in the throes of a heated debate over the intent of allegorical themes in various medieval writings, torturing everyone at the table. Jane, especially.

"No, that's where you're mistaken," said Amy.

"Really? I think Sir Gawain could have pulled it off," said Dr. Bateman, a kindly woman in her fifties. "You never know. If given a chance—"

"That's just ridiculous!" Amy panted, scandalized, turning to Jane for affirmation.

"You don't say," said Jane, monotone, staring down into her drink.

"It's interesting, isn't it, that one piece of literature has room for so many interpretations," said Dr. Bateman.

"So interesting, I could kill myself now," Jane downed her drink. "Truly."

"Well, you're wrong," Amy said. "As long as you know you're interpreting it wrong."

Before Dr. Bateman could retort, Jane begged, "Where's Hannah? Does anyone know where Hannah is?"

"She mentioned something about packing," Amy said. "I don't think she's going to make it tonight."

"Packing? Where's she going?"

"I don't know. Something about Aboriginals in Amazonia."

"There aren't any Aboriginals in Amazonia," Dr. Bateman said.

"Maybe it was something else. I don't know. I really didn't get into it with her."

"Oh," Jane said. She picked up another glass and proceeded to gulp down its contents, not caring who it belonged to.

"How can you say only your way is the right way, Amy? You're one of the smartest here, no doubt. And I'm really looking forward to hearing your defense. More than for most—"

"You're doing your defense?" Jane interrupted and Amy nodded dismissively.

"Because I think you have a lot to offer," Dr. Bateman continued, ignoring the interruption. "But that kind of stubborn thinking is not going to get you anywhere. Nothing is ever simply black or simply white, especially not in literature."

"But—"

"Indeed, it would help you immensely if you could simply remember that no matter how much importance we may put on them now, most books and epic poems and plays were created with one purpose: To entertain. The enlightening is just a by-product."

"But Sir Gawain—"

"Read into it a little less and enjoy it a little more. Open your mind, Amy. You'll see," Dr. Bateman then gave her a warm smile and a supportive little squeeze on the hand.

Amy was about to give Bateman a piece of her open mind when she was interrupted by a familiar baritone voice. "Dr. Bateman," he said. "It's nice to see you here."

"Hello, Dr. Thomas," she smiled, and shook his hand.

"Hi, Amy," he smiled. "You look, um, wow…"

Amy could feel herself turn as red as her shoes and she quickly looked away.

"I'm glad you came when you did, Dr. Thomas. Perhaps you can enlighten Ms. Miller here on literary interpretation and freedom of ideas?"

He looked back and forth between Amy and Dr. Bateman, and then smirked at Jane. "I thought this was a party."

"Good point," said Dr. Bateman. "Nice seeing you, Dr. Thomas. I look forward to receiving your thoughts on the Tolstoy program. Later this week?" she asked.

Deck looked at Amy. "I hope."

"Okay, guys," Dr. Bateman said. "Have a good time," she waved and disappeared back into the party.

"That was a profound discussion between two deep and intellectual people and I, for one, found it to be highly enjoyable," Amy snapped at him.

"Deep, eh," he chided.

"Why? What's wrong with that? Aren't you deep?"

The mischievous grin appeared again. "Why would I want to be deep when I can be happy?" he said.

"Great point!" said Jane. "Finally, someone who makes some sense around here," she downed her drink and turned to Deck. "Hi, I'm Jane."

"Nice to meet you, Jane. I'm Deck."

Jane laughed at him. "I *know* you who you are." Amy glared at her. "Uh, we met at the wake."

"Right, though not formally," he smiled at Amy. She looked away.

"Don't you want to be happy? Let off a little steam once in a while?"

"I guess I never thought about it like that."

"This is because you don't dance enough. Come on. Dance with me," he asked, and she looked at Jane, pleadingly. "I know you *can*," he laughed. "Let's go."

"Uh, well Jane doesn't think she can stay by herself…"

"Who cares what she thinks—I mean no offense, Jane."

"Of course," she smiled.

"What do you *want* to do?"

She smiled. "I want to dance."

"Then let's go."

Deck led her out to the dance floor just in time to catch the tail end of a swing medley, and then the music switched to slow. He pulled her close and she tried to pull away. "I guess we sit now," she said.

"You are so beautiful, do you know that?"

"I don't think…"

"Oh, Amy, come on. Can't you just go with it?" He pulled her closer and as she swayed in his arms, she had to admit it felt pretty good. He was so strong and sweet and tender, and she felt so safe and happy. He smelled so good to her, so fresh and new. And then something familiar started to stir in her, something raw and tingly and more than a little terrifying. She panicked.

"I have to sit," she said, and pulled away from him. He followed her back to the table, and as they sat and joined Jane, the music started to get upbeat again.

"This is my favorite song!" Jane shouted and jumped up.

"Mama's night out!" she screamed and downed her drink in one gulp and kissed Deck on the top of his head. "You're with me now," she commanded.

Deck smiled at Amy. "You don't mind?"

"She had her chance, come on," she said, and dragged him out of his seat.

"See you later," he smiled and let Jane lead him away.

Amy sat back and watched, and soon had to laugh at the sight of six-foot-five Deck twirling around five-foot Jane. She almost expected her to step on his feet, in daddy-daughter-dance style. They seemed to get along so well. She couldn't think of a single time she'd seen David and Jane get along this way.

But lest she be too happy and comfortable this night, just beyond Deck and Jane she noticed David entering the party. With Liz. Then she watched as David leaned over and whispered something to her, and Liz looked right at her. And then they started walking in her direction and she had no way to escape that wouldn't look like she was trying to escape as they made their way to her.

"Hello, Amy."

"David," she said, gulping her drink. "So nice to see you here. Who's your friend?" she managed a weak smile.

"You remember Liz?"

"So nice to finally meet you," cooed Liz in a voice far more feminine than Amy would have suspected.

"Amy's in the English department. She's working toward her PhD"

"Ah yes," said Liz. "But not quite there, are you, dear?"

"Actually, I'm going to make my appointment this week for my defense and—"

"Well, that's okay," Liz interrupted. "From what I understand, Deck Thomas likes them hot and stupid," she said, looking Amy up and down. "Kind of like…"

"Amy's not a natural blonde," David said, and Amy wondered if this wasn't a misguided attempt to defend her.

Liz ignored it. "So when you say you're *working* with Dr. Thomas, does that mean…"

"It means I work for him," Amy said.

"Because you know he has a reputation for," she taunted, "How do I say this? Getting just a bit too close to his assistants."

"He married Marny," Amy replied coolly.

"You *do* know she disappeared, don't you?"

"Yes," said Amy. "She left him. Just ran off for no reason."

Liz laughed. "Really?" she said. "Is that what he told you?" she laughed and conspiratorially looped David's arm in hers. Though David seemed more embarrassed than anything else.

Amy glared at Liz and couldn't decide what it was about this woman she hated the most. As the tension in her mounted, and the urge to punch Liz square in her smug fat face rose high in her, Deck magically appeared with Jane.

"Liz French. What a delight to see you again," Deck said.

Liz looked him over. "You're looking…well…" And she looked away. "Not exactly well, are you, Deck?"

"And you, too. Looking well," he said, a little too cheerfully. And then leaning in and under his breath, for Amy's benefit, "For a sea monster." Except she didn't hear it.

"This is David," said both Amy and Liz at once, Liz boastfully, and Amy in more of a pained whisper.

Deck glanced at both women and then at David, who was looking at Amy. Amy was looking at the ground. He took a swig of his beer. "So you're the reptile man?"

David extended a hand to Deck without looking away from Amy. "David Hayes," he said. And that was all he had to say.

Liz pulled him closer to her. "Apparently he's replaced Heimlich," Liz said. "Strange turn of events, considering their past," she continued to say, now in a loud whisper, still seeking a conspirator and still finding none.

Deck looked at Amy, who was still looking at the ground. David still looked at Amy, and Liz was sneering at David. And as all this was happening around Amy, it seemed the sound of distant drums echoed in her ears as the tension mounted so high, she could feel it in every inch of her. So she was decidedly done when Deck innocently joked, "Well, hopefully Amy won't also poison me." He laughed nervously, looking to Amy for a reaction. But the events of the night had become too much. Seeing David like that. Seeing him actually *with* Liz. It was just too much. Amy burst into tears and ran off.

"Amy, wait," called Deck. "I was just kidding." He turned to follow her and Jane jumped in front of him.

"Don't worry," she said. She stood on her tippy-toes and leaned on his chest to balance as she planted a soft kiss on his cheek. "It isn't you," she said warmly and glared at David. Then she took off after Amy.

Amy arrived at work early the next morning, determined to get Deck's Tolstoy notes organized before he came in. She was so embarrassed and overwhelmed at the events of the night before, she felt that throwing herself into the task would help distract her as she tried to figure out just what the hell was going on inside her head and in her heart.

"You okay?" the familiar, comforting baritone asked. She looked up at Deck, who was standing over her desk with a cardboard tray holding two coffees. He pulled one out and placed it on her desk. "Two sugars, right?"

"I'm sorry I ran out like that. God, what a spaz."

"I don't know about that," he said. "I've never had to face Marny and Lee like that in the flesh. Who knows? I might have done the same in your position."

"I don't know about that. You seem like you could take it."

"You think that? Really?" he said. "Amy, I have no hair."

"Right. Sorry."

"So how about that ice cream now? What do you say?"

"It's ten o'clock in the morning."

"I don't think the ice cream cares."

"But we have work to do…"

Deck looked down at the mess of papers strewn all over her desk. "I don't think you care."

"I care!"

"Let's leave your passion for your job and your performance for another day, shall we?" He offered his arm. "Let's go."

When they entered the cafeteria at the Student Union, Deck was surprised to learn that they were still serving only breakfast until eleven, and as much as he begged them to start up the soft serve machine, the servers wouldn't budge. "There's a vending machine just outside," said a kindly woman who had been nearly worn down to oblige him, until her surly coworker scowled at her. "I think it has ice cream sandwiches, if that helps?"

"Sandwich," he nodded as he said to Amy, "So not only do I get to buy you ice cream, but lunch. Who's a better date than me?"

Once they had their ice cream, they found a table by the entrance and sat down.

"Honestly, I've always been a bit too sensitive. You can ask my dad," he said, and he took a bite that spanned about half the sandwich. "Well, not my real dad. I never knew my real dad. I mean the guy who raised me. Chuck. He's a fireman in Indiana. That's where I grew up, in case you cared." Deck took his second bite, finished the ice cream, and crumbled the wrapper into a ball on the table.

"I care," she said. "Of course I care. What about your mother? Is she still around?"

"Irma? Irma was never around. You could say I never knew her either. Chuck married her even though she was six months pregnant with another man's baby. What can I say? He loved her like crazy."

"What happened?"

"Well, she never loved him. Nor, I guess, me for that matter. She left me with Chuck when I was four and never came back. Chuck explained it all to me in bits and pieces as I got older. It seems like every year there's something new. Anyway…"

"So what happened to your father? Did she leave you guys for him?"

"Nah. He died before I was born. She left because she was crazy."

"I'm sorry."

"Anyway, I guess I didn't handle it all that well. Chuck will tell you that I apparently cried for a month straight."

"Who could blame you?"

He opened his mouth to speak, and then hesitated. "There was something else..." he hedged.

"What?"

"I don't think I could tell you. You wouldn't understand," he said, shaking his head.

"Try me."

"After she left," he started and took a deep breath. She nodded him on. "After she left, I guess you could say I got a little violent."

Now she regretted asking, scanning the room and hoping no one heard him but her. "In what way?" she whispered.

"At first I guess I was just a little destructive. Kid stuff really. Smashing in the neighbors' windows with rocks. Lighting small fires..."

"Kid stuff?"

"This was actually the 'normal' stuff. Seriously. That's what the shrink told us. You'd be surprised to learn some of the things very normal boys will do."

"Okay."

"Then it escalated a little. And then..."

"Then?" she held her breath.

"I kind of killed my goldfish."

She exhaled. "Everyone kills goldfish."

"Uh, no. I creamed the little fucker. Popped him out of his tank and watched him flop around. I can remember that it made me so angry to watch him flipping and flopping like that, and I didn't know why." He stopped talking and this time Amy wasn't sure she wanted to encourage him to continue. Except she did.

"Then he died?" she asked. "He suffocated?"

"I smashed him with a shoe."

Amy gasped.

"I'm sorry. I don't know why I told you that. I don't think I ever told anyone that. Except my shrink. Aside from her, I think it was only Chuck that ever knew because he came in while I was smashing it. And that's when I started seeing Mary."

"The shrink."

"Yep." He paused for a moment as he watched her take it all in. "Too fucked up, huh?" He pursed his lips.

She was quiet as she tried to decide how she felt about all this. Of course everyone does things as a kid they aren't proud of. And the circumstances were extraordinary, of course. "You were only four," she decided out loud. "You were just a baby."

"Personally, I'm horrified by the whole thing, but I guess it could have been worse," he said. "I mean, if Chuck hadn't walked in when he did and I didn't get the help I needed."

Amy did not want to imagine. "If it matters any," he continued, "Mary gave me a clean bill of health. Chalked it up to extreme childhood trauma and swept it under some rug somewhere. Honestly, I really don't remember much of any of it."

"Probably all for the best," Amy said, and she believed it. "I mean, not your mom leaving like that." Her own words dug like a spike in her heart.

"Yeah well, not much damage done. Sure I get a little snappish sometimes, but I think that's more to do with my age than my youth."

"So then, it's just you and Chuck?"

"Pretty much. I did have an uncle actually. My real dad's brother, but—"

"What?"

"You know what? Let's save that shitstorm for another time, shall we? I think you already know too much about me as it is, and here I am knowing nearly nothing about you."

"There isn't much to know."

"What are some of the fucked up things they did to you? You must have had some problems with your parents."

"Oh, no. Not really. They were kind of free-spirited and flaky, but they were there for me."

"*Were?*"

"Yes," her voice cracked. "They disappeared in Brazil. On vacation a few years back. Presumed dead."

"I'm so sorry."

"The worst part of it is I kind of feel like it was my fault," she said, dead serious. He started laughing. "Why is that funny?"

"It's funny, because…it's kind of your calling card, huh? Innocently walking around, killing people?" he laughed some more.

"This is funny?"

"I'm also laughing because like most intellectuals, you think way too much and you drive yourself crazy thinking yourself into things that probably aren't even true."

"You're an intellectual."

"By default, really. But I don't know a lot of intellectuals. I mean, for someone who went into this line of work. I basically grew up in a firehouse."

"Strange," she said.

"That I grew up in a firehouse?"

"There's that. Yes. But I meant because I don't think I know anyone who isn't one."

"Not me. Seriously. You could fit all the intellectuals I want to associate with in a rowboat."

"Am I in the rowboat?"

"Do you want to be?"

There was a long pause before Amy screwed up her face and let out a shriek. "Oh, my God. Eeew!"

Deck shook his head and looked away. "Hey, that's okay. You can just say no. You don't have to do me any favors."

"No," she panted. "Not that. On the table. Right next to you!"

He looked over his shoulder, still confused.

"A spider! A spider!"

He finally spotted the offending arachnid, ready for a tarantula or black widow at the very least, and unimpressed by the small spider that sprawled almost lazily across a student's abandoned copy of *The Turn of the Screw*.

"This?" he taunted, gently lifting the book and holding it before her like a tray. "This is what gets you all riled up?"

"Oh, God!" she shrieked. "Are you going to kill it? Kill it!" she screamed. "Kill it!"

"Quite the sadist, aren't you?" he joked, as he carefully balanced the spider on the book, walked over to an open window nearby, and gingerly lowered the spider onto the outside sill.

He placed the book back on the table and he smiled at her. "Despite my brief era of terror in my childhood, I'm actually kind of a big pussy," he said.

"And I guess I'm the sadist, then?" she said, bitingly, her arms crossed in front of her.

"Forget about it," he laughed. "It was only a joke." She stared blankly at him. "You know. Joke? Ha, ha and all that?" he shook his head. "Okay, so you don't. No biggie," he said. "Should we head back?"

They made the walk back to the English department in silence as Amy stewed and Deck smirked. By the time they arrived, Amy had cooled.

"Hey, do you still have that box?" Deck asked, as they passed his office.

"Box?" she asked.

"Heimlich's trunk?

"Actually, yes," she said. "No one wanted any of his things, actually. Why do you ask?"

"Oh, nothing. Just something Chuck told me. An Elvis song I wanted to hear. Is it here?"

"It's in my cube," she said. "Do you want me to get it?"

"Nah. No worries. I don't need it now."

Deck stepped into his office and Amy stopped at the door. "It's a little strange, don't you think? How no one came to claim any of his things? That in the end, no one wanted to hold on to even a small piece of him?"

"I'm not that shocked about it, actually," Deck said, sliding behind his desk.

"But all those people at the funeral. His family. Surely someone would have wanted something. Even a small memento?"

"For one, Heimlich was about as popular with his family as he was around here. Tolerated, and that's about as far as it went for the mean old crankasaurus."

"How would you know?"

"Look, all I'm saying is that people get weird around death. It's not always real, what happens at a funeral. Some people just like the drama of it," he said.

She considered this. "So, why didn't you like Heimlich?"

"Let's just say he complicated my life."

"In what way?"

"Well, because of him, I almost didn't get my PhD. He brutalized me at my defense, and not in a good way. He was a…how do I say this gently? He was a total dick."

"He was a real ass, wasn't he?" she mused, leaning into the door frame.

"In ways you will never know," he said and he sighed.

She folded her arms around herself again, but this time not defensively. "You're so much nicer to me than he ever was."

He smiled. "It can't actually be a secret that I got the hots for you?"

"Oh," she stammered, a little shaken by his directness. "I just don't think it's appropriate," she lied, her flushed face clearly giving away her deception—to him and to herself.

"Appropriate?" he asked, cocking his head. "Or appealing?"

Amy was confused about what she imagined was starting to happen between her and Deck. She knew she wasn't attracted to him, and yet, there was something about him. Something that seemed so reassuring. Something that put her at ease, but also intrigued her. She was both shocked and honored that he had shared such a dark secret with her, and she couldn't help but want to know more about him. She was filled with questions.

But she couldn't get past the most significant question, which was *why* did she care so much? He wasn't her type. And he was her boss. And yet...she couldn't deny that she was starting to feel something for him. She was still conflicted over David, yes, but with Deck, something stirred. Except the last thing she needed right now was to have more complications in her life. So she decided to bury herself in the tedium of her work and hoped that it would all somehow go away.

Except her work wasn't tedious anymore and her thoughts were still with Deck. How could they not be, especially as she sat here, organizing his conclusions on Tolstoy, his words echoing with meaning as she drank in his interpretation of a story she loved, but for different reasons than he did. She was so caught up in it, in fact, that she hadn't even noticed David standing over her until he spoke.

"Hello, Amy."

"What do you want?" she asked, not looking up.

David cleared his throat. "I wanted to apologize for the other night. It was a little awkward."

"I know," she said. "Anything else?"

He cleared his throat. "Uh. Yeah. Word around here is that you're going to go through with your defense?"

"How do you know that?"

"Uh. Hannah," he stumbled and she narrowed her eyes. "I mean, not directly or anything. I overheard her talking to someone."

"Well, what if I am?" she asked, without emotion.

"Uh, nothing. I mean, well, that's pretty cool. I guess. I mean, if you think you're ready and all."

She glared at him. "I've been ready for years," she said coldly, and looked away again.

"Scruffy... I mean, Amy...are you ever going to stop being angry at me?"

"I don't think so," she said.

He shuffled from one foot to the other, awkward and uncomfortable and not really sure what to say next. "Okay, well, I have some of your things."

"You have *most* of my things."

"I meant your books. I mean, some other things, yeah. But you probably need your books to prepare?"

"You think?"

"We packed up so quickly, I guess I didn't pay attention to what was mine and what was yours."

She sneered at him. "Let me make it easy for you," she said. "All the sci-fi novels and biology textbooks—yours. All the *good* books, mine. Not so hard."

"Right. Well…"

At that moment, Liz stomped over with a box. "Where can I get rid of these?" she snarled, looking at Amy.

Liz was here, making deliveries? Had he really thought this was a good idea?

Amy pointed to a small corner of her cubicle. "Just over there is fine." Liz nodded at Amy and looked away. Amy continued to watch her. *Was she looking for something?* "Right there's good," Amy said.

Then Liz looked at David. What Amy had not noticed, because her eyes had not left Liz since she arrived, was that David's eyes had not left Amy, and were fixed in a gaze that was more than a little uncomfortable for Liz. "David," she called, but he didn't seem to hear her. So she whistled to him, like he was a dog.

"Huh?" he said.

"A little help?" she snapped.

"What? Oh, yeah. Right."

"Thanks," said Amy halfheartedly, as she turned back to her computer screen and slipped on her headphones. She shuffled through the selections on her iPod before settling on an especially angry No Doubt song and blasted the volume as high as it could go.

Exactly how many trips Liz and David each made back to her cubicle, Amy hadn't a clue. So when she finally turned around after about the fifth or sixth song, she gasped. There must have been forty boxes stacked in the corner and overflowing out to the hallway. "Shit," she said as Deck returned from a lecture.

"Moving in?" asked Deck, scratching his bald held incredulously.

"My books."

"Ah," he said and they were both silent for a while. "Why are they here?"

"David brought them."

"Oh," he said. "He brought them *here*?"

"Uh, yeah."

"He couldn't just bring them back to your apartment?"

"I guess not."

"Nice guy," he said. "So how are you planning to get these home?"

"I have no idea," she said and they both looked at the boxes again.

"I guess I could help you. I have a car. I could drive the boxes over in my car," he said, seeming a bit nervous. "And you, too, I mean. I mean, if you don't mind me coming to your house. I mean..."

She turned to look at him. "Deck, are you sweating?" she asked.

Deck smirked. "I am."

She squinted her eyes at him. "Why are you sweating?"

"Uh," he stalled. "You know. No hair to hold it back. Just one of those things."

"I see," she said. "But that doesn't explain why you'd be sweating in the first place. So, why are you sweating?"

He looked point-blank at her. "Don't really know."

"Hmmm," she said, suspicious.

He motioned to the books. "So?"

"Okay," she said finally. "Why not?"

"Great!" he said, with an enthusiasm inappropriate for someone who has agreed to help someone else move four tons of books. He caught himself and cleared his throat. "Let's get to it."

11

How Most Everything Amy Ever Accepted as True Got Turned on Its Ear

Amy's apartment building stood out in her neighborhood of quasi-suburban tree-lined streets, which more commonly featured houses—albeit two- and three-family houses. But it was unusual for a six-story anything to be found here. "Progress" could not be faulted for the building's presence on this block though—nor for its sister structure across the street, a mirror reflection of its rundown, dilapidated twin, as both buildings had stood since before the second World War. And neither had so much as been painted since then. The only way to discern one from the other was that there were different street numbers on the front doors. And, of course, there were the Boys, forever planted on Amy's front stoop. Which was where they were just as Amy and Deck arrived.

"Friends of yours?" Deck asked.

"I guess you could say that," she replied, admittedly nervous about how this was all going to turn out.

Deck expertly squeezed his old Volvo station wagon into a tiny spot right in front of the building, impressing Amy and apparently also some of the Boys, who appeared to be collecting money from some of the others.

As soon as he stopped the car, Deck got out, walked around and opened Amy's car door for her. They headed to the trunk and Deck and Amy each grabbed a box and headed for the stairs. Though Amy had become increasingly uncomfortable as the

Building Boys glared at Deck and she hoped Deck wouldn't notice them staring at him.

"How ya doin'?" Deck smiled as he approached them.

They nodded to him suspiciously. "Everything okay, Amy?" asked Tony, protectively as he edged up to her.

Deck turned to Amy and said, "Why don't I go on ahead?"

Amy smiled embarrassedly. "It's C-9," she said and handed him her keys. "I'll be right behind you." Deck grabbed the keys and walked inside and Amy turned to face the Boys.

"He looks like that guy, from that show," said Tony.

"Yeah, that's right! That old show," said Mario.

Angelo began nodding wildly. "The one on cable all the time. With the bald guy. What was that called again?"

Amy shook her head in her hand. "*The Addams Family*. And that isn't very nice," she chided, crossing her arms in front of her.

The guys looked back and forth at each other. "The freaking *Addams Family*?" asked Angelo.

"What's an *Addam's Family*?" asked Tony.

"*The Commish*," Mario shouted out, like he'd just answered the winning question in a game show.

"Oh yeah," said Frankie. "I love that fucking show," he gushed.

"What the fuck is an *Addams Family*?" Angelo wanted to know.

"Before your time," said Amy, not really bothered by how old this may at one time have made her feel.

Angelo walked toward Amy. "Seriously though, who is that guy?"

"He moving in?" Frankie asked.

"Yeah," said Mario. "What's with all the boxes?"

"Kind of a freak, if you ask me," sulked Tony.

Amy was angry now. "First of all, he's my boss. And he isn't a freak. He has alopecia."

"Alo-what?"

"Alo——" she started to explain, but was interrupted by a shrill, girlish scream coming from her apartment.

"Now what?" she left the Boys standing there, worried that David had been back after all and perhaps Liz had left a stool sample on the floor...

She raced up the stairs and pushed open her front door. There was Deck, frozen in the center of the living room, still holding his box. "What is it? What's wrong?" she asked him.

"What the hell is that?" he asked, with a false calm.

"What?" she asked.

"That."

Amy finally saw what had terrified him. She was annoyed. "Sparky! She's out *again*?" she said. "Shit. You just can't trust these Eastern milks. Total escape artists," she said, bending over and picking up the snake without flinching. "Totally sneaky."

"That's a snake!" Deck shrieked.

"Yes?" she replied, as casually as if he had said, "That's a sandwich."

"There's a snake running loose in your apartment," he said, now barely able to breathe.

She found herself amused at his terror. "Snakes don't exactly run, you know," she giggled. "They—"

"*Why* is there a snake loose in your apartment?"

"You know, for such a big guy, you're kind of a chicken," she laughed. She took a few steps toward him to see if he wanted to pet it, but when that caused the last remaining drop of color to vanish from his face, she thought better of it.

Instead, she headed to the other side of the room, where she pulled open a curtain to reveal a whole wall of snakes, stacked neat and tidy in a series of plastic bins in a variety of sizes. Without blinking an eye, she moved the lid Sparky had tripped and poured the snake back into her enclosure. "Deck, meet the babies. Babies, meet Deck."

"What the—"

"My ex was a herpetologist," she said. "You know this."

Deck cocked his head and began shaking it. "He took all your books but he left the snakes."

"He was being nice," she said. "I guess he knew how attached to them I was and—"

"Sounds like a real prince," Deck said, clutching his box of books like it was a specialized snake deterring shield.

"Honestly, they aren't that bad," she said. "They're just snakes. Are you sweating again?"

"Just tell me this. Would they be here if it wasn't for him?"

She looked at them. "Dunno."

"Huh," he said, calming slightly. "So what do they eat?"

"What? Oh yeah. Uh…" she looked away. "Mice…"

He was aghast. "You drop live mice in there?" He looked around wildly. "Where do *they* live? In the bedroom? What kind of a person—"

"Hey, slow down a minute," she soothed. "The mice are not alive and they are frozen."

"Still."

Now she was annoyed. "What? You don't eat meat from your freezer?" she shook her head. "Honestly, you're such a hypocrite."

Deck put down the box of books and folded his arms defensively. "I am," he baited.

"Do you have pets?"

"A cat. I have a cat. Fluffy."

"Huh," she said. "That's an original name."

He smirked at her. "A *normal* person pet. A gentle, cuddly, loving pet."

"Gentle?" she laughed. "You have mice in your building?"

"It's Queens."

"Uh-huh. And do you have any mice in your *apartment*?" she asked, looking at her fingernails.

"No."

"And why do you suppose that is?"

"I… uh…"

"Just as I thought," she said, triumphant. "And those little mice are still *alive* when Fluffy gets her meaty paws in them," she said. "Now think about that!"

He was silent for several moments. Then he shook his head. "I think you've already given me plenty to think about today." He turned toward the door and started to leave.

"Wait," she called after him, feeling a bit panicked. "Where are you going?"

He turned back to face her. "There are like fifty more boxes out there," he said.

"Right," she said, relieved.

"Why?"

"No reason," she said. "Just, um...just thanks."

"No problem," he smiled and headed down the stairs.

Amy grabbed a knife from the kitchen and began slicing open the boxes. Seeing her books all tucked away inside them, she immediately anticipated reconnecting with long-lost friends. She greeted them warmly as she pulled each one out, caressing their covers, inspecting their bindings. She couldn't wait to rediscover them. And then she heard a commotion on the stoop and she raced to the window to see what was wrong.

She spotted Deck, rubbing his head and then laughing with the guys. She couldn't hear the details of the conversation, but it looked like Deck was telling them something. And then they all laughed and offered him high fives. She headed back to her books.

His first trip back, Deck made alone. The second marked an appearance with Mario, toting a couple of boxes. And then Mario and Frankie. And then Mario and Frankie and Angelo. On the final trip, Amy looked up. "No Tony?"

"I'm here," Tony called from the hallway. "Man, you read a lot," he said, as he dropped the boxes he was carrying on stack of boxes not yet opened. "Here's the last one."

They all stood around a while, looking around at her apartment, with nothing to say. Then Tony spoke, "There's nothing here."

And then Mario, "He really took everything."

And then Frankie, "I kind of like this look. Kind of fresh and minimalist."

And then Angelo, as he walked to the other side of the room and tugged on the curtain string, "Wait a minute. How is there a window here?" He pulled it open to a collective gasp.

And then Deck, "Please, tell me. Tell us. If he hadn't brought them here, would you have them?"

The Boys looked to her expectantly and she shrugged her shoulders. "I don't know," she said. "Actually, I don't think so. No," she sighed. "Not at all. To be honest, I really don't like snakes that much. I mean, these guys I've been taking care of for so long, but, well, I guess, you don't always get to choose what needs your love."

"That's for damned sure," said Frankie.

The guys all nodded in agreement. "Catch you later, man," said Mario as the guys waved and headed out.

Deck and Amy looked at the boxes. "Now what?" he asked.

"Now I pull them all out and shelve them, I guess."

Deck looked around at the empty room. "Shelve them where?"

"Good question. I guess for now I just pull them all out."

"I guess we can stack them against the wall. Too bad you have all those shelves taken up—"

"I think stacking will do just fine, thank you," she snapped defensively.

"Whatever you say."

"I already started," she said, pointing to the books she'd already uncovered. His interest piqued, he walked over to the open box to investigate.

"*Candide*," he smiled. "My favorite."

"Seriously? Because it's also mine."

"Really?"

"Sure. Why?"

"Seems a little light for you," he said, balancing the slender book on one finger like a Globetrotter with a basketball.

She rolled her eyes. "*Candide* is deep and meaningful. I mean, underneath the laughs."

He considered this. "Nothing says comedy like burning heretics."

"And light cannibalism."

"And let's not forget the gang rape."

They both broke out laughing. "So there is a light side to you yet, eh?" he said.

"For your information, I do have a sense of humor. And, like it or not, there is a lot of deep, important meaning in every one of Voltaire's passages. The idiocy of religion and the aristocracy," she said. "The futility of hope."

"I'll give you the idiocy bit, but I'm not sure Voltaire was saying hope was futile."

"He rewarded everyone's hopes and dreams and Herculean efforts with a lifetime of hard labor."

"Well, that's one way of looking at it, yes," he said. "Tending their gardens so they wouldn't have to keep thinking things to death—so they wouldn't *have the time* to think things to death anymore."

"So, you're saying the best of all possible worlds is one in which people don't have to think?"

"Sort of, yes."

"You know you're a college professor?"

"Thinking is fine, smartass. I'm talking about thinking things to death. It's a little different."

"I suppose..."

"Because when they can connect with the land, when they can feel their efforts and really connect to something *real*, that's when they're finally happy."

"And you say you don't think things to death," she chided him.

He smiled. "I guess we're more alike than I'd like to admit."

"Thanks."

They were quiet for a moment as they sat there pondering each other's words. Then Amy broke the silence. "So maybe you can help me with something else then—"and she quickly added, "something about *Candide*?"

"Shoot."

"Every time I read it, and I've read it a ton of time, I can't help but think something's missing, you know? That Voltaire meant to say more, and somehow…"

"I'm not sure. I think he makes his point."

"I still think it's kind of bleak."

"Man, are you thick. It isn't bleak, it's optimistic. It's called "Optimism" for Christ sakes."

"It's sarcastic."

"No, it isn't."

"Of course it is.'"

"Nope."

"How do you *know*?"

"I just told you; it's called 'Optimism'—'Candide, or Optimism.'"

"But how do you *really* know."

"Because sometimes a cigar is just a cigar."

"And sometimes it isn't."

"And there you go, totally missing the point again."

"I beg your pardon?"

"Just like you completely miss the point every time. I think you need to spend some time in the garden."

"But you really don't think it's strange? That it's bleak? That after all they endured, they still believed what they ended up with was really 'The best of all possible worlds?'"

"Things didn't turn out like they thought they would, but at least Candide and Cunegonde ended up together," he said. "Although who would have either other of them in the end anyway?"

She giggled. "True."

"Not to mention that at least they weren't alone—that they lived happily ever after with their freak show of a makeshift family." He placed the book down. "And seriously," he continued, "how could anyone get through any of the crap of life if they didn't believe that what they were living in was indeed the best of all possible worlds?"

She considered this for a moment. "I guess you're right," she said. "But it still doesn't all add up for me."

"No, of course it wouldn't," he laughed.

"What's that supposed to mean?"

"Forget it," he said. "Hey, why don't I get us a drink while you get reacquainted with all your old chums," he said. "Where's the kitchen?"

"That way," she pointed and he headed in the direction indicated.

Amy pulled more books out of boxes as Deck rattled around for a while. He returned with a tray laid out with her antique teapot and two of her little china cups.

"What do you have there?" she asked, delighted that he had not only found her collection but decided to use it.

"A literary tea party, of course. I think there's plenty of madness to go around when it comes to you and I," he smiled. "But no madeleines."

"I must have run out."

"Now how will we properly remember and share things past without our madeleines?"

She grinned. "I'm starting to think the past is overrated."

"So is Proust," he said, as he poured out two cups, offering her the one with the little green flowers. She couldn't help but smile as she watched him take up the other tiny cup in his substantial hand, pinching the delicate handle between two massive fingers. He looked very much the part of Gulliver in Lilliput. "Let's see. What else do you have here?" he asked, scanning through her books with his free hand. "What really gets Amy going?" He looked up. "And why are you staring at me?"

"No reason," she said.

"Fair enough," he said as he shuffled through. "If you don't mind me saying so, I think this is more Faulkner than one person should be allowed to own. No wonder your brain doesn't work right."

"Faulkner's a genius," she said. "He's difficult maybe. But once you understand him, he's incredibly satisfying."

"I guess I have to agree about the genius part. But I never found him to be that difficult. They're really great stories, but they're pretty basic when you get right down to it."

"Are you kidding me? *As I Lay Dying* was such a complex, tragic novel. Brilliant really."

"Tragic?" he asked, almost mockingly.

"Yes," she insisted. "And brilliant."

"I'll give you brilliant," he said, and gave her a serious look. "But Amy, you *do* know this is a comedy, right?"

She gasped. "It is not! How could you say such a thing?"

"Think about it."

"What's there to think about? Their mother is dead and the family sets out on a pilgrimage to bring her home and bury—-"

"They're mountain folk and they're sitting around waiting for her to die," he said. "Her name is Addie Bundren. Get it? Added burden? You don't get it. Okay. Let's go through it."

"Addie's dying and her only request is that she be buried with her family."

"And not the group of yahoos she gave birth to," he laughed.

"So her husband, Anse, builds her a coffin, and sells some of their belongings to finance the trip."

"Why wouldn't he just sell those things to buy her a coffin and just be done with it?" he said.

"And then they head to Jefferson and all kinds of terrible things happen."

He giggled. "They lose the coffin in the river."

"The barn burns down," she said, shaking her head. "And that poor tragic girl."

He smirked. "Who tries to get an abortion from the pharmacist and ends up sleeping with him, too?"

"And the little boy and the buzzards."

"After a week and a half with no embalming and a good soak in the river, I'm surprised there weren't more buzzards."

"I still don't see how any of this is funny."

"Amy, they have no teeth. They have backwards ideas about everything." She regarded him with a horrified stare. "Oh, man.

You really don't get it, do you? You're much too serious." He shook his head. "You're missing out then," he said, holding up the book. "Because it's fucking hilarious."

She stared at him silently for a few moments, a blank expression on her face. "There's something wrong with you."

"Maybe. But I know funny when I see it."

"Maybe we should just drop it."

"Tell me what else drives you. What makes you think?" he asked, moving closer to her. "Fuck that, actually. Tell me what makes you *feel*."

She inched away from him. "I guess…" she paused, unsettled and intrigued at once. "I guess these do. My books. The words. You know?"

"I might," he said, and picked up a collection of poems. "ee cummings?"

"ee cummings is beautiful," she scowled. "These poems are deep and they are exquisitely written and they are nothing to laugh at." She snatched the book out of his hands. "You're not going to ruin this for me, too."

He gazed at her for a moment before he spoke, "I do not know what it is about you that closes and opens; only something in me understands."

She froze. She could feel his eyes on her as he spoke these beautiful words, ones she had always wanted to hear like this. His eyes bore right through her. But she couldn't look at him. She couldn't breathe. She felt a familiar electric current flowing through her and she was very confused. This was all quite unexpected, but then, in a way, not.

"The voice of your eyes is deeper than all roses," he continued, and he moved closer to her, lightly touching her hand. His touch set off a surge of tiny tingles under her skin.

He kneeled in front of her and stroked her face, and only then could she look at him, confused and elated as she was by the terror and delight and comfort she felt, all mixed together, all happening at once.

"Nobody," he whispered, "not even the rain, has such small hands." And then he kissed her. Gently. Sweetly. So many precious emotions tied into one simple gesture. And she kissed him back, feeling a different kind of passion, an all-encompassing passion—a kind of passion she had never known before.

And just as suddenly, he pulled away and clutched his chest.

"Oh, my God!" she gasped.

"Now you're trying to kill *me*?" he said.

"No. Oh God, no. Are you okay?"

He smiled and pulled her close. "Never better," he said as he kissed her again.

Amy had been to some strange places in her life. Before today, she would have said that the strangest place she had ever been was the Northern Berks Reptile Show when she'd gone with David to Pennsylvania one summer . They admired specimens and collected some to add to his menagerie; to their family. But the event was a freak show in and of itself, having nothing to do with the snakes and the lizards and the baby alligators all up for sale. Amy had never seen more mulleted hair. More throwback feathered roach clips. More heavy metal T-shirts and rhinestones in one place. It was as much an event for an anthropologist as a herpetologist; it was hard to say if the reptiles or the humans peddling them were more interesting.

But never in a million years could she have seen herself in the place she was just now. In her own bed, with this enormous bald man quietly snoring beside her.

There was more to it than the visual, though. It was somewhere newly traveled, gladly beyond any experience she had ever had. It was a new feeling of calm. A luscious mix of exhausted bliss and sweet serenity. A place she had only been to with Deck.

Watching him sleep, feeling the way that she did, she knew this was different than anything thing else. And she never wanted to leave this place.

Amy nuzzled into Deck's shoulder and closed her eyes. He opened his, and gently stroked her shoulder with his thumb. "You're not going to report me, are you?"

"I guess it wouldn't look good if the dean found out, no."

"Does that change anything for you?" he asked. "I mean, you could stay working for me and we could forget any of this ever happened. Or…"

"Or I could quit and have more time to prepare for my defense."

"I could never ask you to do that."

"That's okay. I think I'm ready to do just that. We all know I suck at that job and I think this was just the push I needed."

"Good," he said, and lightly kissed her forehead. "Because you are pretty terrible at it. And defending your dissertation will be a breeze, comparatively speaking. I'm sure they'll be so blown away, they'll offer you a new position on the spot." He lay back down and began to drift off again into a peaceful sleep.

"Do you really think that?"

"I told you I read it. There's very little to defend."

She smiled and nuzzled up to his shoulder. "Will you be there?"

"I don't think I'll be allowed on the panel, no," he said, gently stroking her arm. "But I can't think of a single thing that could keep me away."

Amy smiled as she grazed his chest lazily with her fingertip. She was so amazed at the texture of this man. Smooth as glass. Then the tip of her finger rubbed against something wiry, something that bristled her finger as she skimmed it. She jumped up.

"Deck! You have hair! Look! A hair!"

He glanced over and smiled sleepily. "I know."

"But how?" she shrieked with delight, bouncing up and down on the bed. "And why?"

He smiled warmly at her and gave her hand a gentle squeeze. "It's because of you," he said and he closed his eyes again. "Thank you."

"Me?" Amy pulled away. "I don't get it."

"You will," he said, and he took her back into his arms.

12

And How It Flipped Again—and Then Again

Amy managed to make it to work despite the exhaustion she felt at having slept about an hour and a half as well as the conflict and confusion, the ecstasy and the elation, the morning after had inevitably brought. But life was strange like that, or at least it was now.

Barely twenty-four hours ago, she was feeling freshly heartbroken and devastated after colliding with David and Liz. And then all those strange feelings for Deck started to emerge. Then he had ended up in her home and, incredibly, in her bed. And she was really happy about it. But she was cautious. Because despite the magic of the night before, a small slice of David was still inexplicably wedged in her head and her heart. It was all so confusing. Not to mention that Deck was still her boss. And now she was going to quit her job on top of everything else?

Now she was riddled with doubt. What the hell was she thinking sleeping with him? How was she going to play it with him now? How was she supposed to act around him? Should she be cool and aloof and pretend as though nothing had happened? Act as if despite the fact that the very earth shook when they were together, that whatever had happened between them didn't matter that much? Or should she take another approach, and just take what she wanted, pouncing on him the minute he came in? So many questions.

When he'd finally left her place around four, he'd given her a tender kiss, and when she asked him to stay, he'd said he had things to take care of, but assured her he would be back. If he had stayed the night, would she have felt more secure today?

That the light was on in Deck's office threw her as she was sure she'd have beaten him in. She stalled a while, still undecided about what to do. Then Deck came in through the front door, still dressed for the outdoors and carrying his briefcase and two coffees, further confusing her.

"Good morning," he beamed, presenting her with one of the cups. "How are you today?" he asked and gave her a quick, gentle kiss on the cheek.

She relaxed. "I'm good," she smiled. "A little sleepy, but…"

"There's a lot of that going on around here this morning, isn't there," he said.

"Yes."

He started walking to his office, then stopped and nodded for her to join him.

"Sure," she said, and followed him in.

"You're looking strange," a woman's voice said, and Deck froze. "I'd heard about the hair, but I guess it's something you really have to see."

He spun around, shock and fear and that dark something again apparent in his face. "What are you doing here?"

"I could ask you the same," she said as Amy entered the office and looked to the guest chair. She now saw that the source of the voice was a gorgeous woman in her early- to mid-thirties.

"I'm working," he snapped.

"For Heimlich. Even though you——"

"Heimlich's dead," he cut her off. "And I thought you were, too."

"Thought? Or wished?" The tan and radiant woman had shoulder-length, improbably shiny black hair, green, catlike eyes, and lips so round and voluptuous, Amy surprised herself wondering for a quick second what it would be like to kiss her. "And who's this?" the woman asked, looking Amy up and down with an amused expression on her face.

"Marny, Amy. Amy, Marny." He looked at Amy. "Marny is my ex-wife." He looked at Marny. "Amy's just my assistant." Amy wasn't sure which of those blows had hit her harder or hurt her more. *Just his assistant?*

Marny stood and she was like a vision. Ava Gardner in her heyday. A true goddess. Her hair cascaded like silk over perfectly straight shoulders. A sleeveless Lycra dress clung to her improbable curves like it had been cut and sewn around her. Wrapped around her right arm was an elaborate jasmine flower tattoo that reached from her shoulder to the top of the hand that she extended with impossible grace as she spoke. "I'm his wife, sweetie," she said, and looked at Deck. "We were never divorced."

"You're still married." Amy said, very innocently, very confused.

"That's not my fault," he barked.

"Fair enough," said Marny, dropping Amy's hand like it was a bag of worms. "It's a pleasure to meet you," she said, though no one bought it.

Looking as though he'd like to snap her in half, Deck glared at Marny. "What do you want," he asked through clenched teeth.

"I think you know what I want," she said.

"You know I don't have any money," he said.

"Stop playing stupid, Deck. You know Heimlich didn't keep secrets from me."

"Where's Lee?" he coughed.

"Didn't work out," she purred. "Couldn't give me what I wanted. And you know I always get what I want, Deck. So why don't you just give me what I want?"

"What does she want?" Amy squeaked, her eyes filled with concern and confusion and naïveté.

"This is a bad time, I think," Marny said, now eyeing Amy suspiciously. She looked back at Deck and then at Amy again. "I'll come back later, when you're alone. Or maybe I'll pass by…"

"No!" Deck and Amy shouted in unison, of course for different reasons.

Amy was immediately embarrassed. "What I meant was," she stammered, "What I meant was I can go. Don't worry about it."

"Whatever you have to say in front of me, you can say in front of Amy," Deck insisted, confusing both women, though for different reasons.

"Oh," said Marny. "I see how it is…"

"No!" Deck and Amy shouted again in unison, and shot each other annoyed looks.

Now it was Deck's turn to speak. "What I meant was," he said, and took a long pause as he looked back and forth between the two women. "What I meant was that, Marny, we have nothing left to talk about. And what you have to say to me is so insignificant as far as I'm concerned, that I don't care *who* hears it," he said, meaning perhaps not what Amy had perceived: *That she was insignificant to him.*

"I gotta go," Amy said, choking back tears. She couldn't believe that he had betrayed her like this. In front of *her.* In front of Marny. In this way. As she stumbled backward, she caught the heel of her special shoes on the leg of a chair and broke it right off the shoe. "Oh, shit!" she said, as she knelt to retrieve it. "Oh, shit."

"What a shame," Marny smirked. "Those were so cute."

Now panicked, Amy took off the other shoe and tossed them both in the wastebasket before she darted off.

"Not again!" At the very moment that Amy's shoe had split in two, an old shopkeeper in a second-hand store in the eastern part of Queens, New York, clutched her chest and fell off the stool she had been standing on as she searched for an old, dusty clock on a high, forgotten shelf.

Later the diagnosis would be made that she'd suffered a mild heart attack. But for now, as it had been before, the only explanation was that the poor woman's heart had broken in half.

Amy made a mad dash for Jane's apartment and didn't stop until she got there.

"I need a drink and I need one now," demanded Amy from the doorway, looking crazed and sad and somewhat homeless in her bare feet.

Jane motioned her in. "It's only ten o'clock," Jane said.

"Please, just a drink," Amy insisted.

Jane looked down at Amy's feet, bruised and dirty and bleeding. "Of course," she said. "Come on in, kiddo. It's noon somewhere." She watched Amy hobble over to the couch as she headed to the kitchen, opened a bottle of white, and joined Amy on the couch.

"What happened?" Jane wondered, and Amy gave her the whole sordid tale, from the David and Liz dropping off the books to the poetry to the sex to the betrayal.

"This is a lot to process all at once like this," said Jane, sipping her wine.

"Everything's happened so quickly," Amy said, shaking her head. "I can't believe any of this happened at all. Dammit!"

Jane squinched her face. "Are you sure he was dismissing you though? I mean, it seems so out of character. It makes no sense."

"I guess he got what he was after. I must have told you about all his remarks. Always reading into things?"

Jane shook her head. "I don't think he meant anything by that. It was just him thinking he was flirting. I don't think…"

"Well, he got what he wanted so that's that," she said, and downed her wine.

Jane didn't know what to say; luckily, Amy wasn't finished. "It just seemed so different with him, you know?" Amy burst into tears and Jane took her in her arms as she cried.

"Maybe there's more to it," said Zoë, who just appeared, and who tapped her loose tooth with the tip of her tongue after every other word. "He always seemed like a nice guy to me."

"You only met him once."

"Sometimes that's all you need," said Zoë, as she continued to prod away at her tooth. "I mean, I met Uncle David like a hundred times and I never liked him."

"Zoë."

"What? Well, no one liked David. It isn't any big secret."

"Nice girls don't remind their friends of their romantic mistakes, especially in the throes of another one."

Amy caught her breath and looked at Jane. "Then you do think Deck was a mistake?"

"I don't, actually," said Jane. "It's just the situation. You know I only got to talk to him the one time. You know, at the party. But Ollie's known him for so long. He really thinks the world of him."

"What do you know?"

"Probably more than I should," and she put up her hand, "but I'm not sharing. She's a nutjob, trust me."

"She was so confident and elegant."

"And manipulative and crazed."

"And beautiful. Like shockingly beautiful. Like magazine beautiful."

"What makes you think she has anything on you?"

"Seriously?"

"Put it in perspective. She took off. He loved her and she ditched him."

"I saw him look at her. He still loves her."

"Do you still love David?" She looked down. "I don't see where you're going with this," she lied.

"All I'm saying is that it takes time. Always. No matter what the circumstances were. He says he hasn't seen her since she left. You, at least, get to run into dickbag from time to time."

"Mom!"

"I'm sorry. Douche bag. I mean…whatever. You know what I mean. Look, maybe you could give him the benefit of the doubt?"

"For what? So I can lose another seven years of my life when I already know I should be walking away now."

Zoë climbed into Amy's lap and gave her a big hug. "From what you told me, it seems like that woman played a lot of games with him, Auntie Amy," she said. "Maybe he's just confused...dammit!"

"Zoë!"

"Sorry. It's just this tooth. It's making me absolutely incensed," she scowled, as she pushed against it with her tongue. "Argh! I'm never going to shake this thing loose," she whined. "It's such a horrible nuisance."

Later that day, wearing a pair of borrowed socks and sneakers from Jane, Amy arrived at her building. And just as she was dreading, there were all the Boys, standing on the stoop, and looking right at her.

"Nice shoes," said Angelo, as she approached.

"Where's your boyfriend?" sneered Tony.

"You don't mince words," she said.

"We just like to keep an eye out for you," said Frankie.

"Yes, Brendan told me," she quipped. "Thanks for that." They shrugged their shoulders. "How could you know that something was going on with me and Deck?"

They all exchanged glances. "We know he didn't leave last night," said Frankie.

"At least not before we all turned in," Mario added.

"And we know you're not shy about bringing men home," Tony accused.

"What we don't understand is why you look like that," said Angelo. "If it was such a good night."

"And it seemed like it was," said Frankie, jabbing a scowling Tony with his elbow.

"What do you mean?" she asked.

"It's like you just lost your best friend," Mario said.

Amy looked at the guys and burst into tears.

"I don't know why you get yourself involved with all these inferior men when Tony could give you just what you need," said Tony.

"I think she's got it bad for the bald guy. Leave her alone," snapped Mario.

"I guess."

"Head upstairs," said Angelo. "I think you'll feel better about things if you go upstairs."

"Thanks, guys. I think I really just need to go to bed."

Tony stepped forward, a hopeful look on his face.

"Alone. But thanks," she waved as she headed inside.

As she climbed the stairs, she noticed flowers resting on her doorstep. She got closer and picked them up, a giant bouquet of daisies, with a card attached that read:

I know that was horrible for you. I'm so very sorry. I'm taking care of it. Trust me—and please forgive me. All will be well.

—D

And now she was more confused than ever.

13

How Ollie Paid Amy a Curious Visit and How Deck Went Crazy and Left in Handcuffs

"I'm looking it up right now. Hang on…" Jane said, cradling the phone between her chin and chest as she pecked out a Google search on her keyboard.

"Okay," she paused. Got it. Looks like daisies mean gentleness, innocence, and loyal love."

"Well, that would be nice if he was the kind of guy who knew the meaning of flowers, but I'm pretty sure he wasn't thinking that much about it."

"Are you sure?"

"He thought they were pretty, and that's about it."

"I don't know if that's true, because he seems like kind of an introspective guy."

"Who would rather be happy than deep," Amy challenged.

"Right."

"In any case, I don't think he thinks as much as you think he does," said Amy.

"That was a mouthful."

"Sorry. Anyway, I don't know what he thinks. I don't know what to think anymore. I haven't even spoken to him yet today. He's was out all morning and he's been behind closed doors since he got back," she said, her attention directed at Deck's locked door.

"So, go and knock."

"I couldn't do that."

"You had sex. He left you flowers. You can do whatever you want."

"I don't know. The whole thing seems a little weird if you ask me."

"His ex is back. I can see how that would put a wedge in things. But if you want him, you have to let him know."

There was a rustling as Deck approached his door. "He's coming out. Gotta go."

"Call me later?"

"Sure."

Amy quickly hung up the phone but Deck did not emerge. So she turned her attention to her work, scanning through her papers for the notes she had taken at the last department meeting. She finally produced a torn sheet of lined paper with a coffee stain, a doodle of a dragon, and about three coherent words. "Great," she said, and turned to her computer to try and dredge up the main points from memory.

As she typed, Franks came in. "Ollie, hi," she said, getting up to give her friend's boyfriend a friendly hug. "We weren't expecting you. How are you today?" she asked.

"Hi, Amy," he said, returning her gesture with a light, cold hug, as he looked around. "Deck here?"

"Sure. Just locked up all day. You want me to buzz him?"

"That's okay," he said. "I'm actually here to speak to you."

"Oh?" she asked nervously. "Something new come up about Heimlich?"

"Yes and no," he said. "Is there somewhere more private we could go?" he asked, just as Hannah was turning the corner.

"Who's this?" Hannah asked, looking Franks up and down.

"Detective Franks," Ollie said with a wave.

"Oh, right. We've met," said Hannah.

"We have?" he asked, seeming to have no memory of her.

"Forget it," she said, and just stood there.

"It's important," Franks said, nodding to Amy.

"Of course. Excuse us, Hannah. Please," she said, and pushed passed her. She led Franks to the break room and motioned for him to take a seat at the table.

"Marny's back, you know," he said as she was closing the door.

"I did know that, yes," she said.

"What did he tell you about it?" he asked. "About what went down with her?"

"Honestly, I think I got more of the story from you," she said. "He's a little closed off about it, I guess."

"And how has he been acting today?"

"Like I said, I really haven't seen him. Why?"

"Nothing really," he said, with a look that told her he wasn't exactly telling the truth. "Just trying to build a case here."

"Huh."

Just then, the door swung open and Deck walked in. "Ollie. What are you doing here?" he asked, and extended his hand for a shake. Ollie grabbed it tentatively, with about the same enthusiasm with which he had hugged Amy when he first arrived.

"How did you know we were here?" Amy asked.

"Hannah told me," he replied, a little brusquely.

"What can I do for you, Ollie," he asked, eyeing his friend suspiciously.

"Just tying up some loose ends on the Heimlich case," he explained. "How are *you* doing?" he asked.

"I'm fine," Deck replied, tentatively, and the two men stared at each other for a while.

"Okay, I think I have what I need for now," said Ollie. "See you guys later," he said, and he showed himself out.

Deck turned to Amy, and she started to feel a little scared. "What did he *really* want?" Deck asked.

"He told me Marny was back," Amy said.

"Is that all?"

"Pretty much," she replied, but she wasn't at all comfortable in his interest in things or the river of perspiration cascading over his forehead and face. "Are you sweating, Deck?" she asked him. "Why are you sweating like that?"

Deck let out an exaggerated sigh. "We've been through this before," he snapped. "No hair, remember? Nothing to stop the flow."

"Huh," she considered this. "It's just that... It's just..."

"It's just what?" he barked.

"I've just never seen it so bad," she said, carefully.

"I guess it's hot in here," he deflected and then softened. "Look, I know we still need to talk about things, you and me."

"I know," she said, though she wasn't sure she wanted to hear what he had to say now.

"I still have some things I have to take care of. Can we get together at three?"

"Sure," she said, but she wasn't sure of anything anymore. She was feeling full of suspicion and doubt and worry. "But…"

"Hey, just trust me, okay?" he said. "Everything's going to be fine."

"Okay," she said, now not believing either his intentions or her sincerity.

When lunchtime rolled around, Amy wasn't hungry, but she took up Hannah on her offer to join her for lunch at the Student Union because she knew it would be weeks or even months before she saw Hannah again.

"I can't believe I'm leaving tomorrow. Seems incredible," Hannah said, and bit into her turkey club sandwich.

"What did you say you were looking for again?" Amy asked. "I can't keep track."

"Because you never listen when I tell you about any of this?"

Amy felt the color rise in her cheeks. Why didn't she pay attention to Hannah when she talked about all of this? "Maybe."

Hannah stared at Amy for a moment or so before she finally spoke, "I'm looking for El Dorado."

"El Dorado?" Amy asked, incredulously.

"Sure."

"But that's ridiculous."

"Why? Why is it ridiculous?"

"I mean, you *do* know that El Dorado doesn't exist?"

Hannah regarded her coolly. "How do you know?"

Amy laughed. "Because it doesn't."

"But how do you *know*?"

"I guess I don't know," Amy said, and then she was quiet for a moment. "I guess I don't really know anything anymore."

"What's that supposed to mean?"

"This whole Deck thing, I guess. It just seems so crazy. So out of the blue, you know?"

"Hmmm," was all Hannah said.

"Why hmmmm?"

Hannah wiped her face with her napkin. "What difference does it make in your life one way or the other?" she baited.

"Because I…"

"You're *involved* with that maniac now, aren't you? Forget it. Don't answer that. I already know you are."

"He's not a maniac."

"Then why was the detective here asking questions about him?" Hannah asked, now raising her voice.

"I don't know. I guess tying up some loose ends before putting the Heimlich case to bed. Why are you getting so excited?"

"I'm just saying, that detective didn't have the look of a cop putting a case to bed. If you ask me, he just opened up something new and he's ready to pounce."

"On what? You think *Deck* killed Heimlich?"

"I'm not sure how Heimlich is involved in any of this," said Hannah. "I'm just saying it doesn't add up."

"Good, because Deck would never hurt anyone." Then the image of a small bald boy beating a goldfish with a shoe swam through her head and she hated herself for it.

"He's really got you, doesn't he?" Hannah said, and shook her head. "You really are the kind of girl who sleeps with a guy once and then *blam*! You can't see straight anymore."

"How did you know about that?"

"Let's just say anthropologists and archaeologists are like detectives. You know this."

"I don't."

"Okay. Well, it's totally obvious to look at the two of you. But I still don't trust him."

"Why do you say that? You've been suspicious of him from day one and you've never had a reason."

Hannah looked away.

"Tell me. What do you know?"

"It's nothing. Just something Liz told me."

"What?"

Hannah picked at her French fries and tried to avoid eye contact. "Don't worry about it. I'm sure it isn't true."

"Tell me."

"You know they used to work together?"

"Duh."

"Well…Liz said that he used to get, well, physical with his wife. Apparently he has a hair-trigger temper and…"

"What do you mean?"

"I think you know," Hannah said, and paused for a moment. "But seriously, how would Liz know, right?" she looked away. "Probably just heard a rumor or something."

"Probably," said Amy, but the doubt was pretty much already out there and beginning to set in.

"Anyway," said Hannah, finishing the rest of her burger in one bite, "I'm gone as of tomorrow. Anything I can bring you from the jungle?" she chipped cheerily.

Amy wouldn't admit that the only image she could conjure was Hannah's head on a plate, shrunken down to the size of a small apple.

After lunch, Amy returned to her cubicle to find Deck's door still closed and Deck still locked behind it. She started to digest Hannah's words. Was it possible that Deck wasn't what he seemed? Had he really abused Marny and that's why she left him? Maybe something old and buried and raw had triggered within him. So many questions unresolved. She glanced up at the clock on the wall. Only two-fifteen. Three o'clock couldn't come soon enough.

Except that three o'clock wasn't coming—not for her and Deck. Because at two-fifty-five, Detective Oliver Franks stormed into the English department of Charles Stratton University, accompanied by two very serious-looking uniformed officers. Amy stood, subconsciously blocking the path to Deck's door, but Ollie waved her back as he headed toward Deck's office with focused intent.

"Marny's missing again," said Ollie to Deck, who had opened his door at the commotion outside. "Why didn't you tell me she was back?"

"I didn't think it mattered," said Deck, his forehead all a'glisten. "I mean, she *was* back. She came here looking for money—Amy will back that up," he said, not looking at Amy. "But I didn't have anything to give her. So I guess she ran off again."

"Except this time she left a note," Ollie said, as he held up a white envelope.

"A note?" Deck asked, either not aware it had existed or doing a very good impression of someone pretending to not be aware. "Well, what does it say?" he asked, looking away.

Ollie looked at Deck, sizing him up. He opened the envelope. "She says she fears for her life. That she's afraid of you—that you're going to hurt her again."

"That's preposterous. Surely you don't believe—"

"She says here that she left you the first time because you went crazy and burned all your photo albums in a ditch in the backyard," Ollie said flat and serious. Deck and Ollie shared a pointed stare.

"Where did you get that note?" asked Amy. "Where did it come from?"

Ollie looked coldly at Amy. "Do you know a Hannah Lindstrom?"

"Hannah?" she was baffled. "She did..."

"She turned it in."

"But how would she…where did she get that note? This doesn't add up," she looked at Ollie. "Surely you can see that this doesn't add up. Hannah doesn't know Marny. How could she…"

"I'm afraid we're going to have to head downtown to sort this out, Deck."

"But why would she do this?" Amy was dumbfounded. "Why would she…"

Deck sighed deeply. "I understand, Ollie. Let's get to the bottom of it," he said, as one of the officers whipped out his cuffs.

"I don't think that will be necessary, Patterson," Ollie said, not taking his eyes off Deck. "I know this guy. He'll come peacefully."

"We were supposed to have that talk," she said to Deck as he started to leave. "At three."

Deck turned to Amy and smiled warmly at her. "Sorry, Amy, but it looks like I can't do it today."

"But…" she pleaded and stopped, visibly in shock as she watched him walk off between the two officers.

"Ollie, you can't be serious," she said. "You can't do this to Deck. What will Jane say?" Then she gasped. "Does Jane know about this?"

Franks turned around, "Actually could you do me a favor? Could you call Jane and tell her I'll be late—"

"Are you *kidding* me? I'm not telling Jane anything for you."

"Amy, it's okay," Deck reassured, but didn't look very sure of anything. "Ollie's just doing his job," he said, taking a few steps towards her. "There's a note. There's evidence. He's got to check out his leads," he said, and stroked her tenderly on the cheek. "Which reminds me," he said. "Do you still have the dolls?"

"Huh?" she asked, now completely confused.

"Heimlich's dolls. Tell me you still have them?"

"What does that even mean? The dolls? Who cares about the dolls?"

His face went dark again. "The fucking dolls, Amy. Do you have them?" he bellowed, and she backed away. The ferocity of this outburst wasn't lost on anyone.

"On second thought," Franks said, staring point-blank at Deck, "Patterson, why don't we use those cuffs. Until we know what's what."

As Amy watched two uniformed police officers and her best friend's boyfriend take away the man who just hours ago could have been the man she loved, Hannah quietly approached. "I'm so sorry, Amy. I really am. But I always knew there was something off about that guy."

Later that day, Amy Ann Miller met with the department head, Dr. Bateman, to submit her formal resignation as assistant to Professor Decklin Thomas, or any professor for that matter. Three days after that, she set herself to the task of cleaning out her own workspace. This was just what she was doing when David came back into her life. "Hey," was all he said.

She looked up. "Hey."

He didn't say anything for a minute, just watched her, and then, "Sorry about your boss."

"He isn't my boss anymore," she said flatly.

"Oh. All right then," he shrugged his shoulders. "So no biggie."

"He *was* my friend."

"Okay. Sorry. I guess I can't say anything right around you anymore."

Despite everything, she couldn't help but feel bad for David. "No. I'm sorry," she said. "It really isn't a big deal. I'm just a bit overwhelmed by everything is all. Let's start over. How are you doing? How's Liz?"

"Funny you should ask," he said. "She kind of left."

"What do you mean *left*?"

"She said she wasn't happy. She was looking for new adventures or something."

"Seems like a new trend," Amy scoffed.

"What do you mean?"

"Nothing. Don't worry about it."

"Sure," he said.

"There's more," he continued. "She said I wasn't the one."

"Tough break," she sneered.

"I know," he half laughed. "Pretty ironic, eh?"

She had nothing to say.

"So, what are you up to?" he asked.

"Just finishing up here," she said.

"I know. But what I meant was, what are you doing later?"

She cocked one eyebrow at him, suspicious of his intentions but opting to play it cool. "Getting ready for my defense."

"Right," he nodded. "Hey, maybe I could help you prepare?"

"I'm not so sure," she hedged.

"I guess I deserve that," he shook his head. "But hey, maybe you can let me buy you a cup of coffee or something sometime?"

She watched him, shifting from one foot to the other, and looking about as nervous as a junior high student asking a girl out for the first time. It disarmed her. "I guess I don't see why not," she said.

"Great!" he replied. "Tomorrow maybe?"

She eyed him for a minute, this beautiful man who had stolen so much of her heart, so much of her life, and couldn't help but wonder if this wasn't a huge mistake waiting to happen. But she was as curious as anyone is when driving by a car wreck. "Sure," she said.

14

How Amy Visited Deck at the Precinct and How It Didn't Go Very Well

About a week or two later, Amy entered the precinct building from the pouring rain and shook out her umbrella. She had to do a double take, however, as the precinct wasn't like anything she'd seen in the movies or on TV, where they're all beige and gray and dreary.

This precinct was definitely different. It was almost cheerful. At least in the lobby, where the walls were paneled in a rich mahogany hue. There was a square coffee table covered with magazines. A couch and a couple of comfortable chairs surrounded the table. A variety of plants set around the room softened the effect. On the back wall, a giant fish tank was home to a rainbow assortment of saltwater fish. Though aside from a uniformed officer manning the front desk, the space was empty.

She nodded at the officer as she looked around and spotted Deck in a far room, his back to the door. Franks saw her come in; he waved and whispered something to Deck, who didn't turn around.

"Hi, Amy," he said, giving her a much warmer hug than he had the other day as he greeted her in the lobby. He motioned for her to follow him to a nearby interrogation room, but she couldn't take her eyes off Deck.

"What's he doing in there?" she asked.

"Scrabble, of course," he explained. "I'm letting him win."

"I guess that'll help things a little," she said.

"You look different," Ollie said, sizing her up. "What's different about you? You're not ill?"

"No," she replied, puzzled.

"Huh," he said, unconvinced. "Must be the weather then," he said, but she didn't hear him, because she was distracted by the sight of an enormous cat, the biggest cat she had ever seen. She couldn't take her eyes off the giant fur ball as it ventured up to the table where Deck sat and rubbed up against his leg.

"What *is* that?" she gasped.

Franks smirked at her. "That's his cat," he answered, matter-of-factly. "You never met Fluffy?"

"Are you sure that's a cat and not a giant raccoon?"

"It's a Maine coon. She's a big one all right, but she's mostly harmless."

Amy smiled. "Since when are you allowed to bring your pets to jail with you?" she asked and watched Deck lift and affectionately cuddle the enormous animal.

Now she found herself getting angry. "And why is he here anyway? Do you really have to hold him here? You know as well as I do that he didn't harm that woman. That he's innocent."

"And here I thought you didn't care," he smirked. "I'm not holding him here," he said. "He's free to go if he wants. He just chooses not to."

"I don't get it."

"I told you he spent a lot of time here after Marny vanished the first time, right? I think he feels better being here, than at home. Alone." The accusation stabbed Amy right through the heart. It would be too complicated if she chose to defend herself, so she remained silent.

"Anyway, I'm sure he'd love to talk to you," he said.

"Sure," she said, and she followed Ollie down the hall.

"You're back!" screamed Deck as they approached. "Wait till you see what I have for you!" he said jumping up. "Double-letter score for ALL! It's simple and *strategic*!"

Amy and Ollie both shook their heads, both immediately knowing he could have gotten more points had he used the homonym and placed the "W" from his tray on the actual "double letter" square instead.

Deck was oblivious, beaming with pride as if he'd just discovered a cure for cancer, but seeing Amy, his face fell. "It's you."

"Hi, Deck," she said. "How's it going?"

"I guess it's been better. And I guess it's also been worse. Please sit," he said, motioning to the empty chair on the other side of the table.

"Let's give these two some privacy," said Ollie, scooping up Fluffy. "We'll be right outside if you need. Just give a holler," he said, and closed the door behind him.

"You look different," he said, not looking at her.

"Why does everyone keep saying that?" she asked, blowing her drooping bangs out of her face.

"So, how's everything going at Stratton?" he asked, nonchalantly.

"I don't really know. I'm not really there anymore. I resigned, just like I said I would. I even set my date for—"

"Surely you must be aware of some of the comings and goings," he scoffed. "Surely reptile boy fills you in on the daily grind?"

That one took her by surprise. "How did you know about that?"

"I have my sources," he snapped, and looked away.

"What sources?" she wondered.

"Hannah, for one," he said.

"Hannah?" she asked, slightly scandalized, slightly confused.

"Why do you care?"

"For one, it's her fault you're even here," she said. "Not to mention that she's in the freaking rain forest. How would she know anything? And how would she tell you?"

"I know she's in the rain forest. Seems like a pretty incredible adventure if you ask me. Did you know there are hundreds of undiscovered peoples—"

"She called you? You've corresponded?"

"Corresponded?" he smirked. "What is this, 1940?" He paused momentarily. "Facebook."

"Facebook?"

"Yes, you know. Facebook. Social networking? You've heard of it?"

"I know what it is," she replied, slightly defensive as she herself wasn't on it and barely understood what it was all about.

"A remarkable invention really," he said. "A wellspring of useless information that once you tap into, you really can't do without. And did you know you can play Scrabble on Facebook? With anyone in the world?"

"I knew that," she lied.

"I'm really kind of addicted to it," he said, picking up one of his tiles and placing it in the front of the rest of the letters in his rack. "Makes you see things in a whole new light."

"I still don't understand…"

"Look, it's very simple. Hannah friended me, and I accepted her request."

"Okay…" "And so now I've been following her travels through her status updates. A truly interesting person, really."

"Really?"

"So smart and witty and full of insight. And totally freaking fearless," he said, his eyes all alight. "Just an all-around beautiful person. I can't believe I never noticed it before. I can't believe I never gave her a chance."

"Oh," said Amy, her heart and her stomach beginning to tighten. Yet Deck would not stop talking.

"Amazing work she's doing down there," he said, and he smiled in a way that made Amy more than a little uncomfortable, more than a little jealous. She decided to ignore it.

"Well I still don't see how you can know about David and me—"

He shook his head in the manner one would do to someone regarded as having been born yesterday or shortly thereafter. "He's on Facebook, too."

"You're *friends* with David?"

"Absolutely not. But she is."

"She's friends with him? Why would she be friends with him?" Amy stared blankly at Deck.

"Yep. And I can see his status updates through her profile. So I guess," he gave her a sly smile, "that Hannah didn't tell me at all that the two of you were back together. David did."

"This is too weird."

"That, and it's written all over you. Look at you," he spat, disgustedly.

"What's that supposed to mean?"

"He's gotten to you again, hasn't he?" he said, looking her up and down.

"I don't know what you mean," she said as she absently smoothed her hair. She took a deep breath as she tried to change the subject. "How's it going with you?" she asked, sincerely.

"Me? I'm doing tremendously. My prodigal wife came back into my life and ruined me again—and then ran off. Again. So I spend my days and most nights here, trying to figure out if I'm more angry at her or..." he trailed off.

"Or what?"

He shook his head. "Let's just forget it, shall we? Because if things had not turned out as they did, how would I ever have ended up in this glorious place like this?"

"I don't see how—"

"No imagination at all, Amy! Just look around you. *Is this not the best of all possible worlds?*"

"You don't *need* to be here. You aren't being detained here—"

"Ah, but I like it here," he snapped. "What's not to like?"

Amy had no response; she was starting to feel as though Deck had flipped his lid, and wondered if he would now be losing it completely.

"Let's cut the crap, Amy. Why are *you* here? Do you really give a shit about what happens to me?"

"They don't think you killed her, Deck. Ollie—"

"Of course I didn't kill her," he bellowed. "I never hurt another living thing in my life." She opened her mouth to speak. "Aside from the fish," he said, a flash of rage in his eyes. "I don't even know why I trusted you with that. I don't know why I ever trusted you with anything."

She was confused and now starting to feel a little scared. "I just don't know what to say."

He laughed. "Hey, maybe you killed her. Isn't that your specialty?"

She gasped. "How could you say that? You don't mean that."

"No," he cut her off. "I don't mean it. But does it really matter?" he asked, and looked back down at the Scrabble board. "You should know that I'm pretty much done with impossible women," he said.

"I guess I should be going," she said, and she turned to leave.

"I guess you should," he barked. She got up and headed for the door.

"He's pretty excited about taking you to the reptile convention," he called after her. "David is. He's been writing about it all week. I bet you can't wait!"

She stopped and looked at him. "I...I really don't know what to say."

"How about good-bye," he barked, and she turned again. "But before you go..."

She stopped, feeling inside a glimmer of hope that they could turn things around, they could start over again. "Yes?"

"Where are the dolls?"

"The dolls?"

"The dolls, Amy. Where are the damned dolls. Jesus! Do you still have them or not?" he snapped so harshly, his words felt like daggers that tore through her heart.

Her eyes filled with tears. "What does it matter?" she asked, and she stormed out.

15

*How Amy Moped to Jane about the State of Her
Life and How Zoe Finally Lost Her Annoying
Dangling Baby Tooth*

A couple of days later, Amy sprawled out on the couch and watched Zoë play with Heimlich's bisque dolls. For the life of her, she couldn't imagine why Deck was so obsessed with them. Had he truly gone completely nuts? It made her all the more suspicious that he may have had something to do with Marny's latest disappearance. How well did she really know him? How far had he been pushed by Marny? What kind of old grief had surfaced from deep within him? And what was he really capable of?

But this was Deck. Giant, goofball Deck. Deep down, she just couldn't accept that he could be capable of such violence. The man who'd touched her on more levels than she even knew she had.

But of course she could be wrong. It wouldn't be the first time.

"What's this one called, Auntie Amy?" Zoë called up from the floor, interrupting her thoughts.

"I don't know what any of them are called," Amy said. "I really don't know anything about them. But they may be valuable, so please just be careful playing with them."

"Do you really think they may be worth something?" Jane asked, bringing Amy a cup of tea in an oversized mug. Amy smiled to herself, in spite of herself, when all she could think was that this would be a much more suitable mug for Deck. Crazy Deck. Killer Deck...

"I don't know," Amy said, reaching for the tea. "Thanks," she said and took a sip. "Deck asked about them again."

"You didn't mention that," said Jane.

"I didn't?" she asked. "I'm sorry. I'm still a little confused about everything."

"And you look terrible," said Zoe, sweetly, from the floor. "I thought you threw that thing away," said Zoë, looking at Amy's jumper.

"It's comfortable. I guess I just wanted to be comfortable."

"Comfortable, like hanging-around-with-David-comfortable again?" Jane jabbed.

"We're both kind of in the same place right now," Amy snapped. "I don't have to defend myself to you."

Jane and Zoë exchanged a look, but said nothing. Zoë went back to the dolls and Jane traced the rim of her mug with her finger. "Zoë's right," Jane said. "You do look terrible."

"I'm okay."

Jane paused a moment and then took a deep breath. "I have something for you," she said. "Something from Ollie—well, from Deck really."

Amy waved her away. "I don't think I can have anything to do with him anymore," Amy said. "I'm sorry. But he was so mean to me."

"He's going through a kind of rough time right now, Amy," Jane said, placing an envelope on the table in front of her. "Ollie says he wrote this to you after you left. That he felt really horrible about how things went down. He was just so hurt by the David thing and…"

Amy pushed the envelope away. "I don't think—"

"Amy, he *needs* you now," Jane said, pushing the envelope back to her. "If only as a friend."

"He doesn't act like he wants anything to do with me. And besides, I'm busy," she said dismissively.

"Yeah," Jane rolled her eyes. "I know. With David."

"Okay, what's your *real* problem with this?"

"I heard you're postponing your defense again," said Jane.

"How did you…"

"Hannah."

"What the fuck? Hannah again? How would she know anything about anything. And why would she tell you?"

"Facebook," she said. "You *do* know what Facebook is—"

"I get it," Amy said, cutting her off.

"And she also emailed me because we're all worried about you."

"I don't buy that from her. I can't trust her. Did you know she's *friends* with David."

"So she can keep her eye on him," Zoe piped in. "So she can keep tabs on things over here while she's over there."

Amy remained defensive. "You know it's because of her that the note got to Ollie and…"

"Ah, so you *do* feel something more for Deck than anger?" Jane smiled.

"She shouldn't have passed along that note unless she knew for sure that something was wrong—that what it said was true. It's because of her that everything went to hell."

"It's because of Marny, who wrote the note, who showed up at all and disappeared again that any of this happened," said Jane. "Come on. You don't *honestly* believe that he would be capable of what she said. She's a terrible woman, clearly, and—"

"Let's just say there are things you don't know," Amy said. "And besides, why would she set him up like this? She was out of his life. She was free. Why go through all the trouble?"

Jane paused and looked down at her tea. "There must be something in it for her," Jane said.

"Is that what Ollie thinks?"

"I'm not allowed to say," Jane said, and took another sip of her tea.

Jane and Amy sat quietly for a while and watched Zoë play with the dolls, each carefully considering their words before speaking again.

"You really don't look so good," said Zoë, now looking up, her angelic face radiating its trademark warmth and wisdom. "And I think I know why," she said, catching her tongue on her tooth on the last word.

Zoë went back to the dolls, now thumbing the back of one of their dresses. Something wasn't quite right about the way it was laying on the doll, and she started to undo the fasteners.

"Why? Why do I look so terrible? Come on, your turn to take a shot at Auntie Amy," she snapped.

"It's just that," Zoë began, and stopped. "This tooth. I can't take it anymore," she said, and placed down the doll. Zoë started to tug at the tooth with her thumb and forefinger, first slowly and then with an incredible urgency until she finally pulled it out. "Got it!" she exclaimed, as she spit the small incisor out into her hand.

"Oh, baby," Jane cried. "You got the dangler. My goodness. You're all grown up now, aren't you?" she said. She jumped to the floor and gave Zoë a giant hug.

"Congrats, Zoë!" said Amy, joining them. "This is really huge. There's a tooth that could launch your thousand ships."

Zoë's eyes glazed over. "I'm not sure what that means."

"Well, it's not an exact parallel. But you know—like Helen of Troy?"

"Who?" she asked, more than a little confused. "What are you talking about?"

Amy and Jane looked at each other, each about as confused as Zoë seemed. Zoë picked up the doll she had been playing with and regarded it for a minute, as if there was something she was supposed to remember about it, but nothing came to mind. So she placed it down and picked up another one.

"I know what you wanted to say, Zoë. But I don't think it's because of David that things have changed," Amy said, sitting back down on the couch. "I think it's because of the shoes, you know, how they broke and everything," she said. "Must have broken the spell," she laughed.

"What!" shouted Zoë, in the manner of Linda Blair in *The Exorcist*.

Amy was taken slightly aback but decided to continue. "Think about it, guys. I got the shoes and everything was great. I lost them, and everything went to hell."

"Except that you broke your shoe *after* Marny showed up," Jane said. "And you met Deck before you even knew they existed."

Before Amy could come back with a new argument, Zoë started to laugh uncontrollably. "Are you kidding me?" she managed as she gasped for air. "The shoes?" At this she literally rolled on her back laughing.

"Yes. The story. The legend?"

"The what?" Zoë asked, now teetering back and forth.

"The *legend*," said Amy. "Of Rita Hayworth's shoes!"

Zoë stared at Amy for a minute as she prodded the empty new space in her mouth with the tip of her tongue. Then her face took on a maniacal gaze. "That?" she exclaimed, and started laughing again. "Oh, my God. I *so* made that up."

"You made it up?" both women asked at once.

"Magic shoes? Come on, Auntie Amy. That's just ridiculous," she lisped through the new space between her teeth. "You actually believed that? You silly girl," Zoë laughed again.

"I'm sorry, Amy. I don't know what's gotten into her," said Jane.

"It's okay," said Amy, and both women watched Zoë laugh and roll and laugh and roll some more. Then, as though her battery had run out, she came to a dead stop.

"Mama, I'm a little sleepy. Would you mind if I lay down for a little while? I don't really feel like myself."

"Of course, baby," said Jane, concern in her voice. "Go ahead. Just don't forget to put your tooth under your pillow."

"Okay. Night-night then," Zoë said in a four-year-old's voice neither Jane nor Amy could remember her using, even when she was a four-year-old.

"What happened?" Amy asked Jane as they watched Zoë stagger down the hallway. "I don't understand."

"What's not to get?" asked Jane.

"She's acting like a drunk," said Amy.

"No, silly," Jane said. "She's acting like a child," Jane said, her face filled with love.

Amy stood with Jane and watched Zoë slip into her bedroom. "Now what?"

Amy walked home that night, feeling more lost and confused now than ever before. She clutched her backpack where she carried the dolls close to her and wondered what she was going to do with them. Sure, she could give them to Deck, but that might only push him over the edge. She could give them to Zoë, but they somehow seemed to make the child nuts as well. Or maybe she could sell them to Smitty's? At the very least, she could get the old woman's opinion on them she decided and headed to the store.

But when she got to Smitty's she froze. For there, in the window, set between an ancient toaster and a set of Statue of Liberty cocktail coasters, perched magnificently upon their black velvet pedestal, were the shoes. *Rita Hayworth's shoes.*

"What the fuck?" she said, and she headed into the store to confront the woman.

"Amy," the shopkeeper said when she saw her. "So nice to see you again." Amy couldn't help but notice that the woman looked older somehow, more frail.

"What are they doing here?" Amy asked, gesturing wildly to the window. "How did they get back here?"

The woman regarded her with a cold stare. "They were abused," she said flatly. "So they returned home."

"But how did they get here? They didn't just fly over on their own—not from the garbage pail where I left them."

"Well, if you must know," the shopkeeper said, "I bought them back."

"From who? Who sold them back to you?" She gasped. "Not a bald guy?" she asked, her arm raised to indicate tallness. "Fortyish?"

"If you must know, the answer is no," the shopkeeper coolly replied. "It was some Ava Gardner-looking trollop with a giant tattoo," she said with disgust. "She brought them to me and then asked if anyone had come in with a bunch of dolls."

"Dolls? Like antique dolls?"

"I didn't ask. I mean, honestly. Does this look like a toy shop to you?"

"Forget it," Amy said. "And I'll have you know those shoes weren't anything but trouble for me. They're cursed. You should get rid of them."

"How dare you!" the woman accused. "What do you know of anything? Those shoes belonged to Rita Hayworth. Those shoes changed her life!"

"Oh, yeah? Because I heard that story was complete crap."

"That's what you heard," the old woman said, perfectly calm and composed.

"Yes," Amy challenged.

"And that's what you *believe*?"

"Yes, actually. Yes, it is."

A dark shadow fell over the woman's ancient face. "Get out of my store and never come back," she hissed. Amy stood in her place. "I'm not kidding with you," the woman raged, her eyes on fire. "Go. Get out. Now! Go!"

So Amy turned on her heel and left.

And while Amy was navigating the murky jungle of her past and present, of broken hearts old and new and revisited, of the stories people tell and the stories people believe, Hannah Anastasia Lindstrom was navigating a different kind of jungle. Dressed very much like a 1940s archaeologist, in a tight-fitting khaki shirt and matching shorts, she lead her simple team through the rain forests of Brazil, on a mission as important to her as her own life.

As she cut through a clearing, she stopped for a moment. She reached into her belt for her canteen and took a long draw of water. She replaced her canteen, wiped off her chin, and pulled out a map. She pointed to the map and she looked into the distance.

Just then, an improbably large man, similarly dressed, the sun beating down on his shiny bald head, emerged from the thicket. She smiled warmly at him, a smile he returned, and she showed him the map. He looked ahead and she nodded. "This way," she motioned, as the man and the others followed. She was now sure, at last, that she had found what she had been looking for.

16

*How Amy Discovered Yet Again That Things Are
Seldom As They Seem—and Seemed to Ignore the
Message Yet Again*

The parking lot of Little Bay Park is located underneath the south section of the Throgs Neck Bridge. Built in the 1960s, the Throgs Neck Bridge's sole purpose was to alleviate congestion on its larger, more impressive, more glamorous sister-bridge, the Bronx-Whitestone Bridge—known for the most part as the Whitestone Bridge, or simply "The Whitestone."

The Whitestone was conceived and brought to fruition by Robert Moses, the father of road and park development on Long Island and the outer boroughs. In the ribbon-cutting ceremony for this bridge, which was built in less than two years, Moses hailed it as "architecturally the finest suspension bridge of them all, without comparison in cleanliness and simplicity of design, in lightness and absence of pretentious ornamentation. Here, if anywhere, we have pure, functional architecture."

There was no such excitement or enthusiasm for the Throgs Neck Bridge, however; no lavish ribbon-cutting ceremony on record, no fanfare of any sort. Much in the same way some people are compelled to have another child, not because they have a deep-seated desire to love and nurture another human being, but because their existing little lone darling needs a playmate, the Throgs Neck came to be. Even the bridge's name seemed a sloppy afterthought, loosely derived from one John Throckmorton, who settled in the area circa 1643.

159

Now surely Moses, who wanted these bridges, and Othmar Ammann, who designed and oversaw their construction, must have known that the structures might inspire lovers to park under them and admire their beauty, among other things. And surely all the workers who actually built the bridges—some of whom lost their lives in the process, becoming food for the fish or filler for the foundation—must have realized that someday, the blood, sweat and tears they poured into creating such an urban majesty as well as her ugly afterthought of a sister, might attract throngs of lovers to make out in the surrounding parks under the stars as headlights and taillights of cars streaked above them. But had they any awareness of the goings-on inside one particular Dodge Charger, registered to a Mr. David Hayes of Flushing, Queens, at this moment in time, they likely would be spinning in their cement-fixed or watery graves.

"What was that?" asked Amy, as a wave of something not quite water seemed to wash across the front of her dress.

"I'm sorry, Scruffy," David said, making direct eye contact only with the peeling vinyl on the car's ancient dashboard. "I guess it's been a while."

Amy was still straddled around David's lap. Both of them were fully clothed, both of them were considerably wet. Amy wanted also to believe that both of them were horrified and embarrassed at what had just occurred, but when David smiled up at her, pursed his lips and held his hands up in the manner of "oh well," she imagined she was probably taking it all too seriously. Of course this happened all the time. To adult people. Who were not geriatric. Didn't it?

True, it had been a while since they had been together, but it wasn't like he'd been celibate all that time, sexing up the sea monster as he was. Deck had gone far longer and…well, what did Deck matter now any way.

Amy started to feel a quiet, inexplicable rage well up in her, until David softly laughed. "What a mess," he said. She realized then that he was embarrassed, of course, and she started to feel sorry for him.

She started to warm, except she couldn't lie to herself about being disappointed. Though this was just the tip of the iceberg. The real problem this night was that he had forgotten her birthday. Or at least he was doing a pretty good job of pretending he had, not picking up the tab at dinner or making any mention of her having turned thirty today. The dinner bill wasn't such a big deal, she rationalized. He hadn't wanted to go out to dinner, after all. He had wanted to cook for them. He probably had something really special in mind, something intimate and romantic, and she had gone and blown it insisting they go out for sushi. Stupid.

And of course they could have gone back to her apartment after dinner, but this he resisted. It had been his idea to go sit under the bridge and watch the stars, and she'd given in, thinking he'd meant sitting on a bench in that quiet, lovely park under the Whitestone; not cramped into his car in a brightly lit parking lot under the Throgs Neck, right off the main road. And now a new wave of embarrassment washed over her as she wondered if anyone had been watching them. She quickly jumped off his lap and slumped down into the passenger seat.

"I am *truly* sorry," David said, and he brushed her face with the back of his fingers and looked at her with those eyes of his, those shiny amethysts he used to see. "I promise I'll make it up to you. Let me make it up to you?"

She could feel herself melting now with each beat of his eyelashes; with each word he shaped with his gorgeous mouth, but she tried to keep cool. "Maybe another night," she said.

He looked at her over his eyebrows, in that way he had. "Couldn't I at least come over for a little bit. Just get cleaned up. You know…"

Amy wasn't exactly sure what she was supposed to know, or who he would be avoiding having to face back at his own home, caked in his own frosting as he was, but she rationalized. Maybe he had something for her at her place. A gift he had hidden for her somewhere. Of course this was all just a ploy. Of course it was!

"Sure," she smiled. "Let's go."

They drove without speaking to Amy's apartment, David humming a tune she couldn't identify, Amy quietly beaming in anticipation of what could be waiting for her when they arrived. As they approached the building, she felt a twinge of panic that the Boys would be on the stoop and was relieved as they pulled up in front that they seemed to have found something better to do this night.

David stopped the car, got out, and made a beeline for the front door. He turned to face her and nodded in the manner of, *Are you coming?*

Amy let herself out of the car and followed David inside. As they trotted up the three flights of stairs to her apartment, Amy looked down at her dress and noticed that what she had thought was only a small spot had seeped to the shape and possible size of Texas. She was no scientist, but she was a bit curious as to why it hadn't dried yet.

As they arrived at her front door, David held out his hand for the keys. She smiled at this seemingly gentlemanly gesture as he went about the business of turning the locks. Then he pushed open the door, leaving Amy in the prime spot to unexpectedly and horrifyingly be greeted by a loud chorus of: "SURPRISE!"

Everyone was there. Well, not everyone. Not Hannah, at least, who she guessed was probably still in the jungle, but everyone else. There was Jane and Ollie and David and Lauren—and oh God, little Zoe, adorably dressed as a "flapper" fairy with a sash draped around her that read "Goodbye Twenties." There was Aunt Enid and Aunt Clarabelle and Uncle Mort. There was Grant and the ever-unsmiling Ava. There were the Building Boys. All of the Boys. Then her heart jumped into her throat as it occurred to her that Deck might also be there. But as she scanned the room, she saw he was not. Which caused her then to experience an unexpected pang of disappointment, until Uncle Mort yelled out, "What the hell is that all over your dress?"

She turned to David. "Did you know about this?" she demanded, partly infuriated that he would keep this from her, partly delighted that her family had finally included him in something—and wholly horrified that he had let them come home like this, to this, covered by rogue sperm as they were.

"It's your birthday?" he asked, seemingly stunned.

She cocked her head at him. Of course, he was kidding with her. "You knew that. Of course you did!"

He looked down at the floor. "Oh, fuck. It is your birthday isn't it."

She looked away, and Jane swooped in. "The same day as the past seven years," she snapped at David as she pulled Amy through the doorway and into her arms. "And the twenty-three years before she knew you."

Amy felt defensive. "That's not really necessary…"

"Happy Birthday, kiddo," Jane said, and then pulled away. "Is that spot wet?"

"Nice to see you again," David managed.

"As long as we both know that's a lie," Jane said, as Ollie approached, and sized David up as he did such things, by twirling the corners of his moustache. Amy and Jane shared a glance; Amy giggled and looked away as Ollie untangled his hand from his facial hair and offered it to David.

"Ollie Franks," he said. "Detective Ollie Franks."

David accepted Ollie's handshake, though with a slight repulsed reluctance. "David Hayes."

Ollie dropped David's hand and went back to his twirling. "Ah, yes," he said, squinting at David. "I suppose you are."

Everyone just stood around quietly and stupidly watching this until Amy nudged David with her elbow. "You wanted to change?" she asked him.

"Right," David said, now slightly twitching, his eyes still on Ollie. "See you all in a bit," he said, and he sprinted to the bedroom.

"Not if we can help it," said Jane. Amy rolled her eyes and took off after David. They hadn't noticed that Zoë had joined them and was scowling at David as he walked off. "That bastard."

"Zoë!" Jane gasped.

"The little one's right," said Ollie.

"That may be. But Zoë, nice little girls—"

"I know, I know," said Zoë. "But where has being nice gotten Amy anyway?"

Jane had no defense for that, as she quietly played with a loose thread on her dress.

"Uh, huh," said Zoe as she walked off.

In the bedroom, Amy handed David an oversized T-shirt and sweatpants she sometimes slept in and she headed for the door.

"They're not going to be easy to win back, are they?"

Amy considered that David had never really won her family to begin with, so winning back was not technically what he was looking for here, but she decided to keep that to herself. "They're just very protective. Especially Jane."

David approached her and placed his hands on her shoulders. "Amy," he said. A surge ran through her as he looked deeply into her eyes. "I know I've made some mistakes. Some stupid mistakes," he said, "like forgetting your birthday. So stupid," he said, shaking his head back and forth.

"Just forget it," she said, looking away. He lifted her chin with the tip of his finger.

"But I'm really trying here now. I am."

Amy hoped this was true, she wanted to believe it. Especially as looking at him all bare-chested and sexy like that made her want to believe a lot of things. She smiled. "I know you are," she said, encouragingly. "They just need some time to get readjusted. Just keep trying."

He kissed Amy on the forehead and she headed back into the living room.

She took a deep breath before heading back into the fray, sizing up her surroundings. The room had been decorated with great care. Streamers were strung, balloons were hung. Someone had thought to bring in some chairs and a couple of long tables. Both of the tables were covered in festive tablecloths of brightly colored plastic. One was loaded up with bowls of chips and dips and platters of delicious-looking foods, while beautifully wrapped packages covered the other table.

Someone had even though to dig up Amy's parents—or at least the life-sized, cardboard-mounted photo placard of Eric and Shirley. Lauren had crafted it years before and it used to appear at all family get-togethers, decorated in some way to commemorate the occasion. Except one Easter Seder, after perhaps one sip too many of the Passover wine, Lauren got particularly weepy watching Shirley and Eric just standing there while everyone else sat and ate while Joshua, irrationally angry at his friends for disappearing as they had, marched right up to the cutout and punched Eric in the face.

Amy was glad they were back again, no matter how creepy the circumstances. Eric's nose and cheek looked perhaps slightly indented, but otherwise they appeared no worse for the wear. Today, a "Happy 30th Birthday" sign was haphazardly glued to the front of the placard and party hats appeared stapled to their heads. Amy smiled as Lauren approached.

"I'm happy they made it," said Amy and she started to tear up.

"They wouldn't have missed it for the world," said Lauren, as she pulled Amy into a warm hug.

Joshua joined them. "He doesn't look so bad," said Joshua, more than a trace of guilt in his voice.

And then Enid. "You really gave it to him good," she said, and they all laughed.

Then David emerged from the bedroom and came over to them. "Still can't believe they just vanished," he said, shaking his head. "Makes no sense. I mean, who just disappears like that? On vacation?"

Joshua was just about to pull out his left hook again when Enid remarked, "Disappeared indeed," and started looking around the room. "Has anyone seen Grant?"

"Come on, Enid, I'll help you find him," said Lauren, offering her arm.

David, sensing Joshua's displeasure, took the opportunity to flee. "I'll help you," he said, leaving Joshua and Amy alone together.

"So, Amy," said Joshua, not looking away from the cutout. "You think it might be time to change?"

Amy squinted at the poster to figure out what about it Joshua thought they might change. "Change?"

"Your clothes," he replied in a pained whisper, shifting uncomfortably. Though it would be hard to say who was more horrified—him, or Amy, who just then realized she had forgotten all about the mess on her dress. She gasped and raced to the bedroom.

Amy slammed the door behind her and caught her reflection in the mirror that hung over her dresser. She appeared to have been hit with a water balloon filled with snot. She quickly pulled her dress over her head and ducked into her closet to find something else to throw on when she heard a commotion from the fire escape outside her window, followed by a male voice. "Try the pink one," it said. "You look better in colors."

"Uh, thanks?" she said, grabbed a pink T-shirt dress off a hanger and slipped it on. "Who's that?" she called to the window.

Grant stuck his head in. "Just me," he said, and then Frankie and Mario also stuck their heads through. "Uh, I mean not just me, but just me who spoke."

"What are you guys doing out there?" The ensuing silence drew her to the window. She stuck her head out to see Grant, Frankie, Mario, and Jane all sitting on the fire escape.

"Uh, smoking," said Frankie.

"Smoking's terrible for you. You guys really should give it up. And Jane, Grant, I have to say I'm shocked—"

"Not that kind of smoking," Grant said, as he took a long drag on the cigarette in his hand as passed it to his left hand side.

"Oh," she said, somewhat scandalized, somewhat intrigued. "Jane, my God, you have a child!"

Jane took the cigarette and breathed in for a long hit. "Can't think of a better reason," she said and exhaled, her observation provoking a gigglish grunt from Grant. "Besides," she said, and took another hit, "it's not like she's out here."

Amy watched Jane for a while. "Well?"

Jane shrugged her shoulders and shook her head.

"Aren't you going to exhale?" Amy asked.

Jane pursed her lips and shook her head, and finally let out the smoke, which Amy had to admit smelled pretty darn good. Then she caught herself, "Wait. Isn't your boyfriend a cop?" Amy asked as Jane went in for a third hit.

Jane paused. "You have a point," she said, and passed the joint to Mario. "See you guys inside," she said. "I can't promise any Doritos will be left, though."

Mario took a quick hit and passed it to Frankie, who waved it off. "I'm starved," Mario said. He stood up and passed the joint to Grant. "Good stuff, man," he said. "Thanks for sharing."

Grant waved in reply as he took a long toke.

"Wait up!" said Frankie, and he climbed through the window after Mario.

Grant tapped the grate next to him, motioning for Amy to sit down. She surprised herself by complying.

He looked her up and down and nodded. "That's a much better look then when you came," he inhaled, "in," he exhaled, and coughed himself silly on the smoke cracking himself up.

"Oh, ha ha," said Amy, folding her arms in front of her. He held out the joint to her; she paused for a moment and then shook her head. "Frankly, I'm a little shocked at you," she said.

"Why?" he asked and he took another toke.

"Because...well...you know," she stammered, uncomfortably. "What would Enid say?"

He laughed. "She'd probably spontaneously combust. You're right. I should be more sensitive," he said and he took another drag.

"You're being awfully droll for a man who spends most of his life pretty much super-glued to his mother's skirts."

"Yes, that," he said, and smoked some more. "Haven't you ever just given someone something they need, you know, just to give them a purpose?"

"I don't understand."

"Of course you do," he said. "You totally do it with that David schmuck all the time."

"But David's my——"

"Boyfriend, yes everyone knows. But he's also your ex-boyfriend, and if you ask me, your past was a much better place for him."

"I don't see what any of this has to do with you and Aunt Enid," she said, and then added, indignantly, "or how it's any of your business." She reached for the joint and took a drag. The smoke was shockingly smooth. It didn't burn or hurt. It was almost, pleasant... She felt herself begin to relax; he nodded for her to take another drag and she did. She handed it back.

"My mother would have nothing if she didn't have me to coddle. It's pathetic, I know, but it's the way it goes," he said, and he inhaled. "If someone has nothing to live for, what happens to them?"

"What?"

"They die," he said, and he exhaled. "And I don't really need that on my conscience. So, when I'm with her, I try and give her what she needs."

"But you do kind of go for it. I mean, it seems pretty authentic if you ask me. And the way you've been about your wife leaving isn't exactly well, you know…"

"Look, I'm not going to lie to you. I was fucking devastated by that. Still am. That part of it is at least true."

"Okay, but that means then you get it, about me and David. Why I'm back with him. You understand better than anyone else," she said, feeling finally like she'd found someone to connect to on all of this, even if it was Grant.

"Uh, no. I really don't understand what you're doing with that douche bag."

"He wanted to get back together. He begged me."

"So?"

"Oh, come on. You know if *she* ever wanted you back, you would take her back in a minute," she surmised, triumphant.

Grant coughed a good long time. "Oh, for fuck's sake, no. Not on your goddamned life," he said.

"I don't understand. You always say that she broke you in two when she left you. That you're half a man without her."

"Yes. But I'm at least the good half. And I tell you, it's a far better position to be in then stuck with a useless other half. Or worse, a half that slows you down. A half that's just a gorgeous raging bitch with an agenda." He shook his head. "I got none of the bitch baggage weighing me down now. I may be half a man, but I can fly!"

"You may be half in the bag."

He considered this. "You may be right about that," he said. "But I guess this isn't really something you'd understand."

"Why wouldn't I understand? I understand a lot of things."

"Because you gave up being better to be with David."

Amy was enraged and she was about to let Grant have it when Enid interrupted, calling from the other room. "Grant. Grant!"

"Mama calls," he said, getting up.

"I still don't see why you put up with it," she said.

"I still don't see why you do," he said, and handed her the rest of the joint. Just then, Enid stuck her head through the window and began sniffing wildly.

"Grant? Are you out here? There you are!" she said, now rubbing her nose. "What is that?" she asked and she glared at Amy. "Are you smoking? Are you breathing your filthy second-hand smoke around my little boy?!"

"It's okay, Mama. Let's go back inside."

"I just can't believe the nerve..."

Grant pushed through the window and gave a quick backwards wave. Clarabelle, who had accompanied Enid, now stuck her head out and took a deep, long breath. "Ah, the good stuff," she said. And with that she was gone.

Amy stubbed out the joint and headed back inside. She took a quick glance at herself in the mirror and fixed her hair, becoming suddenly conscious of the mousy-brown roots that had started to sprout from her scalp. She quickly ran her hand through, grabbed up a tube of frost pink lip gloss, slathered some on, and headed back out to the party.

She scanned the room for David, but he was nowhere to be found. She spotted Jane and the Building Boys stuffing their faces at the buffet table, and Grant leaning against a wall, dutifully listening as his mother flailed her arms and appeared to be lecturing him. Joshua and Lauren were canoodling in front of the curtained wall of babies, while Clarabelle played patty-cake with Ava and Zoë and the placard of Eric and Shirley. Uncle Mort just sat in a chair and snoozed. But definitely no David.

"He left, in case you were wondering," Ollie then said. "I got stuck with him most of the night. Somehow everyone else disappeared and left me with him. Real interesting guy," he added, the sarcasm obvious.

"I beg your pardon," she nearly hissed.

"You're right. That's not fair. He really didn't have much of anything to add to the conversation. And I don't think he liked those neighbors of yours," he remarked with cool suspicion, as he watched them pig out and laugh about seemingly nothing with his girlfriend.

"Oh," said Amy.

"Why do you suppose those guys are so hungry?" he asked. "I've never seen a bunch of Italian kids go at a bowl of chopped liver like that."

"Uh, dunno," Amy lied, feeling herself kind of desperate to join them.

"Huh," said Ollie, and they stood together quietly and watched the food orgy unfold. "You know who would fit in here well is Deck. Have you spoken to Deck lately? Do you know where he is?"

"Deck and I don't speak. Not anymore."

"And whose fault is that?" he asked.

"I would say it was his, wouldn't you?" she said. "That guy's a maniac."

"That guy's been through the ringer thanks to Marny. You might give him a chance…"

"I gave him a chance. I reached out to him—he blew up at me."

"Well, maybe there's more going on that you don't know about and—"

"Somehow I don't think that's the case."

"I have something for you," he said, reaching into his pocket. "It's from Deck."

"No thank you. I don't want it," she said, thinking it was another letter and feeling a twinge of guilt at having not opened the other one.

"But he wanted…"

She shook her head. "I really need to move on, okay?"

He shook his head. "Have it your way," he said.

"I will," she snapped, adamant, and Ollie walked away.

"Oh, I almost forgot," he said and turned around. "David said to tell you he'd be here at seven sharp to pick you up for your big getaway. Such a lucky girl you are!" he mocked, and walked away chuckling.

Amy then ducked into her bedroom, turned out her light, dropped into her bed, and went to sleep.

17

A Road Trip, a Freak Show, and a Realization
Dawned too Late

Amy turned to watch David as he drove west on I-78. His thick head of stick straight silken hair. His eyes, still magnificent even as they squinted to read the highway signs. His skin, so sexy and rough. Except which now, upon closer reflection, seemed more leathery to her than anything else. Sunburned from his recent Caribbean vacation? Maybe even a little scaly? She shook the thought out of her head.

So many things weren't clear to her these days, but David's looks were not one of them. She was comforted by the fact that at least now there would be no crazy surprises. Not with David. That the worst they would ever share was now firmly behind them.

"I'm sorry I took off like that last night, without saying goodnight," he said.

"That was a little crazy," she said.

"Amy, give me a break," he laughed. "At that party, my taking off was the most mild form of crazy imaginable."

"What do you mean by that?" she asked.

David looked at her and smirked and she glared at him, defensively. "Forget about it, okay?" he said. "I get that that's your family. I mean in the crazy way that they are but those punks that hang out on the stoop, well…sorry. Just forget about it."

They drove along in silence several more minutes. Amy pulled down her sun visor and checked her reflection in the vanity mirror provided for just such a thing. She tugged at her hair, trying to make the blond highlights cover more than was reasonable to desire they would; she created with her hair something that could only be described as a Comb-over of Desperation.

"Your hair looks nice like that," David said, now smiling at her.

"Really?" She blew her bangs out of her face. "I really haven't gotten around to getting it fixed. These stupid roots are starting to get to me. But that's nice of you to say," she said. "Thanks."

"Amy, I said it looked *good*. Why would you think about changing it?"

"Oh."

They drove in silence for a while, until David spoke again. "Did you really sleep with that freaky guy?"

"What?"

"That guy, Tony, at your party…"

"I never slept with Tony…"

"No, that's not what I meant. Tony said that you had been with that English professor guy, your boss. That you had been with him at our place—"

"My place, remember," she shot back. "You moved out."

"Your place. Whatever. Sorry. But did you really sleep with him?"

"He's not a freak."

"You did, didn't you?" he said, and he took a deep breath. "Well, it's okay. I suppose I forgive you, all things considered."

At this moment, even Amy could see the crazy irony of her not-so-distant past infecting her past.

"Can we not talk about this anymore?" she asked.

"Of course," he said, unconvincingly. "Of course." And they drove along in silence again.

Several minutes later, he asked, "So are you sorry you postponed your defense?"

"I guess not," she said. "You had a point that I wasn't really there with my arguments. Probably another six months of thinking it through will help."

"See, Scruffy. I *do* give you good advice. Thank God you started talking to me again," he said, and he tapped her knee.

She stared out the window. "Yeah, I guess you do," she said, as he pulled into a parking lot.

"We're here," he said, and without hiding an ounce of enthusiasm, asked, "Ready?"

"Sure," she said, feeling considerably less excited than David.

"Let's go," he said. He got out of the car, closed his door, and headed toward the building in the distance. Amy sat for a minute, watching him walk away, actually surprised that she was more enjoying the sight of him walking away than the past two hours spent in the car with him, or even the past two or so weeks she'd been seeing him again. She considered staying in the car, enjoying the feeling of being alone, until she saw him stop, look around, and head back to the car. She looked away.

He knocked on the window. "Is this door stuck again?" he asked, and pulled it open with ease. "Gets that way sometime. Liz could never get it open… sorry."

"Don't worry about it," she said, feeling just a quick moment's admiration for Liz, for tricking David into being considerate. She'd have to remember that trick and started to think of some other ways she could also trick him into being more like she wanted him to be as she unbuckled her seat belt, grabbed up her purse and followed. She shielded her eyes with her hand to block out the bright morning sun as they headed to the entrance under the sign for The Northern Berks Reptile Show.

Entering, Amy froze. She was uneasy and uncomfortable even if she couldn't exactly put her finger on *why*. Was it because she was jealous that he'd probably taken Liz to the last event?

As she walked through, she began to remember how much this convention was a freak show in and of itself, having nothing to do with the snakes and the lizards and the baby alligators being offered for sale. Looking around, it all came back to her that she had never seen more mulleted hair. More throwback feathered roach clips. More heavy metal T-shirts and rhinestones in one place. Everything felt wrong again, and a new clarity emerged in her as she wondered if it ever had felt *right* with David.

"Look at this screamer!" shouted David, now a few tables ahead of her. And just like that, it all started to unravel. Like when a person's about to die and their whole life flashes before them, she began to see snippets of her romance with David in rapid succession. Their first date, that terrible action film. His birthdays, filled with love and thoughtful gifts—her birthdays, not unlike the one he'd just blown off, with gifts for her that seemed more for him. All the hours she helped him practice for his defense; all the hours he spent talking her out of doing hers. She could feel herself starting to panic. She could feel herself starting to sweat.

"She's incredible!" David shouted, as the small milk snake slithered around his hand, his arm, his wrist. She imagined it morphing into a giant snake and swallowing David whole. She imagined it becoming a boa constrictor, with David's head, and wrapping itself around her, around her dreams and her passions and her soul, squeezing everything dead. She was starting to have trouble breathing.

"She's gorgeous!" he beamed.

"Gorgeous," she whispered, and she thought about what that meant. She looked down at her clothes, her uniform for David. Drab. Matronly. *Urban Amish.* She whispered the word again as she realized, he had just used a word for a snake that he'd never once used to describe her.

But Deck had called her gorgeous, pretty, beautiful, and had done so effortlessly. He never wanted her to be someone else. He seemed to enjoy her for who she was. He knew who she was—even if she didn't quite know… She was dazed.

"I think I should take this one," he said, as the snake slithered through his fingers. "How are we on room?"

"Huh?" she asked.

"Is there room for more? Could we build another unit?"

She was confused. "You want *me* to take this one?"

"Sure. So she can be with her friends," he said.

"Why would I want more snakes? I have enough snakes," she said.

"I don't know. Because you like them so much?" he dropped the snake back in her enclosure. "Anyway, my place is much too small."

"I don't think I have the room…"

"You don't need new stuff, Amy! When my lease is up, I can just move me and all my stuff back in."

"You're moving back in?"

"Why wouldn't I?" he asked, taking out his wallet. "I mean, we'd definitely have to wait until after the lease is up. I'm not going to eat that security deposit. And then we can go to Smitty's and…"

David was still talking to her as he offered a few bills to the vendor, who slipped the snake into a repurposed takeout container and handed it to David. But she didn't know what he was saying. She couldn't hear anything but the sound of her own blood rushing up to her brain as it seemed to whisper in her ear, over and over, "Flee!" And that's just what she did.

Two hours later, Amy could hardly catch her breath as she raced through the front door of Smitty's. She had made a terrible mistake, and as soon as the vendor handed David the snake, she knew it. She just ran out of the exhibition hall. She ran into the parking lot. She had no idea how she was going to get back home, but all she knew was she had to get there. She had to get away from David. She had to get back to the way things were meant to be. And she knew just where to start.

"I thought I told you never to come back to my store again," the old woman snapped.

"I made a mistake. I'm sorry," Amy said, choking back tears. "I'm so very sorry. I see it now. It all makes sense now. I need the shoes. Please."

The woman eyed her for a minute, then looked away. "Well you can't have them," she said. "They aren't here anymore."

"What do you mean they aren't here? Where are they?"

"They're in someone else's hands now. Someone who really appreciates their value."

"Tell me who. Please! Who is she?"

"Not a woman," the shopkeeper sneered. "A man, actually."

Amy's heart sank. "Was he very tall?" she asked hopefully. "And very bald. Fortyish?"

"What is it with you and your obsession with Yul Brynner?" she chided.

"Well?"

"Nope," she said flatly. "Not even close."

Her heart sank again. "Okay. Well, I guess that's how it is, then. Sorry to have wasted your time," she said as she headed out.

Amy stood outside the store and peered in the window, at the now-empty pedestal where those magnificent shoes once stood. Where she'd fallen in love with them. Where she'd made the decision to change her life. But catching her own reflection in the glass now, her face in the space where the shoes would have been, she had to do a double take. She wasn't sure anymore who this woman was, with mousy bangs and no makeup, looking worn and boring and even a little old.

Walking up to her building, the Boys, reliable as ever, stood and waited for her. Though they said nothing to her at all as she approached.

"Hi, guys," she said, and managed a weak wave. They turned away from her. "Really? Is this how it's going to be now?"

They still said nothing until Mario finally spoke. "We can't know you if you're going to be with that douche bag."

"That freaking guy didn't even know it was your birthday," said Frankie. "What a loser."

"As long as you're with him, you're a loser," said Tony, and he turned his back on her. "And we don't talk to losers." The rest of the guys grunted in agreement.

"Well, that's all over now," she said, and they all breathed a collective sigh of relief. "I'm just not sure what next from here."

They were quiet before a moment until Frankie stepped forward and spoke. "That cop was here, Amy."

"Ollie? Why?"

They exchanged worried glances among themselves but nobody spoke.

"Oh my God, what is it? Something about Deck?"

"Yes," said Mario, and he nodded, solemnly.

"What happened to Deck? Did he go on a killing spree?" she gasped. "Did he kill himself? Oh God!"

They all looked at each other again. "Uh, no," said Angelo.

Frankie stepped forward. "He left this for you," he said, and pulled out a small box. "He said it was from Deck."

She took the package from him and opened it. Inside, was an antique pin, a daisy with mother-of-pearl petals and a yellow topaz center. "Wow," was all she said. There was a note attached, with a very simple message: "Happy Birthday, Amy." She felt something stick in her throat.

"Don't write him off, Amy," said Tony sincerely, surprising Amy and everyone else. "Sure, he's kind of fucked-up to look at, but he has a beautiful soul." To Amy's surprise once again, the guys didn't laugh at their friend; they all nodded instead. "Everyone knows you can't fall in love with a body," Tony continued. "I mean, you can *love* to be *with* a body. But you can only love a soul."

"I see," said Amy, a faraway look on her face. "Thanks guys," she said, and ducked inside.

Once in her apartment, Amy made herself a pot of tea and brought it into the living room. She headed over to the curtained wall where the snakes still lived and she pulled back a corner, revealing the place where she kept Heimlich's trunk. She brought it over to the couch and popped it open, ready to put the dolls back in, but she stopped when she noticed the small locked compartment partially hidden underneath the CDs. She realized she'd never opened it, and the curiosity now overwhelmed her. She ran into the kitchen to grab a butter knife and then went to work at the lock.

After about seven tries, the compartment finally flipped open and there was one thing inside. A simple black-and-white photo. A young man and a small boy laughing on the beach. She had no idea who these people were or what it meant to Heimlich, hidden away in his trunk like this. But, looking at this photo, she somehow knew what she had to do. She picked up the phone and dialed.

"Hi, it's me," she said. "Can you tell Ollie that Deck can have the dolls? Just tell Ollie to come and pick up the trunk."

"You don't want to try and bring it to Deck yourself?"

"I don't think I can see him," she said.

"Okay, I'll tell him," Jane said.

Amy now spotted the letter Deck had written to her. She walked over to it, slit open the envelope, and began to read.

178

18

How Amy Got Reunited with Something Very Special and Rocked the House

Stratton University was established in 1884 as an institute of higher learning, but it had its roots as a much different kind of institution: A sanitarium. From the time the building had gone up in 1816, it had housed the castoffs of pre-Victorian society—the terminally insane as well as an assortment of "Nature's gaffes," otherwise known as "freaks." But with the boom of sideshows in the middle of the century, impresarios began putting a dent in the population of the hospital, instead offering these "gaffes" a profitable way to make a living and gain acceptance, and sometimes reverence in society. Queen Victoria herself was a passionate freak-ophile, inviting her favorites to the palace and bestowing upon them magnificent and opulent gifts.

A decade into the Queen's reign, having lost most of its population to the sideshow circuit, the institute could no longer sustain itself and closed its doors in 1880. It remained deserted until an entrepreneurially-minded entertainer added the property to his already impressive real estate empire. Charles Sherwood Stratton, more commonly known as Tom Thumb, perhaps the most famous little person who ever lived, bought the building so that people such as him could never be imprisoned within its walls ever again. It remained vacant until his death.

When Stratton passed away in 1883, his widow, Ms. Lavinia Warren, decided the building could be used for a higher purpose, in her mind, higher learning. So Ms. Warren financed an extensive renovation to transform the structure into a university, which she named in honor of her late husband. She also used a fair amount of his money to buy up some of the neighboring buildings and plots of land, confident that her husband's name attached to the university could conjure the same passionate interest as had her husband during his days as a performer. The university became accredited in 1904, and in the years since, it had grown to become one of the top universities in the area.

Now Amy Miller, Ph.D. candidate, sat on the very stage that had at one time showcased human anomalies in the interest of science, as she prepared to defend the dissertation that had defined her entire academic career. She watched as judges and supporters filed in. Jane and Zoë, dressed today in a for once age-appropriate cheerleader's costume, waved excitedly from the middle of the room. There they sat among her entire extended family, who had all come to lend their support, including the placard of Amy's parents, with mortarboard and tassels now stapled to their heads and bearing a sign that read: "Our daughter, the doctor!"

One glaring absence, of course, was Deck. While she was still conflicted and confused about how she felt about him and everything else, especially now having read his letter, she couldn't help but think about how big a role he had played in all of this. How his faith in her had helped her to finally have faith in herself. His absence became especially palpable when Ollie rushed in just before the doors closed with a giant panda bear, which he presented to Zoë, who shook her pompons and clapped and squealed with delight at the gift.

Amy rubbed her finger up against the daisy pin that she wore against her heart and thought about Deck. She hoped he would show today. If he really cared, as he wrote to her that he did, surely he would show today. And then, maybe then, she could start to believe in him, believe in them again.

Just before the last of the judges arrived, Lauren and Joshua approached Amy, and Joshua was holding a shopping bag in his hand.

"We're very proud of you, Amy," said Lauren and gave her a big hug.

"We always knew you'd make it here someday," said Joshua. "We have something for you," he said, pulling a wrapped box out of the shopping bag.

"What's that?"

"Open it," said Lauren and she did.

"The shoes?" Amy gasped. "How did you…"

"Long story," said Joshua.

Amy couldn't help but smile seeing them again, beautifully restored and polished, their adorable daisy toes seeming to smile up at her. "That's why daisies," she said out loud. "Of course."

"What's that, dear?" Lauren asked.

"Oh, nothing," she smiled at Deck's thoughtful gesture. "Thanks, you guys. This was really thoughtful," she said. "But these aren't really magical. Apparently, Zoë made the whole story up."

"She did?" said Joshua, seeming as disappointed as a kid who learns Elmo is actually a puppet. "But the woman at the store—"

Lauren cut him off. "You think they aren't magical?" she asked.

"What do you mean?" Amy replied.

"You decide," she said. "Think about the person you were before you decided you were worth having them. And think about how far you've come."

"That's a very good point," said Joshua. "Perhaps there isn't any shoe voodoo, uh, afoot…"

"Oh, God," Amy groaned. "Really? Did you really have to go there?"

"Just think about it, Amy," he said. "Where you are today. What you're about to do. You never thought any of this was possible before the shoes."

"We're not saying it's the shoes, dear," said Lauren. "They're just symbolic, really."

Amy considered this for a minute.

"It's about finding yourself, your true self, and who cares how you get there, really? Indulging in a pair of expensive shoes. A night of knock your socks off sex," Lauren said, and Joshua turned bright red. "It's all about deciding you're worth it and letting yourself have it."

Joshua nodded. "It's not that *they're* magic, Amy. It's that they remind you that *you* are."

Lauren smiled. "So you *do* get it," she said to her husband.

"I'm not completely stupid," he joked, shaking his head at his wife. He looked back at Amy.

"You're going to do great, sweetie," Lauren said. "Your parents would have been so proud of you."

"Thanks, guys," Amy said, a bittersweet rush running through her.

"Knock 'em dead," Joshua said, and he and Lauren headed back to their seats. Amy sat down and slipped on her shoes. She stroked her daisy pin. And she waited to begin.

Within minutes, Professor Ann Bateman entered the room and addressed the group. "Good afternoon," she said. "We're assembled here today to hear the defense of Ms. Amy Miller of her dissertation 'Waste and *The Wasteland*.' Everyone please be quiet so we may begin," she said and sat in the middle of the judges' table.

"Okay, now," she said, ruffling through papers. "Dr. Heimlich is no longer with us. And it seems Drs. Hayes and Thomas have both stepped down over personal reasons, both claiming," she read, and then looked up at Amy, "romantic conflicts with the defendant?" Amy smiled meekly and looked away. "And it seems Dr. French has, well, vanished," she looked again at Amy. "You, again?"

"No," she mouthed.

"Very well," Dr. Bateman said. "So we'll convene with our skeleton crew of myself and Drs. Baron, Nellen, and McGoey, and standing in for our jilted romeos, Drs. Mayer and Mullen. Ms. Miller. Whenever you're ready."

Amy scanned the room one last time looking for Deck, but he was nowhere to be found. So he was lost to her now. He was gone and she couldn't help but shake the creepy feeling that he'd found someone. Someone else. At least now she knew what he really was. That he was just an awkward vessel for beautiful, empty words, none of which he was true to. A man of letters and words and no action to back them up. A man with no real proof for her that what he said he felt for her was real. Her heart would surely have dropped if it hadn't been beating so fast as she stood and walked to the lectern. Now she shook off her disappointment, straightened out her notes, cleared her throat, and began.

19

How All the Pieces Came Together in an Italian Restaurant in Flushing, Queens

It was a popular misconception that Don Corleone's restaurant was and continues to be a popular mob hangout, when it was simply a basic Southern Italian restaurant located in Eastern Queens, New York. It was decorated with plastic grapes on plastic vines and complete with trompe l'oeil murals on every wall of famous spots in Italy, from the Leaning Tower of Pisa to the Coliseum to the Amalfi Coast. Really, just your average Queens Italian eatery. Except that it had received a certain level of unplanned notoriety for its name.

Anyone not familiar with the history of the restaurant might be led to believe that it was named to capitalize on the international success of *The Godfather*. But, in actuality, the restaurant was today owned by a guy named Frank Corleone, who was the grandson of the original owner, who was named, if you can't already guess, Donald—or "Don" as his friends knew him.

Don Corleone's opened its doors in 1958 and enjoyed modest success, serving basic Italian food to a local following, who were essentially all Italian immigrants desperate for a taste of home. But when *The Godfather* movies came out in the 1970s, Don Corleone's, at least for a while, had become more an amusement park attraction, a mob-hungry tourist magnet, than the simple eatery of its intention.

Thanks to the sheen wearing off the mafia in the past decade, Don Corleone's had gone back to being a neighborhood joint. Except for a short while when *The Sopranos* first came out. But an enterprising rival restaurateur opened Fat Boss Tony's across the street, where the tourists now flooded.

The grandson of the current owner, also Francis, happened to be one of Amy's Building Boys, which is why on this day of celebration, a different kind of family was seated in the back party room of Don Corleone's. A mismatched assortment of misfits assembled for the celebration luncheon thrown for their fostered foundling, Amy Miller, who had, that very morning, dazzled the faculty panel ready to pick apart her dissertation, giving more than a few of them something to think about and debate about for semesters to come.

"I have to admit, Amy—I read your dissertation all those years ago, and I really thought you did a fine job in explaining just what Eliot was talking about," said Joshua, spitting out an olive pit. "But today, well, you really made it pop."

"And that it could be funny," said Enid, buttering a piece of bread and placing it on Grant's plate.

"That was surprising," said Grant, who dutifully picked up his bread and took a bite. "Surprising, indeed."

Amy smiled. "It was not my original thinking, no. But it seems to be what tied everything up in the end."

"Well, I'm still not sure I understand any of it, but I like what you said," said Morty, grabbing one of the loaves of bread from the middle of the table, tearing it in two, and taking the larger hunk for himself.

"I know I will never fully understand it," Lauren agreed. "But it definitely makes more sense to me now."

"It's true, sweetie," said Jane. "You have a real gift."

"Speaking of gift," said Zoë, nudging her mama.

"Oh, right," Jane reached into her purse and pulled out a box. In the box was a pen. And engraved onto the pen was a simple, poignant message: "Dr. Miller."

Amy started to cry. "Thanks, guys," she said. "Thanks for all your encouragement and support. You really got me through it. All of you. I wouldn't be here today without you guys."

And while a cacophony of "No, really, it was you," clamored back and forth in the room, a commotion in the front of the restaurant silenced everyone. A familiar shriek carried all the way back to where they were sitting, a request to the maître d' to "Let me back there!" Perhaps this was expected. It certainly wouldn't be out of the realm of possibilities that Hannah had now returned from her expedition, found out about the party and decided she was supposed to be here.

Not expected, however, was the deep baritone of a man's voice that followed, bellowing an urgent plea to "Get back to that room!" Amy took a quick glance at Ollie, and Ollie quickly looked the other way. She panicked as the door to the party room flew open and there stood Deck. With Hannah. They were both still dressed in expedition khakis, and both were panting and sweating and beaming like idiots. Deck, especially, seemed worse for the wear, somehow now bright red and covered in what looked to be hives.

"What are you doing here?" Amy asked, looking back and forth between them. "And why are you together?"

"And why do you look so happy?" Jane was quick to add.

"And what are you wearing?" asked Zoë, who had crept up behind her mother and halfway hid herself behind the folds of Jane's elegant tea length black silk skirt.

Hannah and Deck smiled big at each other, and Amy immediately thought the worst. "Oh, no. Not this. Not you two. Don't even tell me this because I can't handle—"

"You tell her," Deck told Hannah, giving her an affectionate tap on the arm.

"Are you sure?" Hannah asked.

"This is your show," he said.

"Well, only in part. Really it was—"

"Go ahead," he nodded.

"Alrighty, then," Hannah said and looked around. "So, how is everyone doing today?" she asked.

The diners regarded her with blank stares. She turned to Deck who urged her on with another friendly, supportive nod. A little too friendly for Amy's tastes.

"I guess first of all, you may be wondering what I'm doing with this guy?"

"It had crossed our minds, yes," Jane replied coolly.

"Well, you know how I went on that expedition?"

"Yes," said Amy.

"But you never knew why!" she sort of sang. "I mean *really* why!"

"Okay…" Amy said, reaching for more.

"Well, in my research on indigenous tribes in Amazonia, I started to see this weird pattern emerging. A peculiar rash of abductions, not at all typical to the region."

"Abductions?" said Amy, softly.

"Just what are you getting at?" Joshua asked, protectively edging closer to Amy.

"The more I looked into it, the more I began making all these weird connections to this tour company based right there in the rain forest," she turned to Amy. "That's when I asked you about—"

"Jungle Jimmy's," Amy whispered, and there was a loud gasp from the table as everyone looked over at the placard of Eric and Shirley. Clarabelle made a strange attempt to try and cover their ears with her hands.

"We don't talk about that," said Lauren, rising and standing on the other side of Amy, looping her arm around her.

Hannah didn't seem to get the message and kept talking. "Well," she continued. "I always thought it was weird, the way your parents disappeared like that. How they were presumed dead and the case was just closed and all that."

"Be careful, young lady," warned Joshua. "We're *all* family here."

"No kidding. I know all about it," Hannah rambled on. "I sit right over the wall from loudmouth over there," she said pointing at Amy with her thumb.

No one spoke, so Hannah continued. "Anyway, I started to put it all together. And I realized this company and the abductions were definitely connected and I had to find out why. So I secured a grant to head to South America to investigate it."

"You know what happened to my parents?" Amy gulped.

"Better!" shouted Hannah, leaving everyone understandably confused.

Deck stepped in. "Well, maybe not *better*," he interjected. "But be patient. It all does add up." He nodded to Hannah to continue.

"So anyway, where was I?"

Deck stepped in again. "Hannah got a grant and headed down to the Jungle Jimmy's headquarters in Brazil," he said.

"And who do you suppose I found hanging out down there?" she said.

"Oh, my God," Amy gasped. "My parents!"

"No, better!" exclaimed Hannah, pointing in the air. And then she caught herself. "I mean better within the context of the story. Just be patient. Please."

"Marny was there at Jungle Jimmy's," Ollie piped in. "And she wasn't alone."

"Who's Marny?" Mort asked.

"That's Deck's estranged wife," said Ollie.

"Who's Deck?" Morty asked.

"You mean the leper over there?" asked Aunt Enid.

"He's not a leper," said Amy, though looking at him, all red and bumpy, she couldn't quite be sure she was right about this.

"You're Deck," Lauren smiled, sizing Deck up.

"You *knew* about this?" Jane accused Ollie. "Why didn't you say anything—"

Ollie shook his head at Deck. "Neither of them is very patient, are they?"

Deck smiled, and looked at Amy, who was wearing a look of deep confusion as she hugged her arms around herself. "So, I don't understand. Who was with her?"

"A woman you might know, Amy," said Deck. "A woman named Liz French."

"Liz French?!" Amy, Jane, and Zoë all shouted at once.

"Yes," said Deck. "It seems Marny and Liz had mended their old fences in interesting and, well, intimate ways."

"And they were hatching a plot!" said Hannah.

"But how did you..."

"Oh, I had no idea they were there," said Hannah, "or that Liz was involved with Marny in that way. In fact it wasn't until I friended Deck on Facebook that I even started to put it all together."

"I'm on Facebook," gushed Aunt Clarabelle. "I'll friend you!"

"Uh...sure..." Hannah said, and turned back to the group. "Anyway, Marny was after a map, a map of a very sacred place in Amazonia. A map that could only be found in one place."

"And I knew where," said Deck. "Well, I didn't know exactly. But Chuck told me something about my uncle, something special he had. Something..."

Grant looked at Hannah. "Something that..."

"His uncle had the map," Hannah said.

"Yes, we get it. But the map to where?" asked Lauren.

Everyone looked around at one another, both impressed by the mystery and confused as to how any of it related to them or the celebration lunch that had been interrupted before the main course had been served.

Deck looked at Lauren, and then at Amy. And then he smiled at Hannah again, which made Amy's heart sink.

"The map to El Dorado," he said.

Amy gasped. Aunt Enid shook her head. "I don't get it. Why would anyone go through all that trouble for a car?" she asked.

Amy shook her head. "No, not a car. A mythical city of incredible riches, thought to be located deep in the rain forests of South America. But no one ever knew where it was. No one ever found it, so people just assumed it didn't exist. Kind of like Atlantis."

"Well, missy. Apparently, it does exist," said Hannah.

"And apparently a famous French author knew exactly where it was," said Deck.

"You don't mean?" Amy asked, and he nodded his big bald bumpy red head wildly. He was about to tell her everything when Ollie jumped into the conversation.

"Marny planted the seed that Deck was abusive towards her, and that she feared for her life so she could create a distraction to find what she'd come back for, and then have a clean-cut way to disappear without Deck coming after her to get it back."

"Marny wrote that horrible note and passed it to Liz," Hannah added, "who passed it to me. Then I passed it to the detective over there because quite frankly, I never trusted this guy," she said, pointing with that thumb again, this time to Deck. "Seriously. I always thought he was up to no good," she said, shaking her head. "Oh, and I'm *so* sorry about that now," she said directly to Deck, now tearing up. "Because this guy," she choked up as she tried to wrap an arm around him. "*This* is a good guy."

"Well, so far it seems like you've pretty much made up for it," Grant piped in, nodding to Hannah.

She cocked her head curiously at him and smiled. "Have we met?"

Zoë let out a loud, exasperated sigh. "Grant, Hannah. Hannah, Grant. Grant's divorced and a total wet blanket.

"Hey!" he objected.

"And Hannah's also single and kind of a nosy-body who—"

"Hang on," said Deck to Zoë. "Just wait till you see what else she uncovered. You might start to think her being so nosy is not such a bad thing."

"Uh, thanks. I think?" said Hannah.

Zoë looked Hannah up and down. "I'm not so sure I—"

"Zoë, nice girls let people make their point and *then* judge them for it," instructed Jane. Everyone turned in her direction and stared blankly at her. "I mean, you never judge anyone. But—"

Then everyone was uncomfortably quiet until Ollie spoke again. "We finally started to piece it all together after Liz took off," said Ollie. "But it wasn't until we had the dolls back that we knew for sure."

"The dolls?"

"Yep. It was all about Heimlich's dolls," Deck said.

"You gave me some dead guy's dolls to play with, Auntie Amy?" shrieked Zoë. "That's so gross."

"So what's the big deal about the dolls?" Mort wanted to know.

"Well, as some people know, Heimlich and I weren't exactly buddies," Deck said. "But does anyone know why?"

"Sweetie, we don't even know who the hell *you* are," said Enid, taking a sip of her wine.

"Heimlich was my uncle," said Deck, as a collective gasp rose from the table. "His brother, now also dead, was my *real* father. Not the guy who raised me. That was Chuck," he said, as if that last bit of detail mattered to anyone present but him.

"The photograph," Amy warmed slightly.

"Yep," he nodded to her. "Me and the old bastard. When he was still young and kind of nice to me. Anyway, the dolls—my dolls now, I guess—are actually quite valuable."

"Because they're antiques," said Jane.

"Kind of, but the real value lies in what the dolls are keeping under their clothes."

"Their clothes," Zoe mused. "Of course…"

"Under their dresses are the pages of a short, never-published section of a very important piece of literature," he said as he looked at Amy. "A section actually missing from *Candide*."

She smiled.

"And in that section is the map."

"Not the car again," said Enid, clicking her tongue against the roof of her mouth and rolling her eyes. Everyone shook their heads.

"I don't understand," Mort said.

"Voltaire held back a section of *Candide* because it featured an actual map to the city of El Dorado, and he didn't want it ending up in the wrong hands. That section of the book had been kept hidden with the dolls for years."

"The dolls belonged to Voltaire?" Grant asked.

Amy laughed. "That would be impossible considering Voltaire died in 1778 and bisque dolls weren't around until the nineteenth century!" she exclaimed, proud to know all this. Though the looks around the table were more like "Is that really necessary?"

"No, not *his* dolls," Deck said. "The pages were put there by his descendants and passed down through the ages. Heimlich, crazily enough, was one of those descendants. So I guess it follows that, well…"

"So is Deck!" Hannah beamed.

Amy felt like she was going to faint as a gigantic "Wow!" rose from the table.

Deck looked at Amy, but neither spoke.

"So, you're saying you're an heir to some literary fortune?" asked Grant.

He brushed it off. "It's not that important."

Jane looked at Amy. "Kind of a literary prince," she said, but Amy was too stunned about everything to respond to Jane, or even to hear her.

"Unbelievable, right?" Hannah asked.

"This does seem a little bit far-fetched, now that you mention it…" said Joshua.

"Just wait," said Hannah. "Because it just gets better."

"So Marny somehow found out about the dolls and the secret, and realized she wasn't ever going to get them unless I fucked up big time. So she set out to make me look like a killer."

"You can't fuck up worse than murder," Clarabelle mused.

"I don't understand. You *knew* all this when I found the dolls?" Amy asked, starting now to absorb the situation. "Why didn't you ever say anything?"

"Not at all," he said. "All news to me. I swear it. I happened to casually mention the trunk and the dolls to Chuck one day and he told me there was a rumor. But if it was true…."

"How did *she* know about them?" Amy asked.

"Because when I stopped having a relationship with Heimlich, Marny continued hers," Deck explained. "She got it out of him in just the way she does this kind of thing."

"But how was she going to get the map? How was this woman, this Marny, going to get the dolls if she was missing?" Aunt Clarabelle demanded, dramatically. "If she was dead!"

"Aha!" said Deck. "Now that's where Liz fits in to the plan. Marny could not have made it work without Liz."

"Marny needed someone to make sure her note fell into the right hands, but she also needed someone to get those dolls out of Heimlich's hiding spot," said Hannah. "So while she was hiding out, Liz was supposed to be tracking down the dolls."

"But they weren't there anymore because I had them."

"Yep."

"So that's why Liz helped David move my books?"

"Probably."

She gasped. "And that's why David…"

"No, Amy. That was all David wanting to get back with you. And who could blame him really," he said, and she looked away. "You aren't still…"

"Oh, God, no. That was just temporary insanity."

"Oh? Good," he smiled. "Did he take the snakes?"

"Can we get back on point here? I think I see what's going on now," said Joshua, looking back and forth between Amy and Deck, and stopping on Deck. "But who are you again?"

"And where on earth did you contract leprosy?" asked Mort.

"Deck, sir. Decklin Thomas," Deck said, extending a hand, and ignoring Mort. "And you must be Joshua?"

"Ah," nodded Joshua, as he tentatively shook Deck's red meaty paw. "You're 'the boss'," he said, looking to Amy for confirmation.

"*Was*, and that's relatively speaking, sir," Deck smirked and nodded towards Amy. Joshua smirked back. "I know *just* what you mean," he intimated.

Lauren glared at them and shook her head. "So what you're saying is…?"

Deck looked directly at Amy, now beaming. "What I'm *saying* is something you've always known, Amy," he said as he gleefully looked back and forth at everyone present, appearing as though he would burst at any moment.

"That Liz French is…?" Amy tried.

"Is the Missing Link!" squealed Zoë.

"Indeed," Deck smiled.

"Yes!" Zoë said and slammed down a tiny fist. "I'm back!"

"Huh," said Amy, a bit overwhelmed. "I was going for something else," she said, as her mouth curled into a smile, "but I kind of like that."

"I thought you would," Deck grinned. "Marny has always preferred women. I thought I could change her, but… Anyway, I guess after a few months of your ex, Liz remembered that indeed, so did she."

"So when Marny left the first time, she left you for Lee…"

"I didn't tell you it was another woman she left me for?"

"No. You kind of skipped that."

"Huh. Well, I guess it didn't seem that important at the time."

"My husband left *me* for another man!" Jane proclaimed, almost too proudly. "What?" she looked at everyone, now a bit self-conscious. "Well, he did. You hadn't figured that out, yet? Come on!"

"We all knew it, Mama," said Zoë, poking the new space in her teeth with her tongue.

Ollie gave Jane's hand a gentle squeeze and he twitched his moustache affectionately at her. "So now both women are in custody, being charged with attempt to defraud, embezzlement, and, well, kidnapping."

"Kidnapping?" Mort shouted.

"Yes," said Joshua. "Let's get back to that."

"Kidnapping," Hannah confirmed, looking at Deck, who seemed to blush even past his high-voltage redness. "It seems Marny was in cahoots with the Pygmies."

"Wait a minute," said Amy. "There are no Pygmies in Amazonia. They're in Africa."

"There you go again, Amy," said Hannah, with an exaggerated shrug of her shoulders and a light giggle. She shook her head. "You don't know everything."

"But I know—"

"Remember that I told you there were more than forty tribes in Amazonia that had never had contact with the civilized world."

"I guess."

"Well, guess what? Not only does El Dorado really exist, but there are Pygmies in South America. The rash of abductions clued me in to the possibility and now I've proven it."

"Cool," said Zoë.

"Okay, but I don't understand how this Marny had anything to do with the abductions," said Mort.

"And Liz," said Amy.

"Not Liz, at least not the whole time," said Hannah. "But Marny. The first time she disappeared, with Lee, they were armed with the knowledge that El Dorado did indeed exist, and they headed straight for Brazil."

"And took over Jungle Jimmy's," said Ollie.

"Marny believed she could win their secrets," said Deck. "That she could get the natives to lead her to the city without the map."

"She even tried to bribe them with the promise of riches of their very own for their help," said Hannah. "But of course they weren't interested."

"So that's when she started to offer up the tourists," said Deck, carefully.

"Captives being a much more appealing prospect than riches," she said.

"And the more they got, the more open they became to sharing the secrets of the jungle with her," said Deck.

And Hannah steamrolled on. "But it was slow going, and Lee got bored finally and left," said Hannah.

"And then Marny found out from Liz that Heimlich was dead, so she decided to come back to New York," said Ollie. "She figured if she could get her hands on the map, she could find the city herself and get out of the tourism business once and for all."

"Such a horrible industry," Jane mused. "What? I once worked as a travel agent. I know."

"Anyway," said Ollie. "They never made any kind of release deal with the Pygmies for the tourists, so their captives were essentially theirs for good."

"But how did you...how could you..." Grant wanted to know.

"When we found Marny and Liz," Deck said, "Marny wouldn't talk but Liz eventually spilled it."

"We? You mean...Deck, you were there?" Amy asked.

"When we learned all those people were there, that's when we realized we had to go in," said Hannah, and she walked toward the door as she spoke. "And all thanks to Deck, we were able to bring you back a souvenir," she said, and she pulled open the door.

"Mom! Dad!" Amy shouted, as her parents swept in and wrapped her in a giant hug.

"This was what initially inspired my research," Hannah said, beaming. "The other stuff just kind of fell in my lap.."

"That happens sometimes," said the waiter, who had slipped in behind Eric and Shirley Miller to set two new places for Deck and Hannah, and to see if the water glasses needed re-filling.

"Oh Amy, I thought we'd never see you again," said Shirley. "Just look at you!"

"You're a vision," her father said.

There was a huge commotion then as the family rose and greeted their prodigal members.

When everything had quieted down, the waiter set two more places and Eric and Shirley sat down to relay their harrowing tale.

"It was the *best* trip we ever took," said Eric, to a room of confused stares. "Let me clarify," he said. "Although being abducted by the Pygmies I think we could have done without."

"They were actually very nice to us," said Shirley, and Eric nodded. "They treated us like family and shared their customs with us," Shirley continued. "And I have some pretty interesting ideas about how to incorporate some of these into some of our upcoming celebrations," Shirley said, beaming at Zoë.

"Why is she looking at me like that? Mama, don't let her look at me like that."

"But we wanted to be home," said Eric. "And we never would have made it home without this guy," said Eric, smiling at Deck.

"It was Deck who swooped into the camp and demanded our release," said Shirley.

"You can only imagine the visual," Hannah laughed. "They came up to his knees!"

"But he wouldn't lay a finger on them," Shirley said, choking up. "He was a perfect gentleman."

Lauren screwed up her face and asked, "Then how…"

"They apparently play this game called Vinga," said Ollie, "which is kind of like Scrabble, but, well, without letters."

"How does that even make sense?" said Grant.

"He's apparently an expert," said Ollie, a glint in his eye.

"Wait a minute, wait a minute," said Amy, only now getting the whole picture. "You *went* to Brazil? Since I saw you at the precinct?" she asked Deck.

"Yep."

"That's like twelve hours on an airplane."

"You bet."

"To meet up with Hannah?"

"Uh-huh."

"And then you guys found Liz and Marny in the jungle?

"We did."

"All while I was in Pennsylvania."

"Haven't slept in three days!"

"But that's not the only reason why you went down there?"

"No, not really."

"You went for me?" He smiled as she began to understand. "To rescue my parents."

"And you did this by winning some letter-less game of Scrabble?" asked Enid.

"Indeed," he smiled. "Apparently it's the letters that get in my way."

"Huh," said Mort.

"But he didn't only rescue them, Amy," Hannah gushed. "There were others. You'd never believe how many people those crazy Pygmies had collected thanks to Marny."

"He was a hero," said Eric.

"So what happened to the map?" asked Enid.

"Well, we burned the map," said Deck.

"My God, whatever for?" Morty demanded.

"To protect the region, of course," Joshua nodded. "I get it."

"We have to protect those tribes from looters and other crazies," said Hannah.

"Really, it was the only way," Deck said.

"So you gave up all those riches?" Clarabelle asked.

"I guess," said Deck.

"Damned tree huggers," Morty groused.

"But we have all the riches we need right here," said Shirley, as she hugged her little girl.

"And we're so proud of you, Amy!" said Eric, smirking at the placard, and squinting at the sign the photo he and photo Shirley "held". "You finally did it. You earned your doctorate, at last!"

"I did, yes."

Eric squinted more closely at the placard. "Hey, what happened to my face?"

"And you're not with that idiot David, anymore," said Shirley. "Thank God. I think it goes without saying that we really like Deck," she smiled.

"Oh, but Deck and I are just, I mean we were....." Amy stalled.

"Really? After all this you think there *isn't* a future with this man?" snapped Lauren.

"I don't know what to think," said Amy.

"Who cares what you think, Amy," said Grant. "What do you *feel*?"

Zoë started shaking her head. "I really don't really understand any of this. I mean," she said, looking at Hannah, genuinely perplexed. "Who knew that *you* were going to matter so much in all of this?"

"Zoë! Nice girls—"

"I know, I know. Nice girls give props where they're due," she smiled a little toothless grin. "So, Hannah, I'm really glad you're with us. One of us."

"Thanks, kid," Hannah smiled. "Gooble gobble." And Zoë gave her a high five and a great big hug.

"So all's well that ends, well, eh Dr. Miller," said Joshua. "How *does* it feel?"

"I knew you would do it, Amy," said Deck. "I'm so sorry I couldn't be there."

"That's okay. I guess it all makes sense now. And you were there," she said, stroking the daisy pin. "In the way you could be."

"Nice pin," he smiled back at her. "Happy Birthday."

"Thank you," she said, her eyes never leaving his gaze.

"Me too, Amy. I really wanted to be there."

"Oh Hannah, are you kidding? Look at all of this," Amy said, her eyes welling with tears. "I just don't know to thank you."

Hannah looked around the room, and stopped at Grant, who was eyeing her with interest. Hannah smiled at him and while he didn't smile back, he didn't look away either. "You could invite me to stay," she said.

"Of course," said Amy.

"And maybe you could loan me those shoes sometime."

"I'll even give them to you," said Amy. "But not just yet."

"Well, *Doctor* Miller?" asked Deck. "You never answered the question. How does it feel?" he asked.

Amy smiled warmly at Deck as she tried to take it all in.

"Like being in love!" Morty shouted.

Amy took a deep breath. "It feels pretty good, actually. I mean, it's all a little confusing and overwhelming, but I think it's good." Her parents gave her an enormous hug and she cried in their arms.

She pulled away from them finally and looked at Deck. "I really don't know what to say."

"Oh, for heaven's sake," Enid said. "Can't you see that Kojack loves ya, baby?"

"Can we just stop with all the bald references already? We get it," snapped Amy.

"So you do care about me?" Deck said, and she looked away.

"Oh, sorry, dear," Enid said. "But you know, for a doctor, you're not very smart."

"Ah, the way he looks at her," Clarabelle, gleefully twirling her goatee. "Just kiss that boy already," she shouted.

"I… uh…" Amy stammered, not able to decide what she should do next. Deck took her face into his hands, looked into her eyes, and said, "Amy, you're wonderful," he said, and he brushed her two-toned bangs out of her eyes. "And you were the worst assistant I ever had." Everyone laughed, expect Amy, who burned bright red. "But talk around campus is that you're going to be one of the best lit professors there ever was," he said. "And I'm *so* incredibly proud of you." She smiled at him, and he asked. "So forget what you think you should do. What do you *feel* like doing?"

Amy paused for a moment. Then she pulled up and kissed him and everyone cheered.

Deck gazed at her seductively. "I think I know just how to celebrate," he said.

A soft "Oh?" lodged in her throat.

"But first," he began, as he raised a glass and turned to the rest of the group. "A toast," he said, and all the others raised their glasses. "To Amy. To the classics, who now have a new champion. And," he said, with a sly wink to Amy, "To this, the best of all possible worlds," he said. And she couldn't help but agree.

Several days later, after some much-needed rest—and with liberal amounts of sunburn cream and chamomile lotion generously and lovingly applied, not to mention being grateful beyond belief that his enormity had ensured he had not contracted malaria from his thousand mosquito bites—Dr. Decklin Thomas finally began to heal from his jungle adventure. And one afternoon, he and Dr. Amy Miller, entered the Bronx Zoo pushing a large dolly. Strapped to the dolly was a selection of plastic storage containers in various sizes. Drs. Thomas and Miller proceeded to the Reptile House, where Dr. Fish, a smallish man with greasy spectacles and a salt-and-pepper beard, greeted them with a warm smile and a couple of big handshakes.

Later that day, Drs. Miller and Thomas exited the Reptile House, without the dolly and the containers, and stepped out into the warm late afternoon sun. Dr. Miller, especially, was pleased to know that her babies could at last live in a proper home, each in their own naturalized environment, and that Sparky, especially, would have an enclosure with a proper closure to keep her safe and sound.

Still later that day, Drs. Miller and Thomas held hands as they headed towards his car, she standing nearly as tall as his shoulder as she clicked along at a fair pace in a very cute pair of red high-heeled shoes.

"So now what?" she asked.

"Now?" he replied. "This is only the beginning. *Everything* is now," he said. He swooped her up in his massive arms and enveloped her in a luscious kiss that showed just how much he meant it.

20

How Amy Finally Got it Right

It was an unseasonably warm afternoon in the middle of winter as a multitude of elegantly dressed guests began filing into an ancient church, which boasted the most beautiful stained glass windows in the entire city.

Each of the Building Boys were there, dressed to the nines in carefully tailored Italian (naturally) suits. And each walked with a pretty young woman at his side. Except for Tony, who had opted instead to bring his mama.

Colleagues from the university had turned out in droves. Not present, however, was either David, who had left town shortly after Amy dazzled with her defense, or Liz, who was now embarking on a twenty-year sentence at a women's prison in Upstate New York, separated by three states from the women's prison that housed the woman who had stolen her heart, and as an unfortunate side effect, her freedom.

Aunt Enid and Aunt Clarabelle arrived, escorted by Uncle Morty and Grant, hugging a now-smiling Ava close to him, followed them in. Just behind them, a nice-looking man, sixtyish and dressed in a fireman's full dress uniform entered and took a seat on the groom's side, right in the first row.

And just as the back doors were about to close to allow the ceremony to begin, an incredibly old yet strikingly-dressed woman slid into a pew in the very last row. A satin turban was wrapped around her head, held in place by an amazing gem-encrusted dragonfly pin. A single red curl spilled out the front of her turban and adorned her improbably smooth porcelain-toned forehead.

Organ music began to play as Decklin Horatio Thomas walked to the front of the church, escorted (though this time not in handcuffs) by his good friend, Detective Oliver Franks, himself dressed in his New York finest. Deck hugged the fireman in the front row and then took his place at the top of the altar.

Next, proudly donning a white satin yarmulke, edged in tiny white pearls, Joshua Austen-Rabinowitz escorted his lovely wife, Lauren, who wore an exquisite beaded gown, to the front of the church. Their angelic granddaughter Zoë, nestled between them, lovingly sprinkled delicate rose petals as they walked.

Hannah Lindstrom, glowing in silver satin, came next. She caught Grant staring at her and she waved at him and Ava as she passed them—and they both actually smiled and waved back. And then Jane Austen-Rabinowitz, whose own silver gown wrapped her small frame so exquisitely, she looked to be about six feet tall, followed Hannah. When Jane reached the top of the altar, she leaned up and kissed Deck. She and Ollie shared a warm glance as the organ music became louder and more powerful and everyone in the church stood and faced the back.

It was then that Amy Miller, bride and recent Ph.D., sashayed into the adoring fray. As she swooshed down the aisle of the ancient church in a sweeping white gown, glorious streams of sunlight beamed through the exquisitely crafted stained glass windows and made all the tiny sequins on her breathtaking (new) gown sparkle to life.

Flanked on either side by her parents, Shirley and Eric Miller, Amy took long, confident strides, as family and friends shielded their eyes from the heavenly rays as they bounced off her goddess-like visage.

She sashayed to the massive altar, where the man of her dreams stood, trembling at the amazing luck he had been blessed with to have made this ethereal being gliding gracefully toward him actually have agreed to marry him.

And if it was wrong for a bride to wear red shoes under her gown, well, she just didn't care.

ACKNOWLEDGMENTS

Rita Hayworth's Shoes is a project that's been in the works for about ten years (and another twenty years before that if you count all the experiences that inspired it). But it could not have been possible without the group of muses, angels, and impresarios that helped me bring this, the final version, to life.

The first of these are Shawna Mullen and her daughter, Isabelle Dow. Izzy was about five or six when I started writing this book, and the most gorgeously precocious child I had ever known at that point. She was indeed the inspiration for Zoë—and she even named Deck! Her mom is the inspiration for Jane, but so much more. Shawna has put up with an incredible amount of narcissism and nonsense from me, returning only support and inspiration, guidance and glamour, smiles and Sancerre. Plenty of Sancerre.

Thank you to my amazing husband, Christopher LaSala, for taking my author photo—but more than that, thank you, sweetie, for *always* coming through for me. Talk about someone putting up with a lunatic! (And I must also admit that some of Deck's best lines first sprung from his mouth.) A special thank you also goes to my children, Madeleine and Juliana, for inspiring me daily—and for all their delicious distractions.

A huge thank you to the amazingly talented Tricia McGoey for creating an awe-inspiring jacket design. I literally can't look at it enough. And to Anne-Marie Rutella for finding and fixing flaws with skill and wit.

Thank you to all who read drafts of this manuscript, and weighed in with opinions and criticisms, insights and encouragement, including my parents, Paul and Francine

Hornberger, my mother-in-law, Dr. Marie-Agnes LaSala, my aunt RoseMarie McHugh, as well as Judy Jacoby, Dolly Chugh, Karen Costoso-Fernandez (who also helped with the cover copy), Christine Mayer, Diana Shafter Gliedman, Karen Alcaide (with those eagle eyes of hers!), Shane Briant, and Erika Tsang.

This book could not have been possible without the help of so many that lent their support. To all who joined my Facebook page and fan group, for their generosity and faith in me, a huge thank you is in order, especially to Steve Maraboli, who inspired me to "dare" to get out of my own way, and to Virginia Patterson (who also has genius ideas for marketing), Christina Van Tassell and Maria Tahim (for years of necessary shoe-mocking), Stephanie Garcia (for further shaming me into style-consciousness), David Hughes, Maria Yakkey, Michele Contegni, Karen Theroux, Sheila Noone, Derek Hornberger, Don Mochwart, Josh Silber, Laura Chekow, Jeremy Jones-Bateman, Kathi Guarino, Cheryl Meglio, Melissa Hammer, Alison Brew, Denise Gelb, Gia Peterson, Lauren Berkowitz, Pina Adessa, Lee Hornberger, Jonas "Baby Genius" Marijosius, and all who helped crush the final hurdle after we went to press. A special thank you also goes out to Roger Cooper for asking me "the tough questions," which I never seem able to answer, but for always being on my side anyway.

A huge thank you to the folks at Diversion Books, for adding *Rita Hayworth's Shoes* to their list and believing in the magic of the story!

Lastly, thank you to my high school English teacher, Bob Albert, who first encouraged me to write, and to all my former college lit professors for opening my eyes to an amazing world of imagination and interpretation, most especially Dr. Morgan Himmelstein, who first introduced me to *Candide*. I was listening, I promise. I was always listening.

BOOK CLUB QUESTIONS

1. Has a "magical" object ever come into your life and transformed the course of things?

2. *Rita Hayworth's Shoes* is a book about shoes, but with more layers than that. It's soul is classic literature. The book is an homage to Voltaire's *Candide*, but also peppered with many literary references—some obvious, some not—including classic fairytales. What were some of your favorite references?

3. Each of the major players in *Rita Hayworth's Shoes* is a reference to a classic sideshow attraction. Deck's an easy example, as The Giant. How many more can you find?

4. Amy makes a pretty dumb decision in going back to David. Can you relate to choosing the wrong man for all the wrong reasons?

5. Many readers of *Rita Hayworth's Shoes* have suggested it would make a great movie or a Broadway musical. If you were casting this production, which actors would play which roles?

6. Do you think Deck got his hair back in the end? And why or why not?

FIRST LOOK:

The Girl, The Gold Tooth, & Everything

1

It was the kind of day that made Mina Clark feel every breath of her forty-two years—and then some.

It would have been bad enough that the hot water heater had blown out the night before and that today, neither she nor her two-year-old daughter Emma would be able to wash up properly. A problem for Mina who hadn't taken a shower since Tuesday...or Monday? And it was already Thursday. Or Wednesday? No, Thursday.

But a bigger problem for Mina's tastefully decorated home as during a regretful moment's distraction on Mina's part, Emma, with her improbably nimble tiny fingers, had managed to trip the lock on Emma's husband Jack's ancient art supplies. Delicious and dear, dark and demonic, Emma had not only managed to open the long-locked cabinet, but had also managed to unscrew all the tops of Jack's acrylic paint tubes, and was now awash in color, from head to toe. And, alas, so were myriad walls and carpets, fixtures and furnishings. It was as if a Jackson Pollack painting had come to fiery life and "burned" through the bedroom, the hallway, and the living room of the Clark home. A trail of destruction that, like the water heater, there was no budget to correct.

What could she do? Could she wrap the child in plastic garbage bags, haul her down to the community gym, and sneak her into the locker room showers in the locker room where she could rinse them both off? She considered this the only option for a minute until she remembered that her car was in the shop. Again. Hit and run.

Again. And she had no means to collect it from the shop until the insurance adjuster cut her a check.

This time, it had happened in the parking lot of Emma's elitist nursery school. Mina had taken Emma to her classroom, and when she finally emerged after enduring a twenty-minute struggle with separation, she saw that someone had crashed in the passenger-side door of her car. Scum apparently knew no social station. The last time, Mina's car had gotten rear-ended as she sat waiting for a red light to change to green. Without missing a beat, the driver of the other car slammed into reverse and took off. The blood-curdling screams that came from the backseat following the crash, a child seemingly unharmed but frightened beyond words, could have woken the dead. Mina considered that perhaps they had, and that maybe all the bad luck she'd been having lately was the work of one such disturbed spirit who was hot with revenge at being having been disturbed. And she also knew that was ridiculous.

Terrified, Mina had bolted right to the pediatrician—without calling the police or trying to chase after the driver who hit her. It seemed like Emma would never stop crying and Mina was convinced that something was terribly wrong.

Dr. Swenson, a kindly gentleman in his late fifties, had carefully examined the screaming child and concluded: "She's just scared."

"Scared?" Mina near-shouted, as she tried to pull a wriggling, writhing Emma into her arms to console her. A raging octopus with chainsaws for tentacles. "Just scared?"

"Just scared," he said, sweet and soft-spoken, surprisingly audible over the cacophony.

"Well how do I make her less scared?" Mina asked, and they both sized up the still-screaming tot, the mother with a face frantic with worry, the doctor with a cool, matter-of-fact gaze.

There was a long pause before he spoke. "Benadryl," he said.

"Medication?" Mina gasped. "But if you say she's okay, why am I medicating her?"

And just at that moment, Emma stopped had stopped screaming. She gave a little shudder, a big sniff, and she let out a sigh. The drama was over.

"Well, she isn't crying anymore, is she," Dr. Swenson said, and gave Mina a warm, friendly tap on the back. "The Benadryl would have calmed her down. Even knocked her out," he whispered, with a wink and a warm smile.

"Oh," was all Mina could muster.

Later that day, she had sat down with her neighbor, Esther, and told her what had happened. Esther gave her the same warm look and assured, "There's just no way I could have raised my five kids without Benadryl."

Suddenly what the doctor had said made sense. Mina had no idea what she would do without Esther, her octogenarian next-door-neighbor. Esther had been so kind to them. And Emma loved her so much. Her fashion sense arrested in the 1960s. Her curiously black beehive hairdo. Her amazing costume jewelry collection—each day a new piece!

And suddenly, Emma knew just who she should call to help straighten out the mess. Esther Erasmus. The only person who made living where she did bearable.

But as Mina approached the phone, the thing that ruined her day, every day, every week, every month for what seemed like decades. It rang. She checked the caller ID and just as she had suspected, an identifiable 888 number. Her heart stopped, as it did. Her breath trapped in her throat as she watched the phone, praying for the ringing to stop. The machine would have picked it up if it wasn't already filled with messages she couldn't bear to listen to. Messages from people angrily making demands she couldn't honor.

With every ring she was reminded why she couldn't replace the water heater. Why the dryer leaked through the kitchen ceiling. Why her car was still in the shop.

On top of it all, her rear, bottom-left molar was throbbing in pain, and had been for weeks. She hated that she was going to have to make an appointment to see her dentist because she absolutely despised going to the dentist. But more than that was the dread she felt at how much it would cost, the same sense of dread she had felt over not being able to answer the phone. Whoever it was on the other end of that phone wanted money. And Mina had none.

If you looked around Mina Clark's suburban home, the fact that she had no money would make no sense at all; the expansive, well-appointed space pretty much screamed the idea that wealth lived here.

For one, the home was located in the very exclusive enclave of Easton Estates, a gated community of soulless McMansions that all looked pretty much the same—and God help you if you didn't like it that way.

Step through the carved-mahogany double-door front entrance and you encountered a foyer the full height of the house, complete with a dramatic skylight, which splashed sunlight on the terrazzo marble floor and sparkled off the speckled silver bowl with the cobalt blue dragonfly pattern resting on the foyer table. Mina knew she'd had that bowl for years, long before living at Easton Estates, but she had no idea when she had gotten it—from whom or even why.

Downstairs, a fully finished basement was used for pretty much nothing, and again, Mina had no idea why. It was yet another puzzle she was taxed to solve as she wandered daily around this strange house where she lived, desperate to piece back together the life that existed that she couldn't remember before the past two or so years.

To the left of the foyer sat a richly appointed dining room and behind it, a fully outfitted modern kitchen, sleek and cool with cobalt cabinetry and stainless steel appliances. Mina didn't particularly like her kitchen, though. It reminded her somehow of being in a submarine.

Behind the kitchen was a small alcove Mina had gated off and made into a playroom. She wasn't exactly sure why she hadn't decided to make the basement a playroom, except she didn't like having Emma so far away from her. Ridiculous, yes, as there was already the distance of nursery school three hours a day, three days a week. In any case, the room was a crazy, colorful jungle of colors and soft things, a crazy juxtaposition to the submarine kitchen. Already awash in Day-Glo, it now took on a whole new level of color thanks to Emma's "artwork."

To the other side of the foyer was a formal living room, then a family room, and then behind that, another alcove that was purportedly Mina's "office"—though she rarely did anything in that room but surf the Internet and listen to her tapes. She could have paid bills if she had money to pay them. She could have gotten some work done, if she knew what work for her was.

Mina entered the small room and headed for the cassette player. She pressed play and she moved back through the house, heading back to the kitchen to try and call Esther again.

"What do you believe?" the man's voice emphatically implored throughout the house from the state-of-the-art speaker system.

"I have no idea," Mina absently answered.

"What do you want *to believe about* you? *What do you want to believe you are?"*

Mina wanted to believe something about herself. That she was something—was someone. That she had once done more with her life than sit around her house and try and remember who she was, and chase around a maniacal toddler.

"Who do you believe *you are?"*

"I don't know," she said softly. "I don't remember."

The no memory thing was tough and seemed only to get worse by the day. As hard as she tried, Mina simply could not remember anything that had happened in her life before Emma was born. Even Emma's earliest days were a fog. She had no recollection of the pregnancy—whether it was "easy" or not, whether she was sick or not. The birth. The other mothers always wanted these answers. They were obsessed with natural or epidural, vaginal or caesarian, breast or bottle—and they were also obsessed with bonding with the mothers who had done things just as they had, and obsessed with belittling, tormenting, alienating any mother that had done it differently. Mina hated The Mothers.

"You can be WHO you think you are. If you think it, you can believe it!" the voice encouraged.

Then there was Jack. Her "husband." The phantom presence that shared this house and this life with her when he wasn't working late and weekends, or traveling for business. She didn't quite understand how they had no money if he worked as hard as he did; she didn't want to think about what else he might be doing. Mina could not remember meeting Jack or falling in love with him. She could not remember their wedding day—any of the planning or preparation involved. It was hard to get a sense of him even now. She couldn't remember if she loved him, if she ever really loved him. Though she felt she had—and that she still did. Even in the small pockets of time they spent together, she could feel a warmth, a crackling flame, a shared affection and a desire, even if it was seldom if ever acted upon by either of them these days.

"If you feel it, you can know it to be true!" said the voice on the tape, and Mina took a deep breath and as she repeated the words under her breath.

Perhaps the saddest thing of it all was that she had no idea where she came from. No recollection of childhood, of family. She had been able to piece together that there was no one left. But who was her mother? Her father? Did she have any brothers or sisters? It was these questions and a million more like them that distracted Mina daily—and opened the door for Emma to do crazy things like get into paint and ruin the furniture.

"Out! Out! Out! Monny I want out!" Emma shrieked from her "prison," and the phone started ringing again. Mina hoped it was Jack but when she saw it was a different 888 number, she angrily picked up the receiver and slammed it down again. Anyone who she wanted to speak to could call her on her cell phone, she rationalized. At least the vultures didn't know that number. At least not yet.

"If you could, just think for a moment if you could...." The voice paused and started up again with great passion and fury. *"If you believe you could be what you want to believe, would you finally... Would you FINALLY... Would you finally believe in yourself?"*

"Not likely," Mina surmised and dashed over to the playroom to collect Emma. Except she had forgotten to mop up a large puddle of water that had formed under the ceiling from where the dryer was leaking and she slipped, old-film-wipe-out-on-a-banana-peel-style on the Italian ceramic floor.

"Monny! MONNY!"

"I'm coming!" Her whole body hurt as she tried to get up. And then the doorbell rang.

"What do you believe?" the man's voice demanded of her. *"What do YOU believe?"*

"You bad monny. Bad, bad monny. I gonna hit-choo bad monny!"

Mina picked herself off the floor and headed for the door.

"I gonna hit-choo in the head!"

"What do you believe the Universe owes you?"

The toddler just kept screaming. The phone started ringing again and now the doorbell. "Oh fuck, alright, I'm coming!" she said.

"If you know what you believe you need, the Universe will bring it to you! But first you must know what you believe you need!"

"MONNNNNNNNY!!!!"

"I'm coming baby. Hang on!"

"I want-choo now monny! Now! Now! Now!"

Bedraggled, limping, covered in dried paint, Mina pulled open the door. And there, on the other side, stood her opposite. Serenity, manifest in a small-framed, advanced-aged "savior" known as Esther Erasmus, holding a covered plate that held the promise of something sweet, and today wearing a bright, bejeweled pin that reminded Mina of a Tiffany stained glass lampshade. Esther had arrived, as if beckoned by the Universe itself, and now Mina could finally breathe.

"If you want it, you can bring it to you."

"You shouldn't just open the door like that," Esther chided, though with a gentleness Mina had come to depend upon. The soothing calm in the chaos of her life. "You have to be careful."

"Esther, my goodness," Mina laughed as they stood in the doorway. "Here?" She shook her head. "I think the worst case scenario would be that creep that runs the Landscaping Committee.

And I think I could probably take him." Mina then made a pathetic attempt at a laugh, as she and Esther both looked to the planting beds outside her front door—or rather, what had been planting beds.

"Those bastards," Esther said, with a succession of tsks. "I mean, I knew they would do this. But those bastards, all the same."

"You mean that they would do this? To a neighbor?"

"That Charlie Witmore is a pain in the ass and everyone knows it. But the head of a home owner's association holds a lot of power," she said. "Besides, widowers can be assholes in general. Trust me. I've known plenty of them."

"If you want it, it can be yours."

Starting off the seemingly never-ending list of what had been making this the proverbial day from hell was the discovery this morning that the flowers in Mina's planting beds surrounding her front porch had all been brutally murdered. The night before, the entire landscaping committee had come and, with their bare hands, unearthed all of Mina's flowers. As it turned out, peonies, in any shade, were expressly prohibited, as stated in the bylaws of the community. Peonies had been the favorite flower of Charlie Witmore's now-deceased wife. At her funeral, there had been an ocean of purple and orange and magenta peony blooms. And now any time anyone at Easton Estates saw peonies of any kind, all they could see in their minds-eyes was Kitty Witmore, made up like a pasty showgirl in her pink-satin lined coffin.

Shame rose in her face and she looked away. "It was insensitive of me," she said. "I should have gone with Marigolds. No one ever uses Marigolds at a funeral."

"No one uses peonies either," said Esther, and Mina half-nodded in agreement. Esther gently placed a hand on Mina's elbow. "You don't think it was insensitive of them to come here in the middle of the night and massacre your garden?"

"What you welcome will be YOURS!"

"You have company?" Esther asked, a perplexed look on her face.

Mina didn't answer either question.

Esther craned her neck to look inside the house to find the source of the curious voice as she spoke. "I can't tell you what I had done had they messed with my yard," she shook her head and gave Mina a soft, powdery kiss on the cheek. "Honey, you're going to have to stop letting people push you around like this," she said, and she handed Mina the plate.

"If you want it, it will come to you."

"What is that? Is someone here?" asked Esther, now gently pushing her way inside. "Who's that man talking? And where's the little one? Isn't it Tuesday?"

In the time that had elapsed since Mina chose door over daughter, Emma had gone silent. Almost too silent. Now Mina panicked.

"Here," she tossed the plate back to Esther and ran to the playroom. "Emma? Mama's coming! Emma! Are you okay?"

"If you want it, make it yours! Goodnight!"

"Goodnight?" said Esther, befuddled "But it's eleven thirty in the morning."

Mina raced to the playroom and found Emma crunched up in a little ball, holding her knees, rocking and scowling. When she saw her mother had finally come for her, she regarded the woman with a sour grin, and went on sulking. "I'm sorry baby," Mina said, and bent down in front of the gate. "You know mama loves you?"

Without warning, Emma's scowl switched to a smile, the sweetest and brightest smile Mina had ever seen the little girl wear. Instantly, Mina's heart filled with joy; with an intense and incredible sense of love just seeing her daughter like that, smiling at her so warmly, so beautifully. She wanted to scoop up the child, cradle her in her arms and plant kisses all over her little painted body. She wanted to snuggle with her so much, it made her heart hurt. She took a breath and reached out her arms.

"Esda!" cried Emma, and she ran to the section of baby gate that "Esda" now occupied. Jilted by the toddler.

"My goodness, baby, what have you gotten into now?" asked Esther, bemused, looking at Mina, not Emma.

"I paint!" a gleeful Emma boasted, and waved around the playroom to show Esther the extent of her masterpiece.

Esther looked at Mina, and Mina smirked, mimicked her daughter's hand movement, and showed to Esther the "masterpiece" as spread throughout the house.

"Oh dear," said Esther, another tsk in her voice. "Why didn't you drop this child in the bathtub right away? Is it because of that man in the house?" she asked, craning her neck into the next room. "Who's that man in the house?"

"Esther, what are you talking about? No one's here except Emma and me." Then Mina realized what Esther was talking about and she chuckled. "Oh that. That's just some tape I found. I have no idea what it is. Must be Jack's," she lied.

"Huh," Esther said, but yet with a tinge of suspicion. She shrugged her shoulders and seemed to let it go. "Mina, what happened here?"

"Kind of a funny story," said Mina, blowing a strand of paint-encrusted fallen bangs out of her eyes, and lifted Emma into her arms. When Emma nuzzled her small, warm head into the crook of Mina's neck, and she breathed in the fresh sweetness of the small one underneath the paint fumes, she knew in her heart that the look of love that Emma had shown had indeed been for her.

As soon as Esther learned the situation with the water heater, she immediately offered to help out—first by offering for Mina and Emma to take a shower at her house, and then by giving Mina the name and number of a friend who could give her a good deal.

"Except I can't pay anything until the middle of the month," said Mina. "And even then—"

"Don't give it another thought, dear. Bob will help you out, no questions asked. Just pay him what you can whenever you can."

"I don't know how to thank you, Esther," Mina said. "For this. For everything you do for us."

"Not to worry, dear. I was your age once. I know it well. Small children, limited funds. Budget stretched to the hilt. I understand. I'm glad to help."

Mina didn't know what she'd do without Esther.

"Why don't you two walk through the backyard. Lord only knows what kind of fine or punishment that busybody Witmore's going to dream up over the two of you looking the way you do," she said, folding her arms in front of her. "The back door's unlocked. Why don't you two grab some fresh clothes and walk on ahead. I could use your help getting down my old bundt pan from the top left shelf in the kitchen, if you could go on and do that for me. Besides, my legs aren't as fast as they used to be," she laughed. "You could duck in to the shower and be out again by the time I make it over there."

"Sure, Esther," said Mina, warmly. "Downstairs shower then?" Mina and Esther had the exact same home configuration; she had been in Esther's house thousands of times but even if she'd never been inside before, she'd know exactly where the downstairs shower was.

"Of course, dear," said Esther.

Mina ran upstairs and grabbed a change of clothes, first for Emma and then for herself. In her bedroom she noticed Jack's laundry still folded on his side of the bed from the day before. He hadn't made it home last night—had taken the redeye and headed right into the office. A stab of longing pierced her heart as she wondered if he'd be home early enough tonight for them to see one another. Have a conversation even. She never knew these days. Jack working all the time, one day dissolving into the next. She headed out of the bedroom and down the stairs.

"I'm back," said Mina and she scooped up Emma into her arms.

"I'll be right behind you," said Esther. "I'll grab the cookies."

Mina slid open the glass French doors that led to their backyard and cut across the yard to Esther's. With every step, Emma writhed and squirmed to break free.

"I want to walk!" screamed Emma. "I walk!" After taking a couple of considerably painful punches to the face, Mina gave up and set Emma down.

Just as Emma's feet touched the ground, both Emma and Mina were knocked over by a powerful force, which Mina could only identify as water once they hit the ground. She swung her head around to find Esther, wielding a garden hose like some crazed naturist who'd just captured a raging python by the midsection on some wild animal program. The spray must have been on full-force and Mina wondered for a moment how the hell Esther could be wielding such force, and, before that, why Esther was trying to drown them with a hose.

Esther laughed out loud. "You didn't think I was going to let the two of you into my house looking like that!" she said. "I mean, your decorating style is okay, you know, for you," she choked as she chortled. "I myself prefer more muted tones."

Mina opened her mouth to speak and got pelted in the mouth with a hard stream of water. She looked at Emma who she imagined must be terrified at what was going on and Emma looked back at her. Then Emma began to laugh maniacally, and she splashed her tiny hands in the water and now mud puddles that formed in the grass. Mina watched Emma, whose face and hair and clothes and hands were streaked in rinsed paint and brown mud and random loose blades of grass. Emma was now watching Esther, who was continuing to spray away at them with mad delight. "Again!" screamed Emma. "Again!"

As the sun rose in the sky signaling the end of the morning, and Emma and Esther screamed and laughed with the hose spraying away, Mina gave in to the moment and joined in the fun, splashing and laughing spinning around in the grass with Emma as Esther rinsed them clean. And she was feeling, at least for the moment, that maybe this wasn't the worst day ever after all.

Printed in the USA
CPSIA information can be obtained
at www.ICGtesting.com
JSHW031712140824
68134JS00038B/3655